CHRISTINA SCHWARZ
SO LONG AT THE FAIR

Christina Schwarz is the author of the critically acclaimed *All Is Vanity* and *Drowning Ruth*, a #1 bestseller in both hardcover and paperback, which was selected for Oprah's Book Club and optioned by Wes Craven for Miramax.

SO LONG AT THE FAIR

SO LONG

at the

FAIR

A NOVEL

CHRISTINA SCHWARZ

Anchor Books
A Division of Random House, Inc.
New York

FIRST ANCHOR BOOKS EDITION, JULY 2009

Copyright © 2008 by Christina Schwarz

The Library of Congress has cataloged the Doubleday edition as follows:
Schwarz, Christina.
So long at the fair / by Christina Schwarz.—1st ed.
p. cm.
I. Title.
PS3569.C56783S6 2008
813'.54—dc22   2008014600

Anchor ISBN: 978-0-307-27549-3

www.anchorbooks.com

Printed in the United States of America
10 9 8 7 6 5 4 3 2 1

To P,

who made writing companionable

ACKNOWLEDGMENTS

That this book was ever finished is thanks solely to a bevy of superb babysitters, first among them my sister, Eliza Audley, and my parents, Donna and Anthony Meyer, and also including Lisa Huang, Eileen Jinette, Kim Barnes, and Sarah Spoerl. For insight into psychology and behavior, I relied on Jennifer Stuart, as always. I thank Penelope Patterson for her expertise on the advertising industry and on Madison, Wisconsin, Judith Stark for a sense of the job of the landscape architect, and Donna Meyer for details about Wisconsin plants. To the extent that I got things wrong on any of these fronts, it's because I was pigheaded.

As always, Caitlin Flanagan stuck with me through draft after draft and, more than once, kept the whole thing from running off into a ditch. I'm especially grateful to her for insisting that the stories of the two generations belonged in one book. Caitlin, like Charlotte (of the web), is that rare thing, both a true friend and a good writer.

For their generosity with their time and ideas, I'm now for the third time indebted to Barbara Faculjak and Linda Rudell-Betts, for the second time to Amy Halliday, and also this time to Sonja Alarr, Cynthia Davis, and Gina Hahn.

I'm grateful to my bravely honest editor, Deb Futter, who dared to send me back to work when I hoped I was through. And, for her reassurance in the face of that outrageous advice, I'm indebted to Jennifer Rudolph Walsh, my loyal agent and one of the most astute readers I know. I also thank Alison Callahan for gracefully picking up where Deb left off.

Finally, I thank Ben Schwarz, who is uncannily skilled at spotting what doesn't ring true and knowing how to fix it, and who stubbornly always believes that I can do better.

SO LONG AT THE FAIR

1963

"*What are you going to do, then, Clark?*"

Marie crosses her arms and pulls them tight against her body, underscoring, it seems to Clark, the fullness of her breasts. He looks away. He wishes Hattie hadn't told him that Marie is pregnant. Pregnancy strikes him as slightly obscene, the obvious physicality of all that swelling. The obviousness of the activity that had begun it. Not that he objects to the activity itself, although he's not yet had the opportunity to try it. Not really, not all the way. But he doesn't like thinking about Marie that way. Or rather part of him is disgusted with the part that's apparently incapable of thinking about anything else.

"I told you." He forces himself to look at her straight on. "I took her to the police." He rakes his scalp, damp in the heat, with the nails of both hands. "That's the right thing to do." And it is. Of course it is. But his voice sounds squeaky as he says it, as if he's reciting the code of the Mickey Mouse Club.

Pressing her lips together in exasperation, Marie shakes her head and turns away, communing with some invisible, sympathetic presence, someone who knows better, the way she does. "*Yet he's not in jail,*" *she says, focusing again on Clark.* "*Hmmm...I wonder why that is.*"

"*Well, one reason is she won't make a complaint.*"

Both of them look at "*she,*" *a pale young woman in grass-green pedal pushers and a top sprinkled with tiny strawberries, curled into a corner of the couch. She dips her face into the bowl of her hands in response and lets her white-blond hair fall forward.*

"*But they'll investigate. I told them what he did. They'll get him.*" *And now he sounds absurdly earnest, like Joe Friday.*

"*No, Clark. You see, they won't.*" *Marie rises from her chair and goes to the kitchen, which is not a separate room but just a wall of the cabin crudely fitted with a stove, refrigerator, and sink.*

The place is dim, papered in brown, patterned with olive-green fish, and lit by yellow bulbs to discourage insects, the tiniest of which push in through the screens anyway and dance frenetically between the bulbs and the lampshades until they burn. She's prettied it as well as she can, fitting a bedspread, peach chenille, over the couch, dressing up a worn armchair with a striped pillow. As she talks, she arranges a pitcher of iced tea, three glasses, and some neatly ironed napkins on a tray with deliberation. "*He'll say Hattie wanted it, and then afterward wished she hadn't.*"

A sob from the couch at this.

"*Walter Fleischer is very charming. His family is well respected. His father owns the golf course where the sheriff plays. And the bar where his deputy drinks. They'll prefer to believe him.*" *She snorts.* "*Don't tell me they haven't done exactly the same thing themselves and justified it the same way.*" *She sets the tray on the large wooden cable spool that serves as a table. She's painted it a poppy red, but it still looks like the piece of industrial junk it is.*

"*Anyway, they'll believe him over you. Who are you, Clark? The jilted lover. Of course, you'll say he raped her.*"

"I didn't jilt Clark! He broke it off with me! And that was two months ago. This has nothing to do with Clark!" Hattie's skin is blotched with red, her eyes pink as a rabbit's.

Well, of course, it had nothing to do with him, although Clark, whose embarrassment at this outburst causes him to shift his position on the couch, isn't altogether pleased to be reminded of it. Not—Christ—that he wishes he'd raped the girl, but that he never does seem to have anything to do with anything. Drag racing, skinny-dipping, road trips to Madison, love affairs—from all reports, these and more are what people do after he says good night and drives on home to bed. He doesn't really want any of these experiences in particular, although he looks forward to falling in love and thought at one time that he was very close to the brink with Hattie, but he's just sick and tired of being the guy who's told about everything the following morning. He's sick of being the audience.

Marie sips her iced tea and delicately pinches the fabric of her blouse, pulling it forward off her skin, to allow the air to circulate. Clark realizes that she's not, in fact, an attractive woman. Her features are uneven; her nose too large; her chin ill-defined. And yet, even seeing this, he cannot help but think that she's beautiful. Her beauty comes, he thinks, from the certainty with which she presents herself, almost as if she's daring you to question it. "Anyone can see that Clark cares about you, Hattie. Even if he told you he was through with you."

Clark colors. "I never told her——" *he begins indignantly, but Marie cuts him off with an imperious wave.*

"We need to help Hattie now," *she says.*

Clark frowns at the girl beside him, who's wiping her nose with the back of her hand. Sorry as he feels for her, he's also furious with her, furious that she's let this happen, and, now that it's happened, furious with her helplessness. And with his own. "Won't Bud believe Walter, too?" he says. "Last I looked they were best friends."

Marie scissors her fingers, draws them through the thick, dark hair that curls outward at her shoulders. "Bud will believe me."

"Where's the bathroom in this place?" He half expects her to wave him outside, but she points to the bedroom.

"Bud'll make him pay," he hears Marie say, as he squeezes past the bed, trying not to look at it, trying not to think about Hattie and Walt, about Marie and Bud. How he longs to be clear of them all. "My Bud will take care of this for you, Hattie."

one

Over, over, done and over. Finished. Jon Kepilkowski scratched his scalp with his fingernails. He'd shampooed, rinsed, and repeated, scrubbed under his arms and between his toes, soaped every surface, brushed under his nails, squirted into his ears. The water gushing from the showerhead was cooling. Reluctantly, he twisted the tap shut and worked himself over roughly with a towel.

From the bedroom window he watched his wife as she knelt in the dirt, her face obscured by her hat, her hands busy beneath a clump of pink flowers he couldn't name. He'd known her for twenty years, longer even if you counted the first two years of high school when it wasn't so much that he'd been afraid to say "Hello" to her, but more that she'd been so far out of his league that it hadn't occurred to him that opening his mouth and emitting speech in her direction was even an option.

He'd not, he recalled, even uttered "Excuse me" the time he'd accidentally bumped her with his lunch tray, the contact between the orange plastic and the green wool of her sweater so intimate, so electric it had instantly closed his throat and jump-started his heart. He'd pretended at the time, he confessed years later, though she had no memory of the incident, that he'd not even noticed the collision had occurred. When she turned with a slight involuntary gasp to see who'd jabbed her in the ribs, he'd turned in the same direction, as if obliviously searching the line behind him for a friend.

This morning she'd have been up for hours already, taking advantage of the early coolness. He wished he could see her expression under the brim of the hat. As always in these past few months, whenever he'd been apart from her for a few hours, anxiety began to collect around the edges of his consciousness. Between the moment the night before when she'd shoved her book onto the nightstand, maneuvering it among the detritus—the glasses of dusty water, the uncapped tube of ChapStick, the broken earring, the hair clip, the crumpled Kleenex—between that moment and this, had she found him out? What face would she show him when she looked his way?

Impulsively, he twisted the latch and slid the window up with a little too much vigor. The sash banged against the frame. "Gin!"

She turned, tilting her head back, squinting up at him with her hooded eyes, then drew back suddenly, feigning shock. "Hey! There's a naked man in my house! Get out, naked man! Get away from my window!" She kept her voice low, for him, alone.

He sighed, safe. "Maybe you'd like to come up?"

She laughed and turned back to the pink flowers.

He hadn't meant it as a joke. His relief had triggered desire, and he was vaguely, if, he acknowledged, unreasonably, irritated by her response.

He dressed in long shorts and a white T-shirt and Velcroed on the sort of shoes useful for splashing across shallow rivers. Since he'd started working at the agency, he'd decided that the button-down shirts and khakis he'd favored at the start of his career made him look like a little boy playing dress up and had abandoned that costume for one less earnest, one definitely but not too aggressively cool, as much to remind himself of who he was, or was trying to be, as to signal this to others. It wasn't a dull style, but nor was it, he recognized with some disappointment, the least surprising. He'd let his hair grow and curl midway down his neck, wore the jeans the world liked to see on an art director and, on summer workdays, European sandals that would have made his father sneer.

He retrieved the laptop he'd pushed under the bed the night before. One message from Kyle, his brother. Seven work-related messages, beginning with one from Kaiser, sent at four a.m., just before that lunatic had gone to bed, no doubt. Three from Freddi. He felt his pulse quicken. Better to have left the machine cold. Even now it was not too late to let it sleep, snap the cover down, slide the thing into its case ready to transport into work on Monday.

He carried it into the second bedroom, which functioned as his office, and gently shut the door. He fingered the Return key for a few seconds, savoring the anticipation. The first from Freddi was some copy ideas for Ballast Bank, some serious, some silly; none, he saw immediately, workable. The second read: "I hate weekends." The third: "I can almost sense you here beside me on the bed, your warm largeness, your flipper-like feet, your brown-sugar eyes. You are the bittersweet chocolate to which I press my tongue. I send you kisses for your lips and elsewhere. Good night."

He closed his eyes, allowed himself to swell with the thought of her. She resembled a fox, with her pale brown eyes that tended to amber; her small, very white teeth; her smooth, reddish hair; her tight, muscular body. He found the whole combination of sharpness and softness immensely attractive. But it was the way she looked at him that pushed him over the edge; her gaze told him that the two of them were the only ones in on it, whatever it was, the joke, the plan, the skinny. She had chosen him and he'd basked in it, rolled in it, lapped it up. She was like sugar, like nicotine; the more he got, the more he wanted. No, it wasn't over, done, finished. He craved her.

"My lips miss you," he typed, and then paused. "Elsewhere misses you, too." He paused again, absently pulling one of the antique fountain pens from the jarful he kept on his desk. He played with it, capping and uncapping it, rolling its smooth Bakelite case between his fingers. He couldn't think without something in his hands. And then, too, he always felt a little self-conscious writing to her. Words were her thing, not his.

"A kiss on your heart," he typed, inspired, "and one lower down, much lower." It was a line Napoleon had used in a letter to Josephine. He'd heard it on a PBS documentary last night. "You are so . . ." he began.

"Hey."

Ginny, long-legged and stealthy, despite her large bones, stood in the doorway in her garden uniform, the sleeves of one of his discarded T-shirts rolled up to her shoulders, the elastic waistband of her shorts supplemented with a safety pin, her dark hair springing free from its noose.

His heart exploded—the blast of adrenaline actually pained him—and his hand trembled as he reached to close the window of his message. Easy. Not guiltily fast. Stupid to have closed the door and shut out the sound of her bare feet on the carpeted stairs.

"Hey, yourself."

The cover made a tiny metallic click as it kissed the keyboard.

"More orders from headquarters, huh?"

He knew it was a point of pride with her not to allow herself to be suspicious; she would not be one of those women who worried about holding on to her husband.

"Your mother said I'd better keep my eye on you," she'd said just last month, as they drove through the blackness after an evening at Kyle and Paula's. "Like you were some caged bird ready to fly the coop the moment I turned my back on the door." She'd looked out the window as she spoke, her head tipped back, as though she were searching the night sky for a bird that had indeed flown.

"My mother," he'd said, his tone implying a roll of the eyes.

He could sense that she had turned her face toward him, though he'd kept his own eyes firmly on the ever-receding tunnel of light on the highway ahead.

"Does she know something I don't?" she asked.

It occurred to him to confess. Not to the whole of his crime but to a small degree of it. He might say he was worried that Freddi was attracted to him. It would be like opening a valve just a fraction, not so much that it would all escape but enough to gradually relieve the pressure. It would mean the end, of course, of late nights "working," of long lunches during which he could honestly say, "I'm with Freddi," without fear of arousing suspicion. It would mean the end of it all. It was a safe way out. He turned and, while his heart throbbed hard enough to choke him, looked at her full-on for two entire seconds, enough time to kill them both if something unexpected had appeared on the highway. But, finally, he faced forward again. "Of course not."

"I suppose people who've behaved badly themselves tend to be suspicious of everyone else."

"Probably." He wished he could close his eyes to block out the shame.

"Well," she said, smiling, "you'd better never force me to use my wiles."

He laughed. She had always been the most guileless person he'd ever known. It was one of the things he loved best about her.

A near miss, he'd thought at the time. And he had resolved all the way home that it was finished with Freddi, that he'd learned his lesson. He made love to his wife that night with a fierce exuberance released by a nearly clear conscience. The lying was over, he'd assured himself. He loved Ginny. The thought of losing her had filled him with a dark and breathless panic the whole night through.

But by Monday, a bright, cheerful, cloudless day, the panic had seemed far away, a small, irretrievable flutter in the distance. At work Freddi had leaned over him and laughed at something he'd said, and her skin had exuded a scent he wished he could breathe forever.

And now here he was, trapped in his study with the evidence under his fingers and Ginny's large frame blocking the door. How had he gotten ink on his hands? "Just gonna wash up quick, and then I'm ready." He stood up, raising his eyebrows at her expectantly.

"Ready?" She cocked her head, pushing a damp curl behind her ear. Her finger left a smudge along her cheek.

"To go to Summerfest." He frowned. "What we're doing today."

She clapped both hands on the top of her head and made the

face he used laughingly to call "the Lucy." An expression he now thought of privately as "the fuckup."

"What?" He sounded impatient, but what he felt was desperate. He'd conceived of this plan, this revisiting of a scene from their youth, a time when they'd been, it seemed to him now, simply, vigorously happy, because he urgently needed to see her again as he once had, to remind himself of the pull of her, of the way the very thought of her had once possessed him, so that he turned always toward her, helplessly, like a flower on its stalk in the presence of the sun. He wanted to remember how it had felt to be certain that he must have her, her and no other, that only her promise to be with him forever could keep him breathing. Although, of course, he no longer felt this way with any immediacy, until recently, until Freddi, he'd nevertheless been sure that he was still connected to those early impulses, as if by a long, unbreakable, ever-unwinding thread. If he couldn't relive them, he could still see their colors and textures at the inception of all, good and bad, that had come since. Now, though, he was unmoored. Pursuing Freddi, a bright flash in the thickets, he'd let the thread slip from his grasp and he couldn't seem to grab hold of it again.

"Summerfest!" she exclaimed. The surprise on her face made him want to hit something. "Are you sure we were going today?"

He never needed to say anything in these situations. She would play the idea out, letting it loop and twist, until she snagged something solid. "I remember talking about it, but I thought we'd settled on Sunday. Or maybe that we hadn't really decided." She closed her eyes, pressed her palm on her forehead, and exhaled. "Oh, I should have written it down. Maybe I even did write it down. Probably I did. But you know I never check my calendar on the weekends." She opened her eyes, facing the facts. "Shoot, I screwed it up, didn't I? I'm sorry, Jon. I completely forgot."

Her contrition always disarmed him. He reached forward

and put his hand on her shoulder. Her skin retained the warmth of the sun that had been baking it. "No big deal. We can go in an hour. Take your time."

"But I've scheduled two meetings for today."

"Cancel them."

"I can't cancel at the last minute. And one's with Nora. You know how impossible it is to schedule with her, now that she's got Prince Rodney."

He wanted to remind her that she was canceling with *him* at the last minute. "So we're not going."

"Well, how about tomorrow? Couldn't we go tomorrow instead? Is there some band you wanted to see tonight? Did you get tickets?"

No, he hadn't gotten tickets and he didn't care particularly about the bands. In fact, tomorrow might even be better in that Kyle had said something about showing up there today and listening to Kyle go on about paintball and Paula talk about the new drapes in the family room was close to the last thing he wanted for this outing. There was no good reason they couldn't change their plans to Sunday, except that he didn't want to. He'd planned on today; he'd ascribed redemptive powers to today; today was it.

"I don't like this, Ginny. Why should Nora and your work come before me? You're taking me for granted." God, he sounded like a women's magazine.

She stared at him, triumph lighting her face. "You're kidding, right? Mr. I've-Got-to-Stay-at-the-Office-Until-Two-a.m. Mr. I've-Got-to-Take-This-Call-It's-Kaiser." Her tone was light, singsongy, mocking. Never show anger when sarcasm would do, that was her weapon. It made him clench his fists. "Mr. Freddi-and-I-Have-to-Work-Today-You-Go-to-Your-Parents'-Alone."

His blood seemed all to run to his head, leaving his body cold. That had been two weeks ago, a family picnic. And they *had* been late with the McTeague concepting. They had! He couldn't keep his eyes on her any longer. He looked away. There on the desk was the laptop, its secrets crouching under the lid, ready to spring into the light.

Before he could respond, she raised her hand. "No, listen, it's my fault," she said, shaking her head. "I wasn't paying enough attention. I'll go call Nora and these other people. Maybe Sunday will work just as well for them." She turned and started down the stairs. This, too, was her weapon, striking like a snake and then slipping away before they could have it out. He wanted to reach for her, to grab her by the shoulders and hold her there, to beg for her help in fixing this whole mess, but he managed only to follow her to the top of the stairs, where he stood and watched her make her way down.

Stairs, especially going down, were the most difficult for her to negotiate. On flat surfaces, her limp was almost imperceptible, but stepping down she had to lean hard on the rail and her left foot fell onto each tread with a stomp, while her right, the one that belonged to the leg that was now ever so slightly shorter than the other, made no sound at all.

Usually he didn't even notice; he was so accustomed to her gait. Today, though, the sound, the way she jerked her head and shoulder, reminded and reminded him of what he would always owe her, especially when it was beginning to seem that what he had done in an impulsive moment twenty years ago may have cost them a family.

She was looking up at him from the bottom of the stairs, and he could tell that she had changed her mind again. "You know what, Jon?"

He hated it when she used that self-righteous tone.

"I'm not going to rearrange my appointments. Maybe I shouldn't have scheduled them, but I did. You know, I have a job and it's just as important to me as your job is to you."

"I know your job is important—"

"We can go to Summerfest tomorrow."

He came down the stairs then, descending into her hard gaze and meeting it with his own. Halfway down, he felt a twinge, a sort of sizzle deep within his ankle, the remains of a basketball injury he'd sustained, what, six months ago? The older he got, the longer these things took to heal.

"You know what, Ginny?" he said, as he passed her, his voice dishonestly pleasant. "You do whatever you want." It was a relief to feel angry with her, not guilty, not anxious, not sad, just angry.

He kept walking, down the hall, through the kitchen, through the door that led to the garage.

"Where are you going?" she demanded. "Jon! Where are you going?"

But he let her question roll off him. He didn't know the answer anyway.

He backed out of the garage fast and stomped on the accelerator as soon as he hit the street. Next door, the Murphys, raking little mounds of cut grass into city-approved brown-paper lawn-clipping bags, turned to watch him go by, narrowing their eyes. For years, he had tried his best with them. He'd waved and greeted, tossed their newspaper from the sidewalk to the stoop, once re-boxed their recycling when the wind had scuttled it, but they never smiled at him. Fuck them.

"Fuck you and you, too," he said, staring back at them through the side window.

What was this world-music shit? He leaned on the tuner, letting it gallop up and down the stations. Anything, anything, but this.

The Murphys liked Ginny. Even though she laughed when he mocked them in private, checking over her shoulder to be sure the windows were shut tight. Everyone liked Ginny.

two

The car door slamming and the garage door creaking open had pulled her to the window, and she'd watched his Cherokee shoot backward down the drive, hesitate before crossing the sidewalk, and then continue into the street. His tires had shrieked as they spun on the asphalt.

"Watch where you're going!" she'd called, her voice trapped by the window. "Be careful!" In seconds he'd turned the corner and was gone.

She stared at the empty street. She hated it, hated it, when he left angry. It was all right to be the one swept away by high emotion. There was always the anger with which to keep company. But the one left behind in the quiet, motionless space, in a sort of vacuum of waiting and worrying, was in a terrible position.

What if he never came back? She felt a frantic sort of flitter in her gut, almost like mild nausea, a familiar sensation lately, as she sensed him unsticking himself from her. What had he been doing in his study with the door closed?

"I guess it must be his disappointment," she'd explained to her friend Nora several weeks ago, trying to make sense of the changes she saw in him—the distractedness, the irritability, the obsession with work. "You know, about the whole pregnancy thing. Or non-pregnancy thing, I guess I should say."

"*His* disappointment! What about you? He should be rushing to your aid. He should be bolstering you in your time of need, not morosely going off to lose himself in his work. Disappointment!" Nora had spat the word.

He wasn't morose, though. He was just irritable and less focused on her. That was all. But the difference was enormous. It was like—well, this was silly—but it was like an alien had whisked Jon away and was playing his part, playing it perfectly except for the bits that included Ginny.

"He still calls you every twenty minutes, doesn't he?" Nora had asked.

She was exaggerating, of course, but it was true that Jon had always been a caller, checking in several times a day to talk about nothing. She loved that about him, and he still did call frequently, but lately his tone had become slightly formal. He gave her information she already possessed. It was as if he'd forgotten that he knew her better than that.

She and Nora had talked it over while they stood around in Nora's kitchen, watching her son, Rodney, build a sort of web out of can openers and wooden spoons, a whisk and a potato masher, pretty much everything that had been in the drawer nearest the stove. Nora had looked at her levelly, seriously, ignoring the crash and the howl that came from the floor. "Is there any chance that he might be having an affair?"

Ginny had felt her senses intensify in this dangerous environment. The glass of iced tea in her hand was suddenly too slick and cold for her fingers. When she set it on the countertop, the little chips of color scattered through the Formica advanced at her from their creamy background.

"No," she said, bending to retrieve a baster that had rolled up against her bare foot. "He absolutely would never do that." It was a relief to say it flatly, to know it to be true. That was one thing she didn't have to worry about. Integrity was everything to Jon. He might leave her and then take up with someone else; that was conceivable. But cheat? Never. His mother's infidelity had seen to that.

Now, standing at the window, she pressed her fingertips against the glass, sending the power of her wanting through the city after him. "Come back," she whispered. "Come back. If it's so important, we'll go."

But even as she said it, she balked at the thought. Why should she give in to a tantrum? Years ago, she would already have been on the phone, opening the day for him in the hope that soon he'd be pressing his forehead to hers in sorrow and she could present the afternoon to him afresh, a "do-over" for them both. And if he stayed mad and stayed away, she could throw a bucket of self-righteousness at him when he finally showed up again. Something along the lines of "See, I made things right, but, you, you . . ." This sort of thing struck her as childish now, a relic from the days when extravagant emotion had been heady and scenes inevitably recharged their love. By this point in their marriage, they'd locked themselves into that roller coaster so often, said and done so many unforgivable things, hashed out and made up so many times that the ride was no longer sure to be a thrill. Sometimes now it was better to short-circuit the whole thing, bypass the ups and downs, the loud rumble of the rushing wheels, the tear of the wind, and just skip to the end, where in any case they always got off right where they'd gotten on.

Arranged on the windowsill before her were shells they'd collected on a Florida vacation one spring. She dusted a couple with the hem of her shirt. Jon was right, she supposed, when he lamented in fond exasperation the dirt-catching quality of her clutter, but she found it comforting, inspiring even, to be surrounded by the tangible evidence, the accumulation, of their lives. She needed her shells and the smooth black stones they'd picked up on their Door County honeymoon and the antique aqua glass jars of various sizes she'd bought in Oconomowoc and her Pyrex leftover keepers in 1960s colors and her wooden spools from long-closed Massachusetts textile mills to punctuate the long flow of years, to define it in segments she could grasp. There, for instance, lying like a lizard along the porch rail, was a dried length of ocotillo, gray and gorgeously spotted, symbol of a gloriously untethered car trip between jobs that had ended up, somewhat haphazardly, in Arizona. "Even the desert is packed with shapes and colors," she reminded Jon, who preferred his surfaces clear and clean, his memories organized in photo albums. Generally he wasn't a saver, so she'd once been surprised to find, while searching his side of the closet for a pair of shoes he'd asked her to drop at the cobbler's, a chocolate-brown box with red-paper lining full of all the notes she'd written him during high-school study halls and dull college lectures.

She turned from the window (perhaps he would return if she were not watching) and idly surveyed the disorder that was insidiously encroaching on the living room. A throw was wadded in one corner of the couch and yesterday's newspaper was sliding between the cushions. Tumbled shoes and lumpy bags stuffed with overdue DVDs and sweatshirts massed along the hallway. Tidying life's evidence had never been her strong suit. Recklessly, she corralled smudged drinking glasses off the coffee table with one hand, fragile surfaces clinking, and scooped up papers with the other. His attitude toward her commitments was infuriating, she thought, marching toward the kitchen. Hadn't he been the one who'd encouraged her to take herself seriously as a gardener and as a businesswoman?

She'd always had a way with plants. In second grade, they'd each been given a begonia slip in a tiny pot to grow. Many of the other children had flooded their plants or neglected to water them, but Ginny felt the dirt with the tip of her finger and watered just enough. She wiped the chalk dust off the leaves with a damp paper towel. She turned the pot to keep the growth even. She aerated the soil with a pencil. By mid-May, when some of the children had pots of dirt to present to their mothers and others had a few scraggly leaves, Ginny's begonia was covered with pink blooms.

It was Jon, though, who'd helped her to make something of her talent. "It's not just a green thumb," he'd told her. "It's your sense of design, too. You have a real feel for color and form. You're the artist." One day, he went to Agriculture Hall and picked up for her an application for the Landscape Architecture program. In fact, he filled out most of that application, too, when he found it started and then forgotten in a drawer full of expired coupons. "If you could take the energy and focus and creativity you apply to domestic projects," he'd said, his hands sweeping the room to encompass the mosaic-topped coffee table she'd made from their broken crockery and the Marimekko fabric she'd tacked over a hideous mustard-colored armchair and the border she'd stenciled in the stairwell, "and do something in the world with it, you would be unstoppable."

She'd been offended at first. She couldn't deny that her current job fitting eyeglasses was merely a paycheck and a placeholder, and perhaps she squandered too much creativity making Christmas cards and knitting tiny sweaters for friends' new babies, but surely this sort of personal attention was valuable when everyone's lives were crammed with cheap, replaceable stuff, bought with barely a moment's thought.

Still, he'd been right to push her to go. She'd feared that making her art a science would deaden it, but instead it gave her passion substance and legs. Course by course—Research Methods in Landscape Studies, Regional Design Workshop, Plant Community Restoration, Landscape History—she felt herself becoming a serious person, a woman working rather than a girl playing, an expert. She and Jon began to build and rebuild her landscaping business in their talk. They debated the sort of client she would have—she wanted to do private yards, he thought she should shoot for the grounds around corporations and public spaces—wondered whether she should partner with Nora, and, most fun of all, batted around ideas for the company's name.

When she'd earned her master's, he'd presented her with a box of business cards he'd designed in an Arts and Crafts style. They agreed that people in Madison, classy people who might want their yard professionally landscaped, would appreciate that look because of the Frank Lloyd Wright connection.

One night, as she listened to Jon and Kaiser deliver their usual rant about the idiocy and the arrogance of their boss, the uninspired approaches he insisted they take, the conservative clients he preferred, she realized in a bolt that Jon had helped her to get what he most wanted for himself—an independent, creative business—and at the thought her love for him so inundated her that it brought tears to her eyes.

.   .   .

If he came home soon, she would reschedule, make the excuse to her clients that she wasn't feeling well, which, by the way, happened to be true. She'd been feeling slightly ill all morning, probably from the shame of knowing, just under the rim of her consciousness, that she'd forgotten his plans on purpose to make room for her own.

The kitchen, she saw, was more densely squalid than the living room, with this morning's dirty mugs stacked on top of last night's plates. And, as always, the dishwasher was packed with clean dishes, which had to be put away before she could load it again. Daunted by the prospect of sorting the flatware into its proper slots, she boosted herself onto one of the kitchen barstools, pushed to one side a stack of mail and magazines, the "failure to stop" ticket she'd earned several weeks ago, and other bits of paper that possibly had useful information on them, and settled her cheek on her arms. "So handy for casual meals," the real estate agent had said about the bar, when she'd shown them the house. The agent had scratched the lavender countertop with a French manicured nail. "Of course, you can always change this," she'd said. But Ginny loved the purple counter; she'd used it as an excuse for marmalade-colored cabinet doors, which, admittedly, was the sort of thing everyone said they adored when they saw it, but would never actually put in their own kitchens.

It seemed all their dining was casual, because they ate at the bar almost exclusively. Ginny had always imagined herself to be the sort of person who served roasts for two at the dining-room table by candlelight. She'd bought, in fact, several hand-dipped candles in brilliant, saturated colors—violet and hot pink and bright orange—for that purpose. But so far she'd turned out to

be the sort of person who used the dining-room table to pay
taxes and pile newspapers that she would certainly, one day soon,
have time to read, and the candles languished in the drawer.

The Cape Cod, which they'd purchased when they'd moved
back to Madison, was supposed to have been their "starter."
They'd both yearned for something old, with character, and had
coveted as their "someday" house the Victorians and the Crafts-
mans in the Vilas neighborhood. This, with its romantic dorm-
ers and charming front porch, had at least a suggestion of that
world. They jokingly referred to their decor as "eclectic, with a
strong note of Swedish pressboard," but they did have one real
antique, a dry sink, the first example of which they'd spotted in
an Indiana museum shortly after they were married. It was,
they'd agreed, the ideal place to store CDs; the depression in the
surface being just the right depth and the juxtaposition of the
old piece of furniture and the new technology being so satisfying. They'd spent at least half a dozen intensely pleasurable
weekends, at least twice involving drives deep into Pennsylva-
nia and overnights at pretty inns, before they found an afford-
able, perfectly proportioned dry sink with blue-green stenciled
diamonds on the doors, sold by a dealer who was willing to
dicker, so that they could feel canny. A day at Summerfest—
another pleasurable weekend—of course it was worth canceling any number of appointments!

The housewares catalog under her elbow caught her eye—
did their newly wed friends Nick and Shirley need a set of shot
glasses, paisleyed with serrano chilies? What was an appropriate
gift for people who married after living together for twenty
years? Champagne, probably. Or aspirin. His and her revolvers.

Not funny when he wasn't there to laugh.

Against her better judgment, she lifted the cordless phone
from its cradle and dialed.

"This is Jon Kepilkowski. Please leave a message."

She hung up, dialed again. "This is Jon Kepilkowski." Hung up, dialed again. "This is—"

What had he been doing in his study with the door closed?

She slid off the stool, taking care not to wrench her hip, and passed down the short hallway. She climbed the stairs, feeling as if she'd been summoned, but scooping up a pile of clean laundry as she went, as if by doing so, she could disguise the true purpose of her trip.

His home office was a charming room. It had a sunny south window and an oak positioned in just the right spot outside the dormer to give it the effect of a bower. It would make an ideal nursery. She could imagine so vividly a warm, feathery-haired little person, reaching over the top rail of a crib for the squirrel that was just now chasing through the branches, that it was almost difficult to believe that he or she did not, in fact, exist. Might never exist. Dr. Paulson's voice, with its implied accusation, pushed its way in: "There's no *medical* reason why you should not conceive."

She sat down at Jon's desk. She liked to do this in the same way she sometimes liked to wear his shirts; it made her life feel bigger, as if she could not only have her own experiences but could share a good-sized portion of his as well. The few items he allowed on the desktop—a stapler, a tray of pencils and pens, a Rolodex, a small box of paper clips, and a halogen lamp— were arranged in a perfect row. She ran her palm over his laptop. What had he been doing in here with the door closed?

She opened the cover. The oversized screen stared dumbly back. She tapped a key to summon his account. "Password," it commanded. The cursor pulsed tauntingly. Well?

She tried their cat's name, his usual password; then his middle name; then the combination of their names they used when setting codes. The computer shook each attempt off impatiently. Could she keep trying forever or would the

machine freeze up, like an ATM? She slid open the desk drawers and observed, not entirely without smugness, that, as usual,
the inside of his desk was a jumble. She pushed aside pencil
shavings and gum wrappers to sift through sketches, receipts,
to-do lists and half-filled notebooks. She found an appointment
book, but it was a year old.

Through the oak tree, the study had a clear view of the street.
Next door, Michael Murphy raked the blades of grass he'd slain
into piles, while Olga Murphy's behind emerged from a bank of
hostas. A woman ran by, her ponytail sweeping her neck like a
pendulum. Ginny missed running. She could never say so to Jon,
or to anyone for that matter, for fear that he might hear of it and
feel guilty. It was unfair that because he unreasonably insisted on,
indulged in his guilt, she could never express regret, could never
admit aloud that the accident had changed her at all, could not
fear that it may have deprived her of a child, could not even complain about the way the chlorine in the Y's pool was ruining her
hair, lest he be moved to think about why she could not run.

She turned from the window. She had work to do, clients to
see, her own garden to maintain. He'd left a pen lying on his
desk. Willfully, she disarranged other objects, moving the stapler forward, angling the pencil tray, scattering paper clips over
the surface. She shut off the air conditioner and slid open some
windows. Might as well keep the house the way she preferred it.

Where had she left the pruning shears? On the washer. And
her gloves? Never mind. She slipped into her clogs and stepped
back out into the heavy heat. Better to be doing something purposeful, rather than paddling in circles, waiting.

The clematis had begun to curl runners around the legs of
the bistro chairs and the creeping thyme had crept over the
flagstones in several places. She really should move some of
that to the back, but she was inclined to let it spread as it
pleased. Plants in this climate had so short a time to flourish

before the frost crushed them. She was happiest in her garden in these weeks of messy, headlong, irrepressible burgeoning, as it built toward its August climax. This was the time when the sunflower stalks were thrusting recklessly, ridiculously high, but had not yet lifted their heads, and the lilies were spreading open their pointed petals. She ran her palm over the soft spikes of a pot of rosemary and was welcomed by a wave of scent. It was best that she'd not had to spend the hours of this summer day away from her garden. There would be so few.

There were her gloves on the edge of the little wheelbarrow!

The sudden roar of the Lipkes' mower startled her and she stood back to look down the street. Was that Jon's car? No. She waved at Olga Murphy, who was now clipping the grass that grew too close to the trunks of the trees for a mower to handle. The Murphys disapproved, she knew, of the jungle she'd made of the yard, were fearful of the bees it attracted, of the sort of upstart person it implied she must be; she could tell by the wary, tight-lipped looks they gave her house. "Your yard is so different," Olga had once said.

Between the bellow of the neighbor's mower and the bite of her spade in the soil, she missed the sound of her own phone ringing. It was Olga's shout that finally got her attention. "Phone!" the woman shouted, her hands cupped around her mouth. She made little stabbing motions in the air toward Ginny's open window.

Ginny ran, stripping off her gloves as she went, kicking off her clogs as she pulled the front door open. "Hi!" she panted, lifting the phone. And then, more calmly, she repeated, "Hi." Her voice was contrite, soothing as butter. It had to be Jon.

The answer was low; the accent unabashedly upper Midwest. It was a deceptive accent, Ginny knew. It made people sound simple, when they were anything but.

"Virginia? Walter Fleischer here."

three

Jon had driven whichever way he encountered the fewest barriers, turning right when the light was red, choosing always the fastest lane, the air-conditioning and classic rock blasting. This method finally set him shooting west on commercial University Avenue, past the peppering of little stores that were distinctly Madison's—the Wisconsin-based spice shop, the shoe store smothered in patchouli, the artisanal bakery, the coffeehouse smugly dissociated from the ubiquitous chain, the Thai restaurant that featured vegetables grown by local Hmong farmers. And then past the mall, set almost parklike within its border of trees, anchored by the grocery and department stores that could be found in any number of places in the upper Midwest. On his right, a big brown Yukon with a vanity plate—EZRYDRR—and an antiwar bumper sticker kept pace with him mile after mile. Finally, the office- and building-supply stores, red, yellow, blue, and green, like a giant child's giant blocks, rose from fields of baking asphalt. He envisioned the open country that lay beyond those stores, imagined driving on, freeing himself for an hour or two, if not from himself, at least from the emotions and expectations and dependencies and desires he'd snarled in town.

Just ahead, a woman and a girl of about eight or nine waited patiently on their bikes at the edge of a white-painted crossing for a lull in the traffic. The road was way too busy for a cross-walk and should a little girl like that be riding anywhere near moving cars? He pressed hard on the brake and stopped, glancing quickly into his mirror to make sure no one was about to barrel into him from behind.

The woman was the washed-out, no-frills type. Her graying blond hair was pushed behind her ears and a faded pink T-shirt hung shapelessly from her thin shoulders. She could have been a pioneer wife or one of those dust bowl women Dorothea Lange photographed during the Depression. But her smile, meant to thank him, was luminous. He nodded at her and felt a sort of glow watching the little girl struggle to start pedaling, her front tire wobbling for a moment before she gained momentum and cleared his car. It was nothing, of course, but it was pleasant all the same to be the one who was holding back traffic for them.

The horn blast behind him made him jump in his seat, so that he nearly lifted his foot from the brake.

"What the . . . ?" The words flew from his mouth almost involuntarily, and he twisted to look out the back window.

Behind him, EZRYDRR leaned on the horn again. One long, two short, one long again. An aggressive, arrogant, entirely self-ish sound.

Jon slammed the transmission into park, threw open his door, and grabbed the steering wheel and the doorframe to hurl himself from the car. EZRYDRR sat on his high perch, his jaw working over a wad of gum, his eyes obscured by wraparound sunglasses. He was in his forties, Jon guessed, polo shirt over a square chest, bald. He was holding his hands out, palms up, on either side of his shoulders and he thrust his chin forward like a turtle. His lips moved behind his sealed window: "What the fuck?"

He was broader than Jon, although definitely softer. His upper arms were sausage-like, and there was a suggestion of breasts beneath his shirt. He might have been shorter, although it was impossible to tell while he was sitting in his car. Jon approached the window. He raised his hand to tap on the glass and then thought the better of it. Kyle had been charged with assault once for kicking a tire.

Instead, he stood with his arms folded, waiting.

The guy frowned, thrust his face forward again. "What?" he barked.

Jon could hear him through the glass now. He waited.

Finally, the guy pressed the button and the window opened about four inches. "What the fuck are you doing?"

"Why were you honking at me?"

"What?" His voice was loud now.

Jon stepped closer to the door. He pushed his own face forward, nearly into the open rectangle that framed the man's fleshy head. It was a relief to shout, to let the anger rush up from his gut and down from his brain and spew hot and shining like molten gold. "I said, why the fuck were you honking at me?"

The door opened so quickly Jon barely had time to step back to avoid being slammed in the chest. EZRYDRR was wearing running shoes, ankle-high white socks, and khaki shorts, but he was taller than Jon had guessed. He stepped in close, so that Jon had to tilt his chin slightly back to keep his eyes locked on the blue-gray lenses of the wraparounds. He smelled of Old Spice and sweat and McDonald's French fries and the gum, wintergreen. "Get away from my truck," he said, loud.

Other cars were honking now.

"It's a crosswalk, dickhead. People were crossing the fucking street." Jon enunciated each word deliberately. His arms were taut as stretched rubber bands; he longed to send those sunglasses skittering over the asphalt. But he controlled himself, even held his arms slightly back.

Suddenly, EZRYDRR raised both hands and gave a stiff little push with his fingertips against Jon's chest, and then in two steps he was back behind the wheel of the Yukon. "Learn to drive," he said before slamming the door.

"Learn some fucking manners!" Jon shouted after him. Not the most satisfying comeback, but something at least. He threw one finger toward the guy and EZRYDRR returned the salute without even glancing in Jon's direction as he backed up to give himself space, spun the wheel, and pulled away.

Jon got back into his own car. His hands trembled slightly from a surfeit of adrenaline. Best to pull into a parking lot for a few minutes and settle down. You'd think it would be different in a town like Madison, but they were swarming all over the place, the people who behaved however they goddamn well pleased, no matter what it did to the rest of the world.

And what was this? He rolled the window down and gingerly fingered a crack that split the side mirror in two. He must've caught it against the garage doorframe when he'd barreled out. It was a small thing; the mirror still worked. He told himself he could get it fixed the next time the car was in for servicing, no big deal. But it struck him, nevertheless, as a terrible thing that an hour ago it had been whole, a perfect silver rectangle, and he had since wantonly destroyed it. He closed his eyes against the despair that heaved inside him and pressed his forehead against the steering wheel.

The mechanical melody emanating from his pocket startled him, as it inevitably did. He fumbled the phone out and noted the number.

"Hey." His voice was a caress. It was all right, maybe, after all. "I'm glad you called."

"I'm glad you answered." Freddi's voice was light, playful. She'd established that as the predominant tone of their relationship. "I'll get serious, when you're serious" was what she'd said, and he could see why she had to take that attitude, although the way she consistently shook off his sincerity, like a terrier fresh from a bath, could be tiresome.

"What are you doing today?" He ran his free hand through his hair as he talked and sat up straight against the seat. He felt as if he were being put back together.

"Oh, I thought I'd do the farmers' market and then, I don't know. I've had a few offers for this afternoon."

"Oh, you've had a few offers, have you?"

"Yes, I have. I just need to choose from among my many suitors."

"Pick me. Pick me."

"I thought you were busy."

There was a trace of bitterness in her tone. He knew he had to swallow it.

"Well, now it seems I'm not."

She said nothing.

"What if I just came over? We could have a cup of coffee."

The light tone was back. "A rich, steaming lake of coffee?"

They'd worked together on a campaign for a local coffee brand. A rich, steaming lake of coffee had been one of their inexplicably hilarious late-night rejects.

"A rapidly boiling ocean of coffee."

She laughed. "All right. I don't know about the rest of the day, but you can come over. For coffee," she added in an obvious vixenish way that made him laugh but also aroused him instantly.

When they hung up, the thought of Ginny at home, waiting, deflated him. What was he doing, screwing things up like this? But she wasn't at home, was she? Or at least she wouldn't be for long. She'd had appointments to keep. He frowned. Normally, he tried not to think of Ginny at all when he was with Freddi. Anyway, he couldn't call back and cancel with Freddi now. Not after he'd made such a big deal in the first place about not seeing her this weekend. He imagined her opening the door, standing there, smiling, pleased to see him, in love with him. He wanted it badly. He needed it. This would be the last time, he promised himself, one last good day together and then he'd tell her they had to take a break, so he could get his head straight, figure out what he wanted, what was the right thing.

How had he let his car get so dirty? A nearly empty water bottle—Ginny's—lay cloudy with condensation on the passenger-side floor. He picked that up and fished a gum wrapper from between the seat and the gearshift. When he opened the glove compartment for a wipe to dust the dashboard, maps and menus, napkins, receipts, expired insurance cards, and coupons tried to make a break for it. He crammed them back with one hand and shut the door with the other.

To tell a good lie, you had to believe it yourself. They said that a lot, he and Kaiser and Patterson and Freddi, the people at work who were his friends because they were a little cynical—OK, a lot cynical—the way he was. They talked about the problem with advertising all the time. They agreed that it was one of the few fields in which creative people could use their talents to earn real money—as Kaiser said, who else would hire someone

idiot enough to major in philosophy?—but, except for the occasional pro bono project, you were always pushing things like
interest-earning checking accounts or clothes-dryer vents, nothing exactly objectionable, but nothing you could believe in. "I'm
not saying I want to change the world or anything," he'd said to
Freddi, affecting a jadedness he didn't feel, over their very first
lunch (at a Middle Eastern place he'd chosen for its exoticness
and because he liked the owner—the food was mediocre at best),
"but I hate the idea that my loftiest goal is to herd more customers into that bank over there." He gestured with his pita
bread toward the brown-brick institution visible through the
plate glass, which happened to be one of their client's branches.

"I know," Freddi had agreed, flattening her rice with the
back of her fork, as if playing in a tiny sandbox. "I know exactly
what you mean." Freddi had seriously considered joining the
Peace Corps after college and she planned eventually to work
for a nonprofit. But not for a while. "You can accomplish a lot
more in the nonprofit world when you've got private-sector
experience under your belt," she'd explained.

Jon used to complain about his work to Ginny, too. To her, in
fact, he'd never pretended jadedness but confessed that he
longed to do something more meaningful. "Like what?" she'd
said. Which had made him feel ridiculous because he didn't
know. He only knew that advertising wasn't it. Several times
then she'd suggested he quit his job and try this or that. She had
ideas. She thought he might be an artist. Or maybe he wanted to
run an arts program for disadvantaged kids. Or be an art thera-
pist. As well as being an artist, of course. She insisted they could
sell the house and make do on what she could earn until he got
reestablished.

"This is the rest of your life, Jon. You helped me find my
calling. I want to do the same for you."

Of course, he'd never taken her up on that. Quitting a good job without prospects wasn't the way real people, adult people, lived. The trouble was she'd known him before he was an adult, back when he had, indeed, talked modestly but earnestly about becoming a painter. It pained him to remember that serious, unsophisticated boy, whose admiration had clung to the most obvious objects—El Greco, van Gogh, Cézanne, Picasso—based on faded plates he'd studied in library books. Back then, he'd believed the coolest job in the world was designing album covers, for Christ's sake. How vulnerable and foolish he'd been with his big dreams and his profound ignorance.

Well, he knew better now. The first time he'd been passed over for creative director he'd been disappointed, but he could hardly feel insulted. Rich Seymour had been a seasoned guy, with ten years of experience running creative at ICG. "You can count on Jon," Mike Nielson had said to Seymour, hanging a hand on Jon's shoulder in a way that made him want to twitch, "to be a team player." Jon had actually felt proud of that at the time, idiot that he was. But when Seymour hadn't worked out, they'd promoted that slick, hip, entirely talentless asshole Jimmy Ryan.

"Nielson might as well be firing me," he'd said to Kaiser. "It's clear my kind of work means shit to this agency."

"The point is," Kaiser had counseled him, "they didn't fire you. That means you've got an opportunity here to do something big, something daring. Push the envelope, Jon-Boy! Develop that Jazz Age concept you had for Breakneck. If Nielson doesn't go for it, at least you've got something to show Kelsey and White or ICG what you're capable of. As I see it— and I know, I know, you've heard all this from me before—but you just play it too safe. You've gotta be out there once in a while."

Jon had shrugged. It had been a bleak day, he remembered, the sky, the frozen grass, the bare twigs all various shades of gray. They were walking to an early lunch, lunch with a drink or two, because he couldn't hang around after he'd heard the news, news they hadn't even had the courtesy to break to him ahead of time in private. Nielson hadn't even bothered with the "team player" crap this time. "And if I'd been 'out there,' you'd be saying now that I should've played it safe," Jon said. "I'm just not Mike Nielson's guy, that's all. It's just not in me to play those games. But I thought—"

"What? Talent will out? Talent and the fact that you're a nice guy? Talent and nice, my friend, will get you squat."

Ginny had wanted him to quit immediately. "I can't stand the idea of your working another minute for people who don't appreciate you," she'd said, her face flushed with anger.

It had gratified him to hear this, but he knew that in the end he would stay. He was a responsible husband. He wanted to be a responsible father to the child they were trying to conceive.

1963

Bud won't meet her eyes when he comes in, just goes straight for the refrigerator and pulls out a beer, so Marie knows he hasn't done it.

She concentrates on the seam she's started sewing. It's hard to push the cloth through at a steady pace, and she wants the curtains to look nice. They're only renting this place until Bud goes pro, but it's still important to make it decent. There. She cuts the threads and swivels to face him.

"Well?"

"Well what?"

"You know well what, Bud."

He takes a long pull from the bottle, wipes his mouth with the back of his hand.

"Oh, for God's sake," she says. "Don't be disgusting."

He's normally a well-mannered man. That's one of the things

she admires about him. He stares at her defiantly and then trains his gaze out the front window. Outside the trees drip into the lake. The sky is soft and gray like soiled cotton. The water lies still and steel-colored.

"You didn't do anything?"

She might as well have loosened the needle from the machine and pierced his flesh with it, her words are that angry, but he stands staring out as if he hadn't felt the least prick, telling himself the story. "He said that wasn't how it was. It was a loving thing, he said. He was crying, Marie. That's how bad he felt."

She can imagine it, his full lips quivering. His dark lashes clumped with tears. The image makes her want to spit.

"He couldn't believe she'd say it was like that, the way she was on him, her fingers all over, her tongue." He clears his throat. "He said he would have been afraid to try anything with her if she hadn't made clear she wanted it, her being such a pretty girl."

From Marie's throat comes a strangled, choking sound.

"He couldn't believe she'd say it was like that," he repeats, "unless it was…" He pauses. "Unless she had to say it, had to think it that way, so she wouldn't feel like a whore."

"Hattie is not a whore!"

"Of course, she's not. It's just, if she felt like she did something she shouldn't of, maybe she would rather it was done to her, you know, forced on her. Like it wasn't her doing. It explains why she says it that way."

"Bud, he raped her. That explains why she says he raped her."

He sighs. "I just don't know for sure. The way he says it—"

She doesn't let him finish. "The way he says it is a lie and he is a liar. And that you don't know that by now, that you can't see that Walt Fleischer is a snake and a criminal, a rapist criminal… Well, it's just pitiful. That you believe garbage over your own wife!"

"I don't believe him over you! It's your friend Hattie I don't know if I can believe. She's always been a blamer, Marie, as far as I know."

She wants to tell him that he doesn't know anything, but he's right that Hattie tends to fault others. She's told Marie privately, for instance, that if Clark had even "fought for her for one second" when Walt had started in, she'd never have gone with Walt in the first place, which was hardly fair to Clark. But there's something about Hattie's sweet helplessness that makes people want to help her—people like her and like Clark, anyway. She's surprised, but, she has to admit, gratified that Bud seems immune to Hattie's charms.

Still, Hattie has been her friend since freshman year, when they were the only ones in their English class who liked, who even finished reading The Scarlet Letter. Hattie, instantly popular in high school because—Walt is right—she is so pretty, had been the one who drew Marie into the "social" group, the group from which the kings and queens and class presidents were chosen, the group that had no one to fear, not even the teachers. Of course, by force of personality, Marie would have gotten there eventually, but it would have taken longer; she would have lost precious years, and therefore might never have been in a position to claim Bud. She understands her debt to Hattie, and besides, she's genuinely fond of her, and besides, this isn't all about Hattie.

She closes her teeth tightly to stop her tongue and holds her hands over her face so she can think. She'd counted on Bud's temper, on the fact that he knew how to give a beating when it was deserved. She'd seen him fight other guys over insults and injustices much smaller than this one and leave them bloody and hurting, bruised and humiliated, the way she wants to see Walt.

But he doesn't like to fight; she knows that. He fights when he has to, when he can't help himself, his blood burns so. And she'd been crazy to think he'd be able to see through Walt. *Walter Flei-scher has fooled plenty of people with more suspicious natures. Like Hattie. Like herself.* In any case, seeing through people isn't in Bud's nature. That's another thing she loves about him: he believes people are good. Well, she knows better and that will be enough. She can make it be enough.

"Honey, it's OK," she says now, going to him, wrapping her arms around him, enfolding him as well as she can, with his being so much bigger than she. "If you weren't sure, you were right not to do anything."

"I'm sorry." He turns and presses his mouth into her neck. "If he did, I don't like to think——"

"Shhh." She strokes his hair. It's cut so short it looks rough, but it's smooth to the touch, like mouse fur. "We'll wait 'til we're sure. He's your friend, after all. You have to be sure."

four

"Listen, I've got to go," Freddi said into her cordless phone.

When Jon drove up, she was standing on the little balcony that overlooked the street and Lake Monona beyond, flicking maple monkeys off the rail with her index finger as she talked, so she saw his car even before he turned off the engine. Had she really been on the phone so long? The voice in her ear continued, but she interrupted. "I really have to go now. No, I do. Seriously. Of course, I'm remembering. Five o'clock. Of course, I'll be there. But right now I have to go. No, goodbye. Goodbye."

She was in the bathroom by the time she'd severed the connection. She brushed her teeth and ran water over her fingers and pushed them through her sleep-flattened hair, hating herself for it. She wasn't the sort of woman who fussed about her looks, but this relationship made her act like a teenager, primping in the girls' room in the hope she'd pass her crush in the hall. She'd pleaded with him for this weekend and he'd said no. And now, here he was. Which she wanted, but she hated that she'd wanted it. And had begged for it. This whole relationship was driving her crazy. Her nails were a mess, and she hadn't bitten her nails since college.

Another thirty seconds and she was out of her stained robe and into a tank top and shorts, running a palm quickly over her shin to check for stubble. And who cared if she had hairy legs? She would flaunt them. He wasn't supposed to be here, and, after all, he didn't love her for the smoothness of her skin. Her legs weren't too bad, though, thank goodness. But her hair! God! Why hadn't she jumped in the shower the moment he'd told her he was coming over? She grabbed a baseball cap and crammed it over the mess. Fine. Cute, in fact. Whatever!

She was standing in the kitchen, pouring herself coffee with deliberate casualness, when the bell rang. She carried the full mug with her to force herself to move slowly and set it carefully on the occasional table she kept inside the door for keys and outgoing mail.

Obviously, he could hear her. He drummed his fingers softly on the door, the signal they used when passing one another's office, fingertips kissing, in that case, the glass. "It's I," that tapping announced—one, two, three, four—"your secret lover."

She remembered, just as she opened the door, that she'd forgotten to shave under her arms. "Hi," she said, gripping her elbows and pressing them tight against her ribs.

Before he stepped in and fit his mouth to hers, he smiled at her in that quizzical way he had, the way she'd tried once in a moment of weakness to describe to Andrea over beers and a plate of fried cheese curds they'd ordered to be fun and to prove that occasionally they didn't care about prissy, girlish things like health and weight. "It's something about his eyes," she'd said. "The way he holds me with them."

"They all have eyes," Andrea had said scornfully. "That's how they get you."

Andrea's latest boyfriend had just turned out to be a real jerk, like all the others, so Freddi had let it go, even though she knew in a month or so she'd have to smile and nod and wow over Andrea's reports of some other guy's adorably crooked teeth and banal witticisms.

She closed her own eyes, slid her fingers into his hair, and pulled his mouth, his face, against her own. She was climbing him then, her leg wrapping around his thigh, her arms straining at his shoulders, and he lifted her, his hands sliding up, firm and sure beneath her shirt, and carried her backward into the apartment, down the hall, the open door forgotten behind them. Above her bed, the fan whirred hysterically. Their sweaty skins squeaked as they rubbed against each other. She didn't think about where he should have been or how long he would stay. She let herself think only about this.

"When are you going to get AC?" he complained when they'd spread themselves far away from each other and were touching only fingertip to fingertip.

"I told you. Not until I move."

When Freddi had moved into this place seven years ago, she'd had no strong feelings about the apartment. She was in love with its tenant, a mountain-biking, cross-country-skiing, outdoorsy type, who agreed that it was silly of them to pay two rents when they were always together anyway. A month after they'd squeezed her rattan couch and circle chair up the narrow stairs, his employer sent him to Seattle for what was supposed to have been four months. He'd taken with him to the Northwest only a backpack's worth of clothes and his bike, but then he took up sea kayaking and began to talk about oyster varietals in a way that, from a distant Midwestern city, sounded ridiculous. He didn't tell her that his contract had been extended until two

weeks after he'd signed it. He asked her to join him, and she
flew out for a week's worth of interviews, but the rain depressed
her; she froze the afternoon he took her kayaking; and oysters
on the half shell made her gag. Eventually they—first she, but
soon enough he—realized they were no more than good
friends. "I think a lasting friendship is more valuable than a
brief love affair," she'd insisted to Andrea, who'd replied that he
and she would not be friends for long.

Andrea, in this case, turned out to be right, for while still
friendly, they were no longer friends in any valuable way. Gradually, in fact, Freddi came to believe they never truly had been,
and she viewed the apartment as evidence of this. While he had
chosen and loved the place for its creaky quirkiness—its sloping
floors and heavy, crooked, wood-framed windows, its rickety
stairs and jury-rigged shower—she'd despised it. Despised it
but hadn't realized that fact until she'd turned thirty. That was
the scary part, the part she and Andrea had spent several pleasurable evenings scrutinizing.

"It's like I had no mind of my own back then, like my skull
was a vacuum waiting to suck up the boyfriend's opinions." She
put the term "the boyfriend" in quotation marks with her voice
to indicate that she didn't mean a particular boyfriend. She
meant any boyfriend, all boyfriends. She'd been anti–nuclear
power because of one boyfriend and became a vegetarian
because of another. She'd turned up her nose at *Citizen Kane*
because a boyfriend had thought Orson Welles was overrated.
"And it would be one thing," she'd said to Andrea, "if I'd recognized that I was following them. But I didn't, not at all. I always
convinced myself that we simply agreed. And that our agreeing
meant we had a terrific relationship!"

"If two people truly love each other," Andrea had said, sipping delicately at a Seven and Seven through a swizzle straw, "it
doesn't matter if they disagree about everything."

It was a little irritating to hear Andrea, who had once dyed her hair solely because some man liked the idea of dating a redhead, deliver this as if she were bestowing pearls of wisdom polished at her own throat, but Freddi thought she was probably right.

Now she stared out her bedroom window where leaves hung in thick swags, nearly touching the glass. Even as a child, Freddi had found the exuberant growth, the chaotic and excessive sprouting and thickening, the sheer bullying green push of the Wisconsin summer, disturbing, almost frightening. She preferred the clean angles, the openness and clarity of winter. She despised secrecy and indirectness, and yet here she was, hiding in a back room, not daring even to ask her lover his intentions for the rest of the morning, let alone the rest of their lives. She felt resentment, like a geyser, rising in her chest as she reminded herself that she could not count on anything with him. She sprang off the bed.

"Where are you going?" His eyes were nearly closed. He, the one with all the power, all the control, could relax.

His somnolence infuriated her, but with an effort she kept her answer breezy. She even smiled. "About my business. I've got to get some things done today."

He pushed himself up until he was sitting with his back against the pillows. "I thought . . ." He hesitated.

So she'd surprised him. Good. "What?"

"Well, I don't want to screw up your plans."

They'd had this out. He was not to assume, she'd said, in the straightforward, not shrill, not whiny, not bitter nor angry tone she'd practiced with Andrea, that she was free to cavort—she'd thrown that word in at the last minute—with him whenever he happened to have some spare hours. She, too, had a life to lead. She wasn't just lying around like a glass-eyed doll, waiting for him to decide it was time to play.

She hadn't rehearsed the last sentence with Andrea, although she'd expressed it and many sentiments like it under her breath in the grocery aisles, behind the wheel of her car, loading laundry into the machine, and in myriad other venues. That line came out bitter and angry. She couldn't help it.

But he'd understood. For weeks, Freddi had savored the unexpected minutes that had followed her anger. He'd looked pained, stricken even, and cast down his brown, intriguingly slanted eyes. "Of course, you're right. You're right," he'd said. "I'm sorry. I should have thought, been more aware . . ." She didn't interrupt him. Such a show of emotion, especially involving the eyes, which appeared even to be dampening, was the stuff that sustained her through lean evenings and weekends. "It's just that I want to be with you so badly. All the time." He sat down then on the couch, or really let himself nearly collapse onto it, and lowered his face into his hands. "Listen," he said, looking up at her finally. His eyes, yes, definitely damp now, tenderly searched her face as he spoke, as if he was both hopeful and fearful of her response. "I know you don't want to talk about this. I know we said we wouldn't talk about it, until I was ready to make a change. But I just want to say"—he held his hand up to stop her objections, although she hadn't been about to make any—"that I love you. I know it's hard for you to believe because I'm not with you, but it's true. It's just that I've been with my wife for such a long time." He hardly ever used Ginny's name, Freddi had noticed. Was that a good sign? Or a bad one? "So, it's hard, you know? She's had things happen to her . . . she's been hurt. I don't want to hurt her again."

Freddi had looked away. She'd stared at the pattern in the throw pillow, an Escher-like optical illusion of brown geese against a cream sky or cream geese against a brown one. We've all been hurt, she wanted to say, *I've* been hurt. It hurts me to hear about the "long time" you've had with her. The things she knows that I can never know. Why doesn't anyone worry about not hurting me? But she bit her tongue.

He grabbed both of her hands and slid off the couch, so he was kneeling at her feet. "It's different with you," he said. "*I'm* different with you. You've just got to know how special you are to me. You've just got to believe me!"

And she did believe him! Still, when Andrea phoned, Freddi had evaded her questions. She'd told herself that she wanted to treasure Jon's opalescent speech for herself, but even then, the very next day, she'd known that she also feared sharp-eyed Andrea might prick those sentiments like a soap bubble. Certainly she knew that Andrea would shake her head over his attachment to his wife, but Freddi appreciated it. After all, she didn't want to love a heartless man. If he needed to stay with Ginny for a while, she could endure it. As long as she, Freddi, was his real love. And that's what he'd said, hadn't he? That she was the special one? Too soon she was no longer certain; she'd stroked his words so often that they'd begun to fray around the edges.

She wished she'd asked him that afternoon to describe exactly how it was different with her.

"I was going to take Ginny to Summerfest today," he said now. "I thought I owed her. I've been so distracted lately. Thinking about you."

"So why are you here?" She tried to keep her voice neutral. Since the beginning, they'd talked a lot about what he owed Ginny, and for a while, such discussions had pleased her. They assured her that he was honorable, for one thing. And they'd made her feel that he and she, Freddi, were the team, with Ginny the odd woman out. She'd even suggested things he might do for his wife; she wanted, after all, for both of them to do this fairly, compassionately. But it was starting to seem that no matter what he did, his debt to Ginny never diminished.

"Oh, we had a fight. I may have started it. I'm not sure. This fighting, this feeling guilty; I can't take much more of this."

He couldn't take much more! When she was the one who had to fit her life into a few stolen, vacant cracks of someone else's.

"I don't want us to be together because you had a fight," she said. "You should go home."

"You think?" He sat up, swung his feet off the bed. "Yeah. Maybe you're right."

She turned away. Sighed. She couldn't help it: she clicked her tongue disapprovingly against the roof of her mouth. "Yeah. OK. Bye."

"Hey, I thought this is what you wanted me to do."

"It's what I think you should do. That doesn't mean I have to like it."

He put his arms around her and began to press against her, to burrow into the flesh of her behind. She could feel him stiffening, herself softening. "Fuck that," he said. They laughed. "I'd rather do what you'd like."

"Why don't we go?" she said suddenly.

"What do you mean?"

He looked nervous. Did he think she was proposing they go together to his house? "To Summerfest. I've never been. I think it's time I was exposed to that piece of my cultural heritage."

Exposed. That was what she wanted. At least sometimes it was. Sometimes she wished they'd just go ahead and get caught, get it over with so they could move on, one way or the other.

But what if they moved on one way and not the other? Or what if she got what she wanted? Then she'd be responsible for some other woman's unhappiness.

"What you don't seem to understand is that it's her or you now," Andrea said. "Why is her happiness more important than yours?"

five

When Walter Fleischer had called for the first time about two months ago, Ginny had had to scramble to reorient herself in that old world. She'd been an eighteen-year-old hostess at the country-club restaurant when she'd last spoken to him, and then only to say "Hello, Mr. Fleischer" and show him to a seat in his own establishment. Why would he be calling her?

She'd felt, too, that out of loyalty to Jon, she ought not to talk to him; she ought to hang up the phone. Better yet, she should say something cutting about her disinclination to have anything to do with him—he had, after all, as much as ruined Jon's family. But, in the end, she couldn't bear to be impolite, and so she waited through his talk, interjecting murmurs of acknowledgment and agreement from time to time, so as to ease her own awkwardness.

Did she remember the little nine-hole golf course? He was

developing that land, building "very exclusive residences." The smallest lot would be two acres; the houses would be architecturally distinct. He planned to preserve the clubhouse. It had hardly been touched since the 1930s, except for the addition of that hideous green-and-gold carpeting, which was coming right out, so all the place would need was some refurbishing, some updating of the systems—copper pipes, two-twenty voltage. Anyway, that wouldn't concern her. He was also adding a pool with a slate deck, six tennis courts, and a lawn for croquet or boccie ball. Had she heard of boccie ball? It was the new craze, apparently, that's what they told him.

She'd half suspected senility, until it became clear that he intended she should do the landscaping for the project.

Oh, no. Obviously, she couldn't. Again the opportunity arose for the cutting remark. But she prevaricated. She was awfully busy at the moment, so many projects under way and in the queue. She was just too overbooked.

He understood. He was very disappointed to hear it, but he understood. Could she possibly, though, as a very great favor to the man who had given her her first job, visit the site? At her convenience, of course. Just for a consultation, a one-time thing, to give him a sense of the direction he should take. He would feel so much more confident about the whole project if he had the opinion of an expert who truly understood the area, a local girl made good, a woman who maybe even loved the place as much as he did. Who would be as sorry as he to see it lose its character, which was, admittedly, very likely in the face of development, unless it was done very, very carefully.

He took a gamble. For all he knew, she had no attachment to the place of her childhood. For all he knew, she wanted to keep well away from that town and particularly from that specific treacherous piece of land. But, in fact, she was perversely drawn to it. She dreamed of its clipped dark-green expanse under a summer evening sky, of its hummocks, like the remains of an ancient fortress. She dreamed of the deep, weedy bowl that protected the first green like a moat. If she could somehow do it over, how easy it would be not to fall.

What she hated were the developments, which had transformed the fields and woodlands and marshes into miles and miles of sweeping, soulless, centerless exurbia. She'd met Walter Fleischer at the golf course the following week for one meeting, propelled by the desire to do whatever she could to minimize the damage his plans would certainly cause.

He looked better in his sixties than he had in his forties, she thought, as he came toward her on that windy April day. His body had changed from squat to dapper, and his features, always too large for his face, had softened. He no longer had what she'd always considered a slightly lascivious look. Although it may have been she who had changed, Ginny realized. Maybe it was she who felt more at ease, less threatened by a man's regard.

"Virginia!" he exclaimed, taking her hand in both of his own. "I'm so happy you came."

"I wanted to see it again." She'd intended to stay cool, brusquely businesslike. She couldn't put out of her mind how hurt and angry Jon would be if he knew she was helping Walter Fleischer.

What she'd told herself was that she would not, in fact, be helping Mr. Fleischer at all. She'd be thwarting him to the best of her abilities. What she'd suggest would probably not attract the sort of people he needed to buy his houses. It would certainly not maximize his profits. She was sure it would not be what he wanted to hear.

He gestured toward the old clubhouse. "It's changed, hasn't it?" His tone was wistful.

He was right. She remembered the place as brightness, the buildings so white that at night they seemed to glow; the grass so brilliantly green that it might have been plastic. And she remembered it as noise, the screen door incessantly slamming, car engines flaring, tires rumbling over the gravel lot. It was desolate now. The sides of the building had been used for target practice. The paint and the wood beneath it was gray.

"Remember those window boxes you did? The geraniums and the lobelia and the ivy? My father loved those. 'So Bavarian,' he said."

Unbelievable that he would remember those. She'd lobbied for the chance to fill the boxes and had been very proud of her work at the time, although she hadn't thought of that juvenile effort in more than a decade.

"So you've obviously come a long way since window boxes," he said. "I saw you won some big award for one of your designs."

"You did?"

"Well," he said sheepishly, "after I saw your name in that *Madison Magazine* piece on gardens, I Googled you. Just to see what else you'd done, if you had a Web site. I was impressed. Especially with your use of native plants."

"Well . . . thank you."

"See, that's what I have in mind for here. Preserve what woodlands we've got and then maybe put in a prairie. Sort of in the center of everything. Like the village green, except not squared off, of course."

They were skirting the bowl, now overgrown with honeysuckle and box elder, that had made the first hole tricky. On the far side, the old green was still faintly visible, the growth pattern of the grass and thistle that covered it slightly different from that which surrounded it. Behind them, through the trees, the lake glowed in blue snippets outlined in black branches like an expanse of stained glass.

And there was the slope the flatbed trailer had been heading down, obediently following the tractor, tilting at such an angle that everyone was screaming in happy terror. A bottle had rolled off—there'd been a keg; who would have a bottle?—but she remembered a bottle distinctly, dark-brown glass, tipping over the edge just beyond her hand, landing safely whole upon the thickly growing weeds, but then exploding under the tractor's wheel, the pieces flying every way like shrapnel.

"What do you think of that idea?" he was saying.

"A prairie? I think a prairie would be perfect. You'd want to get a good mix of flowering plants—bee balm and Indian paintbrush. Actually, I know where you could get some wonderful seeds." They were past the bowl now and the vista of what had once been the rest of the course opened before them. "You really want to put in a prairie? What sort of developer are you?" she joked.

"I always hated golf," he said. Here in the open, the sharp, damp wind overwhelmed the weak April sun. "It was my mother's game, you know. I think my father hoped I'd take after her, but I was always a lousy player, dismal when it came to athletics, a disappointment to him." He smiled at her, ruefully. "He loved the course itself, the perfection of it, the way it could be tamed and groomed, kept just so, not a blade out of place." He swept one hand through the air, Carol Merrill style, indicating the whole of it—the matted grasses and briars, the volunteer trees and patches of thistle and burdock. "Nature always has the last word, doesn't it?" He paused. "Anyway, to answer your question . . ." He cleared his throat and said in a pretentious, self-mocking tone that made Ginny laugh, "I'm the sort of developer who would like to retain the wild quality of the meadows and the stands of oak and hickory, the red vistas of dogwood and sumac, the smatterings of sugar maples."

Ginny had always found ludicrous the idea that Jon's mother

had once been so attracted to this ugly man that she'd cheated on her husband, but she was beginning to understand it better. She reminded herself that it had been an affair, so Marie had been as much to blame as Walter, or maybe no one was really to blame, or everyone, including Bud, who ever knew the real story behind an affair? She could feel desire for this work—she would never have another chance like this!—licking at her like flames.

"Right here in my hand," Mr. Fleischer was saying now, over the phone, "I've finally got some of that preliminary material we talked about, some figures indicating lot sizes and a sketch of the proposed changes to the clubhouse. Just wanted to let you know, in case maybe you wanted to schedule some extra time over here this afternoon."

"Extra time? Well, actually . . ." She paused. Why not? Her day with Jon was ruined already, wasn't it? Even if he were to roll into the driveway right now, they would have to soldier through the raw period, then the debate over whether it was still worth going, by which time it wouldn't be. "Ya, sure," she said. She tended to slip into the accent herself when others were using it. "I've got nothing scheduled after our appointment."

"Oh, ya? That's great! That will be fine! Just fine!" He had a habit of booming, she'd noticed, when he was pleased.

Almost immediately, Fleischer's project had engrossed her. Well, that was the way she always worked, all-out, full-on sprint, the minute the gun went off. She'd quickly finished two other gardens to clear the decks and turned down three new ones. They were talking to a potential client today, but only because Nora had insisted and because it was Heidi Dubchek, Kaiser's ex.

Nora didn't approve of putting all their eggs in one basket. What if Fleischer folded? What if he fired them? And they needed to maintain their presence in Madison. Who cared about some little town thirty miles away where no one would ever see their work?

But Nora was not an equal in this business and Ginny was already devoting ninety percent of her time to Meadowwood. She'd spent many full days there, tramping around, getting a feel for the land, for the way the development would be laid out in relation to the sun, examining the spots where the water would naturally drain and where it would tend to bog, checking the health of the stands of red and white oaks that Walter had promised to preserve, collecting soil samples. Her happiness in this work was marred only by her fear of telling Jon where and for whom she was working. He might very well ask her to give it up, which she would understand but which she was deeply unwilling to do. It had been easier than she'd expected to hide it. He didn't seem curious at all lately about what she was doing with her time.

"Nora!" As soon as she hung up with Walter, Ginny called her friend. "Can you go out to Meadowwood with me this afternoon?"

"Meadowwood? Rodney, honey, don't . . . oh, Rodney, why would you do that? Hang on."

Ginny hung on.

She'd met Nora in her Wetlands Ecology class; Nora of the loose, long, springy hair—the kind Ginny's father called "bedroom hair"; Nora of the jingling sandals and jangling bangles;

Nora, who wore vintage slinky jeans that showed off her hips, while the rest of them still wore the style that primly cinched their waists. "Nora the Unkempt," Jon called her at first, and Ginny recognized and appreciated this as an attempt to tame Nora's obvious sensuality. Nora had chosen Madison for college, she told Ginny over vegetarian chili that first day, "for the radical politics," and hadn't realized until she'd arrived that she was about fifteen years too late.

"I picked Madison because my father worked at the capitol," Ginny offered. "It seemed like Madison was where you went, if you wanted to be an adult." She didn't add until she knew Nora much better that her father had insisted that she live at home and commute with him every day, not to save money but because he knew what went on in college dorms. And, being unable to buck his disapproval and his disappointment, she had, sick with disappointment herself, done as he wished for three years. "What can I do? Clark's paying my tuition," she'd argued to Jon (they called her father by his first name when they complained to each other about him). It wasn't the tuition, though, that kept her from bucking her father, or at least that factor was only superficial. She'd been afraid since the accident in high school, since she'd come to understand how easily she could be hurt, of pushing herself into the world. Staying at home, much as she hated the idea, was safe.

Within a year of their meeting, Ginny and Nora had agreed that they would be business partners. Ginny knew the horticulture and was good at translating people's errant notions into plant installations and hardscape. She could deduce, for example, from a woman's obsession with a particular wrought-iron bench, the vine-laden trellises and winding paths she craved, or from another's wedding picture, an affinity for neat, well-organized flower beds. "Something just like this," one client had said, opening a book to a photo of Versailles. Her design for him was as grand and formal as his tract ranch house could handle.

Inevitably, there were gaps between what people believed they desired and what Ginny knew would truly make them happy (and could thrive in zone 5). Those gaps were Nora's territory. Nora, cool-headed and confident, reassured customers, extracted energetic work from crews, finessed relationships with nurseries, and kept the irate from sowing salt and ruining the project before Ginny could see it through. Nora was also outgoing: she could come away from a trip to the grocery store with the names of two new clients in her purse.

"OK, I've tied him to the TV with a length of clothesline," she said now, having returned to the phone.

"I highly doubt that you own a clothesline, Nora."

"Well, with the lamp cord then. It'll give him something to stick in the outlet. So what do you want me to do?"

"Come out to the development with me after Heidi's."

Nora sighed. "Oh, Ginny. I've been meaning to call you all day."

"Don't tell me you can't go to Heidi's. I don't even want this job!"

"No, no. I can go. It's just that, well, Peter changed his mind about taking care of Rodney. He's got a pile of papers to grade by Monday and he just has to have the time to work. I've tried a couple of babysitters, but I'm not having any luck. Do you think we could take Rodney with us?"

"Of course, Rodney can come with us. He's a vital member of the team."

Being hobbled by a three-year-old was in some ways an asset, Ginny thought. Clients took them less seriously and expected less. They also assumed they wouldn't be charged the highest rate, but Ginny never felt comfortable asking top dollar for her work anyway.

"Does he need to come to Meadowwood too?"

"Well, I could ask . . ." Nora's voice trailed off uncertainly.

"No, just bring him."

When she married Peter and produced Rodney, Nora stopped being mistress of her own life. Peter's was the salary the family depended on, so no matter how poorly he managed his time, his work always came first. Ginny and Nora had long ago silently agreed to accept the comfortable fiction that it was Rodney who was doing his best to scuttle their business, or at least Nora's part in it.

So the day was going on then without Jon. She felt half shaky and half resolute as she washed her face and brushed her hair, transforming herself into the Ginny who made her way in the world. She stood still for a moment, trying to sense the onset of the monthly cramping she'd been expecting but did not feel. She pulled open the drawer beside the sink and looked again at the plastic wand sealed in its plastic bubble. She couldn't bring herself to open it either to confirm or uproot her suspicion.

Twenty years ago, her mother's hand had squeezed her own, competing with the soft current of the anesthesia for her attention. Her mouth had been so close to Ginny's sixteen-year-old ear that Ginny could feel her words, the message that had to be communicated privately, woman to woman. "Don't worry, the doctor says you'll still be able to have children."

Jon had talked of a baby from the time they'd settled in Madison. For the first several years it had been easy to deflect the idea, to laugh and say lightly, "Soon enough," to imply that they were enjoying their freedom, sexual and otherwise, as adults too much to shackle themselves to mundane family life. Eventually, as Jon became more insistent, she'd found herself developing arguments. She had, she told him, no desire for children. She reminded him of their friends' endless complaints about their offspring, drew his attention to tantrum throwers and whiners, flattered him with talk about the pleasure of being with him alone. She'd been cruel, although not altogether dishonest, when she insisted that Jon wanted children only to complete the picture he envisioned of a perfect life: a boy and a girl, born three years apart, to add to the air-conditioned house, the museum membership, and the stationery tastefully monogrammed in gray.

In truth, she was scared of what might happen to the child once it was born, once she loved it, once its well-being meant everything to her. Because she knew the sort of thing that could happen when people were careless. And she knew that she was careless.

But in one way she couldn't manage to be careless enough. For years she wished she could have forgotten to swallow that pill even one single morning. Ironically, although she feared to expose a child to all the dangers she knew she couldn't guard against, she wished for an accident of a very different sort, a happy accident, as it were. Faced with the prospect of a child, certainly she would rise to the occasion. But to actively choose to make a baby when she knew she didn't have the requisite vigilance to raise it seemed too wrong to contemplate.

And now, as it turned out, she was weak as well as careless. For, ultimately, as years passed and it grew clear that if she stayed the course she truly never would have a baby, her greed for a child overwhelmed her. So for many months now, she had neglected to fill her prescription.

Maybe the doctor who had reassured her mother had been wrong. Or maybe her mother had lied. In any case, something within her womb, so near those bones that had been mangled and had grown crookedly back together, obviously knew she couldn't be trusted to take care of a baby, just as she hadn't been able to take care of herself. They'd called it an accident. But accidents, as her father had told her time and time again, were almost always avoidable, if only one took enough care. Jon blamed himself, but she knew, in a place she could barely admit even to herself, that it was not his fault. If she had not acted in the way that she had, it never would have happened.

She slid the vanity drawer closed again and went into the bedroom to change from her gardening clothes to khakis and a boxy T-shirt, the uniform she wore to talk about gardens. While digging for the T-shirt—she could never remember which drawer she'd stuffed things into!—her fingers brushed the shawl Jon had given her last Christmas. Its texture was so delicate, so impossibly soft, that each time she wore it, she feared her perpetually ragged fingernails would snag it. She'd assumed it was cashmere, but he'd been almost offended by the term and assured her that it was something much better, something far more refined. In other words, it was something like his car, which had to have the sunroof and the leather upholstery; and their bedsheets, which she was almost afraid to wash for fear of ruining; and their toaster, which could, if one could only master the controls, prepare a Thanksgiving feast for twelve; and their stereo speakers, which were precise enough for a recording studio. In other words, it was something nominally practical but really much more than they needed, that cost, if not technically more than they could afford, more than they should have been spending on such an item.

He'd binged on purchases like these even back when they'd earned barely enough to eat and pay the rent. He was as generous with others as with himself when these impulses grabbed him; he'd bought his mother a condo, for instance, which was why they were still living in their starter house, and Ginny had approved that decision wholeheartedly. But she also knew that, while he refused to return anything, he felt sick with worry over what he'd done for months afterward. She tried to tell him that throwing money away on luxuries would not make up for the deprivation of his childhood, that what they needed was a steadily accumulated nest egg, a value her parents had taught her. But while he agreed in principle, sometimes he just couldn't help himself.

She pulled the shawl out to refold it, but it was unbearable to touch in the heat, especially now that the air conditioner had stopped pumping. She flipped it quickly back into the drawer and returned to the bathroom to wrestle with her hair, which was an in-between length that resisted being gathered into a ponytail. She snicked a portion of it back as well as she could with a device Nora had given her—a little plastic jaw that resembled a wild-animal trap. Then she went downstairs to wait for her friend and willed Jon's car to appear at the corner. She would cancel everything were he to come.

By now, if they'd gone to Summerfest, they'd be passing St. Coletta—they liked to take the old highway rather than the interstate when they weren't in a rush. Her bare feet would be on the dash; his hand would be over hers on the armrest. He would be obsessing over a stop for a root beer float. It was summer, he would argue to himself, and the float was a summer treat. It might be their only chance to have one. On the other hand, shouldn't they save their appetites for brats or Italian sausages? They would stop, probably. And he would eat more than his share of ice cream. And he would regret it later when he couldn't force down a funnel cake. She knew him so well.

She knew, for instance, even if he wouldn't admit it, that something had changed in him in the past few months. For one thing, she seemed always to be waiting for him. He worked late or he went out with the guys from work for drinks and wouldn't get home until midnight. She liked that he had friends and she didn't want to be shrewish, the sour wife in curlers and housecoat, tapping her foot just inside the front door, but finally, on the fourth or fifth occasion, she couldn't stop herself from asking, "Didn't Mark and Freddi and Dennis have to get home?" But Mark was divorced and Freddi was single and Dennis's wife was a sales rep, out of town half the week. So then it was up to her to impose spousal restrictions, and she wasn't sure what was all right.

What bothered her lately wasn't so much his absence but his vagueness about it. He'd call to say he'd be another forty-five minutes, and she'd be relieved to have the time to apply to whatever project she had on the table, but then an hour and a half would pass and she would have had enough, frankly, of site plans and elevations, and she would turn to writing grocery lists, and paying bills, and skimming through a *House & Garden* article about the advantages of milk paint, but she could not keep herself from looking up every few minutes, hoping to see his lights swing over the windows.

It wasn't that she wanted him there all the time. But she wanted him to give her the feeling that he would mostly, not always, of course, but mostly rather be with her. "You mean you want me to get a bumper sticker made with your name—'I'd rather be with Ginny?' " he'd said, not unkindly, but not taking her seriously.

"There was a time when you *would* rather have been with me," she wanted to say. "What's changed?"

The cordless phone's handset was never where it was supposed to be. She pressed the intercom button and followed the insistent chirpy ring to the window ledge behind the couch, where she'd left the phone after talking to Nora. Her fingers knew his cell-phone number. She let them dial it while she watched another car, the wrong make, model, color, and year, the wrong everything, glide down the street.

"This is Jon Kepilkowski. Please leave a message."

six

Freshly showered for a second time that day, Jon trotted easily down the rubber-treaded stairs. All he had to do was push his feet into the thick, cabbage-coated air. The pain he'd felt in his ankle earlier in the day was entirely gone; he sensed only the suppleness and strength he'd been able to count on all of his life.

He loved Freddi's building, even this dim stairwell with its perpetually blowing bulb on the third-floor landing, its boxes crammed to overflowing with empty diet-cola and light-beer cans on the second-floor landing, and, on the first floor, the three plastic tubs, one of kitty litter, one of sand, and one of rock salt, ready year-round to combat the full range of step- and walkway-glazing ice. He loved it for the Indigo Girls that wailed up through the uneven floorboards, for the wavy glass in the windowpane over the kitchen sink, for the odor of decades' old linseed oil rubbed into more than half-century-old wood.

"It's so relaxed here," he'd said to Freddi, the third or fourth time they'd gone off-site in the middle of the workday, ostensibly to concept, but, in fact, to end up on the king-sized bed that filled almost every inch of her bedroom.

She'd rolled her eyes. "Yeah, too relaxed. This is glorified student life."

"But this place has a pulse—people going in and out, little dramas going on all around—and it's got a history. Think of all the people who have passed through here!"

"You don't have to live here," Freddi had said drily.

She was the least-sentimental person he knew and her apartment was furnished sparely, which he also loved, the couch a clean-lined knock-off of a Florence Knoll; the dining table, an unornamented rectangle of glass. She had a special drawer in which to store mail she didn't want to deal with immediately, a solution he'd guiltily suggested to Ginny, who'd pointed out that all of their drawers were full. Every night, whether she'd read it or not, Freddi put the day's newspaper on the recycling pile. At her house he luxuriated in the lack of clutter. It seemed to allow for more oxygen.

What if he were to live here? What if he were to give up that other life and slide into this one instead? She sometimes served him tea in fragile white Japanese cups. He imagined sipping it with her on the porch in the soft gray of the early morning. The lake was just across the street, through a line of trees and down a steep bank. After midnight, when the rest of the street had been long asleep, they could shed their clothes on the rocks and slip into the dark water. She thought this place was uncivilized, but he knew it was merely sensual. Although he tamped down the thought as best he could, it reminded him of the apartment he and Ginny had rented just after they were married.

What he'd wanted then was to be grown up. He'd wanted to

be a good man, one with a respectable job and responsibilities, a man, in other words, entirely unlike his father. To that end, he had, until now, done everything right. He'd married a classy girl; he'd worked his way, if not to the pinnacle of his profession, then at least to a decently high ledge; he maintained a nice house in an excellent neighborhood. He did not yet have children, but at last Ginny had agreed, and therefore soon . . . well, what he'd realized, not all at once, but slowly, over the course of the spring months in which Freddi began to intrude on his attention in an increasingly insistent way, was that soon the door to a fresh life, a life unsullied by compromise and untethered by promises, a life whose driving forces and accoutrements he couldn't even clearly imagine from his current vantage point, would be locked against him forever.

There should have been a more significant reason behind the course he'd embarked on than panic over the contours of the future he'd established for himself and the appearance of a woman with whom he could fall in love. But nevertheless it was too late. Now he couldn't bear to give up either woman, either life.

"Sauerkraut!" Freddi whispered behind him. She pulled her lips wide and touched her finger to her tongue.

Jon grinned. It had become their habit on the stairs to make fun of the dishes with which the elderly landlady in the first-floor apartment attempted to poison her husband, the controlling partner in a lawn-care company consisting of three old men, two well-oiled mowers, and a clutch of rakes. This couple habitually left their front door half open when they were at home, for air, for information, for company, who knew? He and Freddi tried not to look in, but it was impossible not to observe the old man, white hair sprouting from the V-neck and under the arms of his undershirt, in the moss-green easy chair, awaiting the meal he and his wife still called "dinner."

When Freddi had gone by, but while Jon still had a full view of the living room, the old man winked. Jon looked away, trying not to have seen and understood. Maybe the old man had only been trying to expel from his eye a bit of leaf mold, a curl of gasoline fume, the sight of his wife's eight-hooked brassiere dripping in the bathroom. But Jon knew he'd meant a slimy congratulations. He was probably even offering the secret handshake of the adulterer's club. The taste of the morning's coffee and its now curdled cream rose suddenly from his stomach to his throat and he had to push it back down with a forceful swallow.

"Damn," Freddi said, stopping halfway through the screen door and then stepping back to let it slam. "Forgot my sunglasses."

He would have run back up, too, to keep her company, but he couldn't face the old man again. "I'll be on the porch," he said to her slightly roughened heels as they disappeared up the stairs.

They'd never intended this, but he wouldn't try pleading that case to Ginny. She'd tell him that that was what they all said. And she'd be right. But he'd be right, too. Because they really hadn't intended this.

It made him feel guilty when he called it love. But that's what it was. Not, as it turned out, such a miraculous, once-in-a-lifetime event as he'd once supposed. But he was a romantic and so he wondered: Was this the real thing? Or was that? And if he honestly loved two women at the same time, well, then what?

"That's when you convert to Mormoncy, Mormonness, whatever they call it," Mark Kaiser had joked.

That was at the beginning, back when he'd been able to talk

about it with Kaiser, when the both of them had assumed it was a fairly harmless flirtation. A helpful flirtation, in fact, in that Jon's crush had made him wildly productive. At work he was charged with so much energy that he was up and going full throttle every minute. And he was so eager to please Freddi, to amuse her, to wow her, that he churned out great stuff, brilliant stuff, pow, pow, pow, one idea right after another.

He'd always talked plenty to Ginny about work, Freddi included, but a couple of months ago he had started to censor himself. Freddi was in his thoughts every moment; was he bringing her up too often? As a safeguard, he began to criticize her. Wasn't she fooling herself with her big talk about a nonprofit? And the way she sucked up to Nielson! If he'd hoped thinking about her and exposing her to Ginny in these terms would dampen his ardor, he was wrong. The criticism was merely a way to indulge in the thought of her without revealing his infatuation.

"The way we work, it's bound to happen now and again," Kaiser said. "The wee hours, the creative juices. You expose an idea; she caresses it in her hot little hands before tossing it back to you. You push it, knead it, spank it lightly, panting with exertion—"

"Stop," Jon laughed. "You and I never fell in love."

Kaiser grinned. "Speak for yourself."

Of course, the building, the flowering, the exploding, whatever, of a really great concept did generate a euphoric intimacy. There were the hours, the days, sometimes the weeks of frustration and lassitude, the pounding of hands against heads and sometimes of heads against walls and desks, as if that might somehow jar an idea loose; the grasping at whatever flotsam and jetsam happened to be passing through the mind: Light beer! Lightning rods! Debby Boone! There was the application of methods that had worked before and theories never previously tried. There were the pages of bad ideas, and more pages of modifications of bad ideas, and pages upon which what at first appeared to be good ideas were flogged until they revealed themselves to be only more bad ideas. And then, somehow—this was the part he couldn't explain—there was the idea that began to work. He had heard that for some teams an idea emerged full-blown, but for him it had never been love at first sight like that. For him it was more like following the clues, clues he knew somehow in his brain or in his heart were the hot ones, the right ones. A drawing of a dog in a chair got them closer; a dog on a unicycle set them back; a dog on a tricycle—now they were onto something!

They were still in the head-beating stage that May night, and he would have given up and gone home had he not been working with Freddi. Instead, ostensibly for a change of scene to jump-start their brains, but in reality to prolong the evening, he'd suggested a drive. He'd known the moment they stepped out of the building into the balmy dark air that it would have been wiser not to go. Nevertheless, he drove out Mineral Point Road, until they were clear of the city and all around them was only the darkness of newly planted fields and the surprisingly loud pulse of the spring peepers when he cut the engine.

Freddi handed him the Coke bottle into which she'd trickled rum from one of the little bottles she carried in her purse. The rim was still wet from her lips. They got out of the car and leaned against the hood, Freddi casually letting herself slide against him and then turning slightly toward him, her thigh against his. He'd had to answer her invitation, had to pull her to him, had to bury his face in her warm neck, had to move his lips upward until they were against hers.

He felt like he had when he'd run down steep hills as a child, the thrill of plummeting forward almost faster than he could thrust his legs out, the delicious fear of the asphalt, the sense that he was as close as he could physically come to flying. They'd kept kissing there on the spring-damp hillside, their bodies pressed tightly against each other, first his on hers and then hers on his, fully clothed because they were not meaning to do it, until he could stand it no longer and had to scramble to his feet and walk around to settle himself. In the car on the way back, she snuggled against his shoulder as well as she could without injuring herself on the cup holder, and he turned his face to hers and kissed her as often as reasonably safe driving allowed. In the parking lot, they held each other fiercely and said "Good night" and kissed again and said "Good night" and kissed again and again, and one final time, because that was to be all there was, and they squeezed each other's hands as they stepped apart in tender acknowledgment of what they might have had, had things been different, but now never would.

That night he'd managed to feel almost innocent. What crime, really, had he committed? He was obviously attracted to Freddi, but he didn't love her. His feelings, he told himself, had probably very little to do with her specifically, and were more owing to the circumstances: the warm night, the intensity of their collaboration, maybe even the sugar in the Coke, and, of course, the rum. And they'd stopped themselves, hadn't they, before any real harm was done. It was only a crush, a flirtation, indulged a little too far maybe, but still, what really was the harm? In fact, by acting on his desire, he'd gotten her out of his system. Now he wouldn't have to think about her so much and want her so badly, as, he admitted, he'd begun to over the last few weeks. He'd been there, done that. He was lying to himself and he knew it, just as he'd known in the previous week or two that working late would be dangerous, and just as he'd known as he'd slammed the car door and turned the key in the ignition that driving into that night would be fatal.

"Why are you doing this?" Kaiser had asked.

Jon might have asked the same thing of him, since they, the last two left in the office at nine-thirty, were standing beside a desk that didn't belong to either of them and Kaiser was idly, but carefully, so as not to disarrange anything, lifting the corners of various papers so that he could read what was on the ones underneath, and sliding open drawers. Snooping on random people, even people he hardly knew, was a habit he'd indulged in ever since his wife, Heidi, had cheated on him.

What Kaiser really wanted to know, Jon understood, was why Heidi had done that. The nearest Jon could come to explaining his own behavior to himself (he didn't attempt to explain it to Kaiser, who, he knew, would have sneered at any explanation) was simply that he wanted to. His feelings for Freddi sprang lightly over the earth—he doodled, as he thought about this—a small gazelle in mid-leap, all four legs parallel to the ground. What he pictured when he thought of his feelings for Ginny— something he lately tried to avoid doing—was a root ball, the tough strings of love tangled with those of dependence and habit; the whole, heavy mass clotted here and there with disappointment and accommodation, as well as satisfaction and joy. He loved her, deeply, solidly, he had no doubt of that. He was easy with her. She "got" him, got his humor, got his thinking, and he got hers. Knowing what worked—what news story the other would find outrageous, what the other was likely to order in a restaurant, what would make the other laugh, or come— was a little predictable, but such intimate knowledge was mostly a pleasure. He respected her, admired her, would have felt, if not for the constant itch and worry of Freddi, mostly happy when she was near. If he were in trouble, it was Ginny he'd call out for.

But he wasn't in trouble. He was at the top of his game, more juiced than he'd been in years because of Freddi, Freddi,

Freddi. What he felt for Freddi was as pure and uncomplicated as an illicit relationship could be—he just loved her, loved to be with her, to touch her, to please her, to talk with her, to play with her, loved that she loved him. Of course, it was all on the surface; he reminded himself that there was no substance to it. But, oh, this feeling! That he'd experienced it before only made him more aware of how precious and ephemeral it was, of how regretful he would be if he didn't catch hold of it for as long as he was able. Even if they were to go a little farther—which they didn't intend to, of course—but even if they did, it would still be only the smallest portion of their lives devoted to this tiny flash of happiness. How bad could that be?

She'd stood beside him in a full elevator, her arms at her sides, and he couldn't resist surreptitiously running one finger down the inside of her palm. Her fingers had fluttered and then closed briefly around his. The next time they were alone she'd locked the door and they'd pressed against each other fiercely, urgently, until the phone rang. Not Ginny, but an account exec. If it had been Ginny, would it have been over? Would he have had to come face-to-face with what he was doing and been unable to continue? Two evenings later, they'd gone to Freddi's apartment. By the end of the week he'd lain awake at night beside Ginny, listening to her deep breaths, terrified that he might vomit or shriek, so violent was his guilt and shame.

With Ginny, he'd always been tender, gentle. He couldn't help but feel she was fragile. He'd accidentally broken her once, after all. But Freddi was strong as a cat; she pinned him to the bed and lapped him up like cream.

The sunglasses were taking a very long time to fetch. He expected that sort of thing with Ginny, who was always misplacing one item or another, but Freddi was organized to a degree he found almost disturbing. He was conscious of the old man staring at him through the window, and he turned to look up the staircase where he'd watched Freddi disappear, her shorts snug enough to emphasize the swell of her buttocks. Maybe they should forget Summerfest; he'd be happy just to spend the day here.

Against his thigh, his phone burred. He slipped it from his pocket and shaded the little screen with his hand to read the number. Kaiser.

"Hey."

"Yeah, hi. Listen, do you remember that stuff we did for the Lacey thing? The second version? The one with the rabbits?"

"Yeah."

"Do you have that?"

"It's on my laptop somewhere. I'm sure I can find it."

"I've got to drop Anthony off at Heidi's later. I could come over right after that. Will you be around this afternoon?"

"Can I e-mail it to you tomorrow? I'm on my way to Summerfest."

"Oh, well, good for you. That's right, Ginny loves Annie Lennox. Isn't she playing tonight?"

"I guess."

Kaiser began singing. Any normal person would've stopped after the first couple of phrases, but Kaiser had to keep on line after line, amusing himself. "Would I li-I-I-I-e to yeew?" At least, Jon thought, he didn't have to watch the air guitar.

"Da-a-d." Anthony's reproachful voice was clear in the background.

"OK," Jon said, when the verse was over, "tomorrow then."

But Kaiser kept going. "My friends . . ."

"I'm hanging up," Jon said, and he did.

Kaiser could be, was often, irritating, but he was someone whose respect Jon was deeply sorry to have lost. It was too bad that Nielson Gray insisted on its policy of mixing creative teams up. True, they probably got more decent stuff that way across the board, but they'd never get anything really great. Together, he and Kaiser had produced some work that was well beyond what either one of them could ever do with the people they were matched with now. It wasn't just that Freddi was more junior, although that was part of it, it was a chemistry thing. He and Freddi worked well together; they could build a decent, a more-than-decent ad, but professionally he and Kaiser sparked.

"What about Ginny?" By the time they'd had this conversation in the Big Burrito, Kaiser had known the extent of what was going on with Freddi. He was balancing three taco chips edge to edge to make a pyramid and he kept his eyes on that project. Kaiser liked to confront people, to, as he put it, "get in their faces." He called it "telling it like I see it." Jon had been waiting for Kaiser to tell it like he saw it for weeks now, and he'd felt a surge of impatience.

"Oh, for fuck's sake, say it. Tell me, already, what a jerk you think I am."

Kaiser shrugged, his gaze still focused on the precarious structure between his large hands. Suddenly he brought one palm down on top of it. Bits of broken chip shot across the table. "Honestly," he said, looking Jon straight in the eyes, "you disappoint me. Sure, you've got some talent, but so do seventy-five percent of the rest of these jokers. Talent's not as hard to come by in this business as you'd think. You've got a decent personality—you're reasonably funny, easy to work with, and all that—but there again, so are at least half the people I know. What was special about you, Jon, is that you had integrity. I've never seen you scramble to cover your ass; I've never seen you poach someone else's idea; I've never seen you promote yourself at another's expense. You were, in short, a trustworthy son of a bitch. And now, quite frankly, you're no better than the rest of them." Kaiser paused and dipped a chip in salsa. When he brought it to his mouth, his canines, weirdly, wolfishly sharp, flashed. "Is that what you wanted to hear?" he said.

It was, in a way. Part of Jon was hungry for punishment. A part of him, though, was surprised. He'd half imagined that Kaiser—Mr. Honesty—would have, if not approved, at least understood his feelings, the impossible situation he was in. He hadn't considered the way Heidi's cheating would probably have colored just this sort of behavior. Jon closed his eyes now against the memory of the disgust he'd felt emanating from his best friend. They'd smoothed it over by not talking about it, by confining their conversations to work, about which they always had plenty to say to each other. They'd become cordial, even jokey again, but their relationship had suffered what might still turn out to be a mortal wound. Adultery was a lonely business, it seemed.

"Ready?" Freddi was behind him suddenly, and he jumped, startled.

"I believe I was waiting for you," he said, smiling.

She leaned into him, gazing into his face expectantly. Impulsively, he grabbed her up, spun her around as he bent to kiss her. He loved how light she was; her bones seemed almost hollow, like a bird's. When he set her down again, he glanced over his shoulder at the old man's window and then also up and down the street. You never knew who might be watching.

1963

"*Just say you saw us together.*"

Clark and Marie are sitting on the end of the unpainted dock that the cabins share, their feet dangling in the water. She says it as if it's the easiest thing in the world to sidle up to a man he hardly knows, a man who's the town's closest approximation of a movie star, and insinuate that his wife is cheating on him. Bud Kepilkowski had been the quarterback of a team that had made it to state, for God's sake, when Clark Otto had been a freshman bantam-weight wrestler, too inept even to warrant a uniform. He'd had to wrestle with his skinny white legs sticking out of gym shorts. Sure, they're both adults now. They're peers. If anything Clark, by virtue of the fact that he'd be sitting for the bar next summer, should have the advantage. But here in Winnesha, Bud is still Bud and Clark will always be Clark.

Social niceties are not the kind of problem Marie has any

patience with. Actually Marie never admits to obstacles, period. When she wants something, she goes after it, no matter what. Her wanting is all. At least that's what she'd been like as a child, when he'd known her well, and he can see that in that way, at least, she hasn't changed.

Marie and Clark had become friends because their grand-mothers had been friends and neighbors, with piers side by side down at the swampy end of the lake. He'd loved her for a couple of years, too, and she'd let him moon over her a little. She'd laughed at him, but not in a mean way. Once they started at the district high school they were reincarnated—he into one of the "smarts," she into one of the "socials"—and for the duration they were not allowed back into their former, more flexible lives. Sophomore year they were assigned to the same gym class and, come the dance unit, with the girls' ring circling left and the boys' ring circling right, it was more comfortable to dance with her than with most of the other girls, but that was pretty much all he'd had to do with her until he started dating her friend Hattie.

He was surprised around Christmas when she called to sug-gest he come along with her and Bud to Lawrence of Arabia, *even vaguely mistrustful when she said she had a friend she wanted him to meet; that is, if he wasn't serious about someone else. Maybe he'd met someone off in Madison and she hadn't heard.*

He'd gone only because Marie had summoned him. He had no interest in a fluffy-headed Winnesha High prom queen. But Hat-tie, shy and very pale, delicate-looking as a snowdrop, with the fine white-blond hair of a child, turned out to be sharper than he'd assumed. Over coffee she pronounced the movie he'd immensely admired "much too long," and, as she made her case, lightly, humorously, but with conviction, he found himself beginning to agree. When she playfully touched his arm with two long, thin fingers to keep him from interrupting, he suddenly remembered seeing her play the piano once on the high-school stage, her hair glowing under the spotlight. Her touch had been lively, but she'd snarled a phrase, more than once. He remembered seeing her shake her head, her face reddening, and then plunge on and finish the piece with a flourish. He'd not only applauded but whooped for her, uncharacteristically, so much did he admire her for toughing it out. Yes, that, he remembered now, was Hattie Sorenson. Later, as he ushered her into the cold that immediately pinked her cheeks and brightened her eyes, Marie gave him a look from the door, as much as to say that, of course, she'd been right; he ought to know better than to doubt her.

Now she gives the waves an impatient little kick. She's looking at him intently. It's exactly the way she looked more than a decade ago when she told him to dive in after his decoder ring. He'd been full of excuses—he'd never find it in the muck, it'd be ruined already, it was a stupid toy anyway. "Just go get it," she'd said. She wore a gold chain around her neck that summer, and she played with it as she waited for Clark to do as she instructed, pulling the metal away from her neck and rubbing the links against the ball of her thumb. He could see the pale-green line the necklace had drawn on her skin. "Just go on." Finally, her patience exhausted, she dove in herself and came up with the ring on the third try.

He'd put it on, but he hadn't thanked her. It was his, after all. If he preferred to let it stay lost, that was his right.

And this is Hattie's business. If she wants Walt punished, she has the legal means to do it. And if she doesn't want to avail her-self of those means . . . well, he doesn't want to question her, but it makes him wonder what exactly had happened that night. He doesn't doubt Walt took advantage; the guy is a creep. But Hattie had liked him, had flirted with him at that party in April, even though she'd been there as Clark's date. Well, he'd been right to *break up with her. She isn't his problem. No way is she his problem. Except that Marie is making her so.*

"He'll be at the Dew Drop tonight. There's a bachelor party for Jim Vetter."

"I wasn't invited."

"You don't have to be invited to go to a tavern!"

"He's not going to like it."

"That's the idea." She's drumming the board beside her with her fingertips.

"He's not going to like me for telling him."

"Oh, for Pete's sake. He's not going to think about you for one second. Just do it, Clark."

That he might as well be a stick of furniture in this drama is depressingly accurate. "What if Hattie's version isn't the strict truth?"

"Clark, I know Walt Fleischer and you know Walt Fleischer. I think we both know it's true enough. Walt is poison for Hattie and he's poison for Bud. You think Walt doesn't take advantage of the way old Mr. Fleischer loves Bud, getting Bud to take the blame for the stunts he pulls—the T-bird he smashed last year, that speedboat he put a hole in? You think he doesn't hate the way his father'll forgive Bud anything? Bud's just too nice to see it on his own. It's my job to show him."

"Won't Bud be angry with you, though, Marie? Won't he hate you, too?"

"Bud! No. He knows me better than that." The look on her face is almost dreamy. "I can make it all right with him. Don't worry about me."

But he does worry about her. He worries about all of them, even Walt. That's his nature.

seven

It bothered Ethan that Winifred had hung up the phone so abruptly, without even saying goodbye. Maybe she hadn't yet agreed to spend the rest of her life with him, but she could at least be polite. Their relationship was such that he could rightfully expect a certain minimum of manners.

Just a few weeks ago her head had been resting on his shoulder. They'd been watching *Apartment Zero*, his choice, but he wouldn't have been able to follow it if he hadn't seen it a couple of times before. He was distracted by such an insistent longing to embrace her that he had to concentrate on pressing his arms against the wool of the couch to keep them from rising.

"You're a good friend," she'd said, her eyes never leaving the shadowy rooms on the screen. He'd winced at these words, tightening his shoulder, so that she'd lifted her head and he'd had to reach around with his left hand to replace it.

No matter what she said, they were more than friends, he thought, as he turned the key to engage the dead bolt in the front door. Friends, for instance, did not hang up on friends.

Ethan was pleased, as he always was, when he glanced at his house from his driveway. Certainly it was small—a living room, separated from the kitchen by what the realtor had called a "dining bar," and two snug bedrooms—but large enough for starting a family. He'd spoken to the realtor about that specifically and she'd assured him that his wife would be pleased with the smaller bedroom as a nursery and that the backyard, perhaps with the addition of a low fence, would be ideal for a toddler. He hadn't meant to suggest that he already had a wife and a child, but the agent seemed to like him better for it, so he didn't correct the impression.

He'd set up his computer and file cabinet in the nursery, but he wouldn't hesitate to move them. Give him half a day and he could set up an office in the garage with a fan in the summer and a space heater in the winter. He'd be just fine.

Or, if his wife wanted the garage for her own study, Ethan would be willing to do the work he brought home at the dining bar.

"She," he dreamed, would be Winifred. He was pretty sure she would be. Well, to put it accurately, sometimes he was positive—he could imagine her so vividly in that house, doing some of the things she actually had done there, like washing mesclun, and also some things she'd never done, like brushing her teeth in the cornflower-blue-papered bathroom or putting her head on his pillow. She'd once rested her arm on one of the burgundy accent pillows he'd propped on the couch. He'd taken that pillow to bed, but after a couple of nights it had lost the indentation her elbow had given it, as well as the scent of her lotion, so he'd put it back on the couch again. Other times, terrible times, he was less sure, and he had to stay up all night building a case to reassure himself.

He wasn't sure why he was driving to her house now. Of course, they'd been having a conversation, there was that, and he wanted to finish it. That was what he would say when she opened her door to his knock: "I just wanted to finish what I was saying about Saarinen and his influence on postmodern architecture."

Possibly that was reasonable. (At least, it didn't seem entirely unreasonable.) Still, he knew he didn't care just then whether she understood his views on that particular subject, or on any subject for that matter. What he wanted was to assuage the unbearable feeling that she was pulling away from him, that her eyes and her thoughts were somewhere else. He wanted to put himself right in front of her to remind her of his value. Waiting in neutral for the red to give way on Park Street, he kept his left foot on the brake and he pushed and released the accelerator with his right. He shot forward when the light changed, crowding the minivan in front of him.

As always when he drove toward her apartment, he thought about how she should not be living on the east side in that ramshackle place. It was not her.

They'd met during her sophomore year of college, his first year of law school. He'd noticed her standing at a library copy machine. So many undergraduate girls collapsed into sweatpants and halfhearted ponytails, but she was wearing a kilt and a soft gray sweater, textured tights, and loafers. Her hair was neatly bobbed, sleek, the color of cherrywood. If she'd not been pounding the side of the copier with the flat of her hand and if her face hadn't been red with near tears of frustration, she'd have looked very like the girls pictured in his social studies texts in elementary school. He'd never before seen a girl who looked exactly as a girl was supposed to look.

Ethan had spent a summer working at a copy shop. He unlatched the front panel of the machine, moved some levers, gently tugged at the accordion-pleated page that had jammed the works, and extracted the pages that had piled up behind it. She made a joke about her compulsion to make a copy of her work before turning it in. He laughed, but assured her that he, too, had little faith in the power of a TA's Guatemalan drawstring bag to retain the papers stuffed into it. He offered to get her a discount rate at his former employer's store.

She never took him up on that, but for a few months, with minimal maneuvering—more a matter of being alert to her presence than of significantly altering his routine—their paths intersected fairly frequently in the Rathskeller, where they would share a bag of popcorn, or on the path along Lake Mendota, where he would slacken his pace for a mile or two so that they could run together. She complained of being unable to find a decent research topic for an anthropology class, and he suggested the methods of conflict resolution practiced by the pre-nineteenth-century Potawatomis, a topic one of his law courses had touched on with annoying brevity. She got an A. She changed her brand of running shoes when he recommended it; they had long conversations about possible careers she might pursue—she'd considered politics, advertising, and public relations; he'd argued for editing, and law, of course. He suspected that no one had ever offered her advice before; she seemed ravenous for his guidance and approval.

During the following fall, he became aware that she was seeing a certain boy who affected an unkempt look, the laces of his sneakers loose, his trousers creeping down around his narrow hips, his hair, always dirty-looking, falling into his face. Ethan remembered feeling more surprised than jealous; after all, his own relationship with her was avuncular, not romantic.

At that point in his career, he had to spend so much time and energy maintaining his position in his class that he had little left to spare for romance or even friendship. And, frankly, he'd never had much luck with girls. He was disappointed—maybe that's what it was—that this was the sort of person she'd choose. He'd also noted that she was taking a late-afternoon class, and he began to make a point, as the days grew shorter, of timing his run to finish as the class let out, so he could escort her, if she happened to be walking alone afterward. It was a safe campus, but after dark, one could never be too careful.

That he saw her meet the unkempt boy outside of Science Hall one evening, then, was no coincidence. Obviously, she didn't need his escort services and because he'd gotten a late start and had curtailed his run to be there, he decided to do another couple of miles.

He was already well on his way, up the hill and down the slope on the other side, past the Ag Building, heading at a good, clean pace toward the barn, when some uneasiness made him loop north toward the lake and back along the path toward which he'd seen them headed. It was the way the boy had been walking, or rather the way they were together, him crowding, her pulling away. The way he'd twice hooked his elbow around her neck. Maybe it was nothing. Maybe it was affection. Just because he couldn't imagine himself behaving in that way didn't mean she didn't welcome it.

He wouldn't have heard her voice if he'd not been listening for it. They'd gone off the path onto a small spit of land, so hidden by evergreen shrubs that they were invisible. He could tell by the sounds that they were tussling. But whether in a way that called for privacy or intervention, he wasn't sure.

He turned out to be right to risk embarrassing them all, and, luckily, the boy was a physical coward, as well as a moral one.

Ethan, who was tall but inordinately gawky, hardly appeared threatening as he pushed through the shrubbery in his running tights, his cap plucked off by a branch, but the boy, exposed and taken by surprise, had run off, trailing obscenities. Winifred had cried in his arms, an experience he was startled to find himself fantasizing about afterward. She'd broken up with the boy, she'd explained, the night before, and, as a consequence, he'd drunk too much that afternoon. He'd just wanted to be with her one last time, he'd said. And she'd consented, although she hadn't thought he meant there, right then, behind half-frozen bushes. She sniffed, wiped her eyes with the heel of her hand. Being in his running clothes, Ethan hadn't had a handkerchief to lend her. It was sort of funny, really, when you thought about it, she'd said, the ridiculousness of the scene. How lucky that Ethan had happened by to rescue her.

He urged her to press charges, but she'd refused. After all, she hadn't told him no. Not really. Not, obviously, clearly. And the whole thing was just so embarrassing, unseemly. In the bushes, for God's sake! She seemed to avoid him after that, and he understood. It *had* been embarrassing, after all.

By the time he graduated, second, thanks to the true salutatorian's psychotic episode in the home stretch, she was no more than a vague regret, a woman he wished he might have met at a different stage in his life. And then, this spring, he'd been presented with a second chance.

He'd gone to the fancy organic market to buy only free-range chicken and sugar snap peas, but some other products had made their way into his cart, peach salsa and smoked salmon spread, a package of little crackers laced with rosemary and a four-pack of locally brewed ginger beer. He found it morally troubling to shop in that store. Organic farming was obviously desirable—it was healthy and good for the environment—but it was also so elitist! Those eight-dollar slabs of herb-scented soaps and four-dollar jars of pollen-infused mustards! They were absurd. But so sensually satisfying. He could scoff at the soaps, but he'd feel significantly impoverished without a selection of vinegars in his cupboard. Still, the peach salsa was overkill; his refrigerator door already supported at least three partially consumed varieties of salsa. He was heading back to the condiment aisle to replace this jar when he saw her. She was using the bottommost shelf as a step and was clinging to an upper shelf with her left hand, while swinging a cracker box with her right in an attempt to dislodge a bag of blue tortilla chips from its aerie.

"Winifred?" He'd never used her masculine nickname.

When she turned, he observed a momentary blankness in her features and knew she was scrambling through stretches of time and contexts, trying to place him.

"It's . . ." he began.

"Ethan," they said in unison.

She smiled. She stepped off the shelf, came toward him, and encircled him lightly with her arms. He was taken aback. They'd never, except for that single traumatic evening, been on hugging terms.

They exchanged numbers in the parking lot. Ethan didn't know whether he would ever have called her—he didn't yet realize the import of this meeting, that this was not merely a pleasant, casual encounter but was indeed an opportunity for lifelong happiness—but she called him the following week.

He'd heard the phone begin to ring as he was coming in the door. Normally he would not have picked it up but would have waited to hear the voice leaving a message on the machine. He preferred not to talk to people without preparation. But when he'd made it to the kitchen and had not yet missed the call, he was overcome by an impulse to beat the machine and lifted the receiver.

"Hello?"

"Ethan, it's Freddi."

"Freddi?"

"Yes, Freddi. Winifred."

"Winifred." The idea of her coming right into his home like that, albeit through the telephone, made him uncomfortable. He picked up the sharpened pencil lying by the phone and pressed the point against the countertop.

"Yes. I thought you might want to have dinner with me tonight."

"Tonight?" Press, release, press, release, press, release went the graphite point against the laminated surface.

"Right, tonight. It turns out I'm free and I thought . . . well, I just thought of you. So-o-o . . ." She drew the word out, as if speaking to a slow child. He'd forgotten the teasing way she had with him. "Do you want to?"

"All right." The lead snapped and shot off the counter. "I have some work, but I could do it later. Or I could do it now and meet you later. Or I could just skip it. Maybe that's what I'll do. Or get up early. I could do that, too. Sure. Yes. I'd love to have dinner with you tonight."

"OK, good," she said. "Good. You're just what I need." And she told him to meet her at a nouveau Italian place on his side of town in an hour.

She was giddy, almost, when they sat down, giggling at nearly everything he said. She was different from the way he remembered, more girlish, less serious, at least through the bruschetta and the baby greens. She'd ordered a cosmopolitan, which she finished before the first course had arrived, and she asked him to choose a wine.

Her mood began to change in the middle of the roasted Amish chicken, which he'd recommended and they'd both ordered. She became preoccupied, asked him the same question twice, looked to the door whenever a new party came in. After the chicken, he ordered coffee, although she'd already asked for the check. He'd sipped it, trying to enjoy it, though it was both weak and bitter and though she was obviously waiting for him to finish. She kept her head bowed over her purse for the entirety of the walk to her car, searching for her keys.

"Is something wrong? I shouldn't have had the coffee, huh?" He laughed a little to cover his embarrassment.

"No, no." She put her hand on his arm. "I'm just thinking about something at work."

"What is it? Maybe I can help. I know I'm no expert when it comes to advertising, although, of course, I am a consumer, so maybe I know more than I think. We all know something about advertising, I guess, these days. It's everywhere, isn't it? Subliminal messages in our coffee." He stopped, embarrassed again at the mention of the coffee. "I've watched my share of *Bewitched*," he added.

She smiled, but he could tell she didn't mean it. "No, I'm afraid it's nothing like that." She looked up into his face. "You're a dear, Ethan," she said. "You know that?"

As he stood there, holding the edge of her car door to be polite, she rose up on her toes and kissed him. And then she slipped into the car and he swung the heavy door closed and that was that.

Driving home, he thought about her kiss. What had it meant? He pulled his teeth over his lips, top and bottom, as if they were artichoke leaves. And then, idling at a light, the inside of his car a lurid red, he was seized, as he had been on that evening years ago, by a sudden intuitive fear that she was in trouble. That old car had broken down; she'd been in an accident; or—and he knew this was far-fetched, but it was possible—a maniac had sprung from his hiding place in the well behind the seat and was raping her with a knife pressed against her throat. Once he'd imagined that, nothing would ease his mind but to turn around and drive to her place.

He didn't know her building number, but she'd mentioned her street, and when he turned the corner and spotted the Mustang parked at the curb, he thought he could guess which place was hers. Obviously, the car being parked there meant she'd made it home all right. He could relax, go home himself. He glanced over his shoulder to pull away, but then hesitated again. Her getting home didn't rule out every danger. He studied the windows of the three-story house.

There. He spotted her on the top floor. She seemed to be moving in a leisurely way, not the way a person would move if a man with a knife or a gun was crouched under the windowsill, ordering her around. Although who knew how someone would move in that situation? It would help to be able to read her expression.

Ethan turned off his engine, extracted the key, and leaned to insert it into the glove compartment's lock. On weekends he sometimes drove over to the Arboretum for a hike, and though he wasn't fanatical about bird-watching, still, he liked to carry his binoculars and Peterson's guide along.

A light came on in a different window. He adjusted the focus and could see her clearly, staring forward, presumably toward a mirror. She looked unperturbed. She touched a finger to one of her eyes. Contact lenses.

She disappeared and he scanned the windows for some time,

waiting, wondering whether it was safe to go. He was about to lower the binoculars, when a movement and a lightening of the color in one of the windows at the back of the house caught his eye. Instinctively, he swung the glasses that way, and then nearly dropped them as he slouched as low as he could, hiding behind the doorframe.

She was standing in the window, practically right up against the glass, wearing only a bra, which he wasn't even sure was a bra at first; it wasn't white, but confusingly close to the color of her skin. He hadn't intended to spy. To peep! But that was what it looked like, obviously, and she'd caught him, was teasing him, in fact, with this display. "You want to see? Take a look," she seemed to be taunting.

Except that she wasn't. Even without the binoculars, he could see that she didn't register the presence of his car. Certainly, she didn't notice that he was in the car looking up at her. She was just staring straight out into the air, or maybe into the trees with their fresh, nubby leaves, or maybe over Lake Monona, but definitely not at him. She lifted her arms up over her head, stretching so that her ribs showed, and then she turned and was gone.

Guiltily, he slid the binoculars back into the glove compartment and turned the key in the lock. He would take them out of the car when he got home and hang them in the basement stairwell, where they could do no harm.

But they were still in the glove compartment this Saturday morning as he pulled along the curb in what he'd come eventually, in the months since that initial night, to think of as his usual spot. Composing himself, he looked away from the house for a minute, across the street toward the lake. A line of thick undergrowth and trees blocked what should have been a view of pretty water. That was the way all over Madison. In summer, when the lakes would have been a refreshing sight, dense greenery choked every vista. And then, in the winter and spring, you longed for a few leaves to soften the hard, gray bleakness. It was all or nothing here, Ethan had often observed.

When he looked back, the man he always thought of as "the guy" was sitting on the porch steps. Ethan had done his research; he knew the guy worked with Winifred, so it was all right. Ethan himself often had to work on Saturday mornings and late at night; he understood. And the guy's presence explained why she'd had to hang up—it was awkward to conduct a personal conversation in front of a colleague.

The guy pulled his cell phone from his pocket, frowned at it, talked for a while, and then put the phone back into his pocket again. Why didn't he just move along?

Why not go right by him up to her apartment? Ethan's hand closed on the door handle. He was about to push the door open when the guy stood up and started down the stairs toward him.

What if he came over and said "May I help you?" in that tone that really meant, "What the hell are you doing here?" Well, he was waiting for his girlfriend, wasn't he? No crime in that. But he wasn't waiting, really, since he had no reason to believe that she was coming down.

The guy was squinting toward Ethan's car, trying to see in. Ethan started the engine and pulled away from the curb. He would wait around the corner, come back when the guy was gone.

eight

"Beth made me come." Those had been the first words Ginny had ever spoken to Jon.

They were wrong. Idiotically wrong. Ginny felt redness seep into her cheeks, which was embarrassing in itself. She looked down at her Tretorns. She'd only meant to make clear that she knew she hadn't been invited, that it wasn't her fault she was crashing his party. She didn't even know Jon except by sight.

Beth had sulked and teased when Ginny said she didn't think she should go. "It's not that kind of party. It's not like 'we request the pleasure of your company,' " she'd said in her English-butler accent. "Besides, I get the feeling the whole reason he asked me was because he thought I'd bring you. Which sucks, obviously, since I'm the one who thinks he's cute. Anyway, don't make me go by myself."

When they'd turned off the sunny main road onto the shady

single lane that sloped and twisted toward the water, nervous excitement had skittered through Ginny. She'd been resting her elbow out the Pinto's open window, and she'd lifted her palm to catch the cooling air.

When she was seven and eight, she'd had a friend who'd lived in one of the cabins down this way. Daisy's mother tapped her cigarettes into empty Fresca cans, instead of a real ashtray. Roy didn't even smoke cigarettes. He chewed tobacco. The back pocket of his jeans had a white circle, where the tin rubbed.

Roy wasn't Daisy's father. Ginny had found that out one day when she and Daisy were riding bikes on the packed dirt road that ran between the two rows of cabins. Ginny's bike was a standard Schwinn, a little old-fashioned looking with its red frame and white vinyl seat and hand grips. Her mother, who had bought it at a rummage sale, said it had "classic design" and "good workmanship." Daisy had a banana bike. Its hot-pink seat had glitter stuck right into it. Ginny had shed her training wheels the year before, but Daisy still had hers. Her bike listed from one side to the other as she careened along the rutted track.

From behind, Ginny saw the right wheel angling in and then out, like a top in its final spins. "Your wheel!" she yelled. "It's about to fall off!"

Daisy braked and both girls got off their bikes.

"Maybe your dad can fix it," Ginny said, seeing that Roy had raised himself off the stoop where he and Daisy's mother had been watching and was coming toward them.

"My dad?" Daisy looked up. "Oh, Roy's not my dad." She said this matter-of-factly, as if it were something any doofus would know, like that babies grew from eggs in their mother's stomachs, a fact similar to this one about Roy in that Ginny was uncomfortably aware that there was more to it than she understood.

Roy laughed. "The kid thinks I'm Daisy's dad," he called back to Daisy's mother.

Daisy's mother let out a snort.

They all were laughing at her now. Chuckling, Daisy's mother leaned forward to tap her ash into the Schlitz can at her feet. She was wearing a bikini top that tied around her neck and you could see pretty much right into it when she folded herself over her thighs.

"Shit!" Roy said. "That can ain't empty!" He was grinning, though, when he said it; you could hear it in his voice.

"You've had plenty," Daisy's mother said. She giggled and tossed her head so that her long, ragged-edged hair rippled like water.

Roy started back to her. "I'll say when I've had plenty."

"Shit, Roy. The girls." She was laughing now, pushing herself up from the stoop with her free hand. And then she was running toward the pier that the cabins shared, the pier with the high-diving board, where the big boys threw each other off playing king of the hill and where the big girls stretched themselves head to head to tan. Daisy's mother held her cigarette in the air as she ran. Her fingers said "peace," but she was shrieking when Roy grabbed her around the waist and lifted her so that her feet kicked out helplessly.

"No, no, no," she screamed, but it was the same giggly way Ginny's little sisters screamed when their father turned them upside down and tickled them. Roy's heels thumped loud as hammers on the pier, and the platforms sagged under both their weights and then sprang back. He threw her in the lake and then jumped in after her. Their two heads bobbed in the water; she hung around his neck and kissed him, and then they both took a pull on the cigarette she had held all this time above the waves.

Finally, they climbed back up on the pier. Daisy's mother twisted her hair to squeeze the water out. Ginny could see it was hard for her to walk in her tight, cutoff shorts now that they were wet. Harder still for Roy, who was wearing jeans. Daisy's mother went into the house, but Roy came over and squatted beside Daisy's bike. Water streamed from the bottoms of his pants into the dusty rut.

With both hands he wiggled the wheel. It came all the way off. "Hmmm . . ." He frowned at it, turning it over in his hands.

"I think maybe if you tighten this," Ginny said, plucking the nut off the ground where it had fallen and holding it out to him.

He looked at her, then he snapped the wheel like a Frisbee so that it flew into the tall grass. "Nope," he said. "Sorry. I ain't gonna be able to fix it. I guess you're going to have to ride without 'em, Daze. Like your friend here." He winked at Ginny.

Ginny looked away. She didn't like him using her to make Daisy feel bad. And that he couldn't fix the broken wheel was a big strike against him. Her father fixed everything, or at least he stacked broken things under his workbench to fix later. Fixing was obviously the difference between a man who was your father and a man who wasn't. Roy had also littered. Dads didn't do that, either.

Ginny's father had somehow made clear that, while he loved all three of his daughters equally, she was the one he was closest to. At least she'd believed that growing up, although now she wondered if he'd managed to communicate the same message to each of her sisters as well. Certainly she and he spent the most time together. On weekends, she would ride with him when he went to interview witnesses. She'd wait in the car, reading or doing her homework. She could listen to anything she wanted on the radio, as long as she switched back to 88.7 when he returned.

Once, one of the interviews had been down in these cabins, she remembered. It was November, pouring. The windshield wipers were breathless with their frantic labor. The sky looked like lint; clumps of sodden brown leaves lined the road.

"I used to come down here all the time when I was a kid," he'd said, putting the car in park. "That was back when this place was a nice vacation spot. These cabins were in good shape then and Chicago people would rent them from the country club for the summer. They had this huge raft with a diving board."

"They still have that," Ginny interrupted.

"No, this wasn't the high-dive you're thinking of, although they had one of those, too. This was a low board, stuck way out over the water." He spit his gum into its foil wrapper and jammed it into the ashtray that already overflowed with crumpled silver pellets. "Some kid was waterskiing too close. Took his head right off."

"Oh!" Ginny covered her face with her hands.

"That's why I'm always telling you, you have to be careful. One minute you're having a great time, wind in your hair and all that, the next minute . . . sslltt." He pulled his finger across his neck. "The fun's over."

The cabins weren't what they once were; that was obvious even without her father's lecture about the increase in air travel, the completion of the interstate system, and the proliferation of two-income households, which meant weeklong vacations to Disneyland and the Grand Canyon, and the end of summer rentals on Wisconsin lakes, with their aimless days of swimming and fishing and their evenings of sheepshead and euchre, with maybe a tournament of horseshoes or a Saturday night dance thrown in for thrills. They'd been cheaply winterized, their plank walls covered in shingles meant to resemble brick. Sheets of plastic were tacked to their windows for insulation, and they were rented year-round to people who couldn't afford anything better, people who let their Novas and their Dusters and their lidless Kenmore washers rust in the yard when they quit running, people who might even be on welfare. People like Daisy's mother and Roy, and people, apparently, like Jon Kepilkowski's parents.

The steep road down to the lake seemed to Ginny to be narrower than she remembered. The branches meeting overhead formed a sort of tunnel, and honeysuckle, the invader—she'd appreciated even then the distinction between native and imported plants—had been allowed to grow unchecked, so that its branches scraped the doors of Beth's car.

"Ain't fell in the paint," Ginny's teacher had told them, not that Ginny had ever said that word anyway. But Daisy went to a different school, so maybe she didn't know. Her not knowing was part of what made Ginny aware that there was something undesirable about living in the cabins. After a while, she'd stopped asking her mother to take her down there.

Now, in high school, she was ashamed of that reaction. She wished Daisy hadn't moved away. If she hadn't, they could be friends again, she thought, now that she knew better than to care about such superficialities. It was different in high school. People were less where they came from, more where they were going. Those with enough force of personality could negate their backgrounds. The head cheerleader's mother used food stamps; everyone knew it; nobody cared.

The road leveled off at the bottom of the hill and the asphalt gave way to two lines of dirt with a wide space of grass between them—there was still no real road down here. Had Jon been one of those boys who pedaled their bikes furiously down this track and then stood on the brakes at the bottom, their back wheels skidding crazily as they looked over their shoulders, admiring their rooster tails of dust? She stroked the braid that hung over her shoulder, nearly to her waist. She wondered if his brother would be there, the one who had been arrested.

A Frisbee sailed above their roof as they pulled over. Lots of people were already standing around on the grass, plastic cups dangling from their fingertips, cigarettes held furtively close to their thighs. Despite the heat, most were wearing jeans long enough to step on with the heels of their hiking boots. Jon was wearing shorts and sneakers, though, like she was. He was standing by the keg, holding a stack of plastic cups in one hand.

"Hi," he said, when they went over. "Glad you could make it. How about a beer? Or there's Coke or Sprite." He tapped a blue-and-white cooler with one rubber-capped toe. "Or Tab, if you want."

"Beer's good," Beth said. She slid a cup off the stack he held out to her, positioned it under the tap, and flicked the lever. Foam dribbled into her cup.

"Here." He tucked the stack under his arm and took the cup from her hand. Ginny noticed that when he pumped the keg, a muscle made a ridge along his tan forearm. He looked at her, as he angled the cup under the spigot. "See?" He smiled. He had a nice smile. "This way you don't get the foam."

He drew a cup for Ginny, too, even though she hadn't said to; otherwise, she probably would have chosen the Tab. The rule was that you could have beer if the parents said it was OK, but Ginny didn't see any parents. Also, she could be kicked off the tennis team if her coach found out she'd taken so much as one little sip. The team stood in a circle holding hands before every meet and prayed to God to keep their "bodies free from harmful substances." That meant "no smoking, no drinking, no drugs," at least during the season, which had started two weeks ago.

She would just hold it, Ginny decided, just carry it around and then maybe accidentally on purpose spill it somewhere on the grass, or set it down and forget where she'd left it.

She took the cup from his hand, her fingers pressing for a moment against his thumb. The sensation made her chest constrict suddenly, unexpectedly. That was when she'd said it: "Beth made me come." The entirely wrong thing.

"Oh," he said. "Well, I hope you have a good time."

"I knew I liked Beth." That's what he should have said. Or "Good work, Beth." Something like that. Jon thought of it after they'd wandered off, but then it was too late. He couldn't go and work it in—"Say, you know how Beth made you come? Well, I knew I liked Beth." He would sound like an idiot. Also, he regretted pointing out the Tab. They might have thought he was trying to say they were fat.

He'd planned the party for Ginny. He'd spent the whole spring going out of his way to pass her locker several times a day and forgoing rides home so he could be sitting on the steps when she hurried past, her knapsack bulging on one shoulder, her braid bouncing against her back. He'd even joined the track team—her spring sport—hoping it would give him a chance to approach her, but in a matter of weeks the school year was over and he'd done nothing more than mumble "Good race." And then he'd had to endure the long, barren summer, staring out the open doors of the garage where he slid section two of the semiweekly local paper into the fold of section one, dreaming that she might walk by, planning what he would say if she did. By September, he felt he'd go crazy, the thought of her buzzed so continually in his head. He was giving this party, spending a good portion of his summer earnings, so that he could invite Beth, so that she would bring Ginny. "Hey, and bring Ginny," he'd planned to say casually, but didn't, because he'd never said her name before and he knew he couldn't make it come out casual. Well, he'd gotten lucky and it had worked out as he'd hoped, only now he was blowing it.

"Jon-Boy! Head's up!"

A Frisbee flew at him and his fingers closed neatly around it with a clomp. Had she seen that?

Beth had drifted over to Tracy and Kim, who were sitting on the porch steps.

"That sucks," Tracy was saying.

"I know, can you believe her?" Kim tipped her head back and gave it a little shake to perk up the wings of hair that framed her face.

Ginny stood beside Beth and gnawed on what she'd said to Jon. So rude! What was the matter with her? Well, she barely knew him anyway. They'd have nothing to do with each other now this year, just as they'd had nothing to do with each other for the previous three, and then they'd never see each other again. Chalk it up to practice. To experience. Shake it off. But she felt bad. Maybe she would say, before they left, that she hadn't meant it that way, had meant it as a joke, ha, ha. Except she couldn't imagine how that would play out. How could it have been a joke exactly? No, better to say she'd had a great time and pretend the other had never happened. He'd given a great party; she'd had a great time; that's what she'd say; that might fix it. She glanced over at him. He was talking, laughing, doing a little balancing act with the stack of cups. He hadn't given her a second thought, she told herself, so it was all right. Disappointing, but all right.

"Hi, Kyle." Beth knew how to make it sound natural. They'd kept standing at the bottom of the porch steps talking to Tracy and Kim, because Beth had seen Kyle go into the house when they pulled in and figured that sooner or later he'd come out again. Kyle, Ginny realized, was the main reason Beth had come to this party.

"Hi," he said. "Having a good time?" He was wearing flip-flops. Probably half the school would show up Monday wearing flip-flops now. He stood on the step smiling down at them, the Kyle smile, they all called it privately, full-lipped and languorous, and then he moved past them, nodding at Beth as he went by.

Ginny felt a little tug on her braid and turned instinctively to look. Kyle Kepilkowski winked at her and then he was off, flip, flop, already nearly across the yard.

She'd been growing her hair since sixth grade, braiding it down her back since eighth. She'd resisted pressure to layer. Boys were always tweaking the braid. She was aware, without articulating it even to herself, of its usefulness as a sort of bridge between her and them, a chance to touch without commitment. Her mother was aware of this, too. She was always after Ginny to cut it: "Don't you want something stylish? A perm, maybe. Something to show off your pretty face, honey?" But Ginny didn't. She liked being different, enjoyed those few moments of safe attention. Now she pulled the braid forward over her shoulder, her fingers caressing the spot his must have touched.

It's just the hair, she reminded herself, but still, she was glad now that Beth had made her come.

Jon had never pulled her hair. He'd never been very flirty, not with her, at least. But then the circumstances under which they'd gotten to know each other had been so serious. And she'd cut her hair off, too, as soon as she got out of the hospital. She was someone different after that.

1963

Clark gets to the tavern too early. Only the hard cases are there, three men propping themselves along the bar and an emaciated woman dragging on a cigarette at a dark corner table, all of them human islands, concentrating on getting and keeping the drink in their veins. He orders a Rob Roy, a drink he's read about in a novel, and is close to the bottom of his second when Bud and the others finally begin coming in, in twos and threes—nine of them in all. They're slapping Jim on the back, calling him a condemned man. "Life sentence, Jimbo!" "Life without parole!"

The attention's on the guest of honor, but Bud stands out nevertheless. His Indian blood helps to set him apart, the blackness of his hair, the darkness of his eyes, but he also has an ease about him, an openness. He greets the bartender as a friend and ushers the other men inside, obviously playing the host. Clark knows that Bud has done grand, impulsive, exuberant things. He "borrowed" a train one night, drove it to the next station. That's the story any-way, although it's hardly plausible. How would he know how to operate an engine? How could he escape prosecution? He climbed a water tower and painted his initials on its side. He swam the length of Lake Winnesha. Clark can't decide whether feats like these are heroic or silly. He knows himself to be almost capable of vanishing into the paneling if he doesn't make a conscious effort to articulate himself, and he sees that Bud is the opposite—he seems to generate electrical impulses, luring others to him.

Not one of them orders hard liquor, only beers from the tap, except for Jim, who orders a Coke. They're friendly: "Hey, Clark." "You know Clark." "Yeah, hey, howya doin', Clark?" They fill in the bar around him, offer him a pool cue. Bud sits on a stool facing into the room, his arms generously spread along the top of the bar. After Clark loses his game, it's easy to slide onto the stool beside him, to mumble that he has something he wants to talk about. "Sure, Clark. Geez, you want to talk, I'm your man. Another of these for my friend, here," Bud says, lifting Clark's nearly empty glass by the rim and giving it a little shake. "What'cha drinking anyway?" He squints at the dregs, sniffs, then sips. "Whew, strong stuff! Make it two," he shouts to the bartender, pointing at Clark's glass. And when two fresh glasses of brown liquid have been set on the bar, he says loudly, "Put 'em on Jim's tab!" He looks around to be sure his friend has heard the joke, while pulling out his wallet. "I'll get 'em," he says, which is a lucky thing, since Clark's down to small change. "So." He sips and pulls his lips back like a chimp to show nearly straight white teeth, the way actors swallow a stiff drink in the movies. "What did you want to discuss?" He frowns slightly and tips his head, as if to cup Clark's words in his ear. His oddly formal diction seems to mean that he'll take the matter, whatever it is, seriously.

Around Bud, though, there's a constant ruffle of men vying for his attention, one trying to get him to take his turn at the pool

table, another wanting him to listen to a story. They're like chil-
dren. Bud's hands, palms open, rise and fall, as he wards them off
when they try to interrupt.

"It's kind of something private. Do you think we could go out-
side for a minute?"

"Let's go out back. Then we can take these along." Bud raises
his glass and slides from his stool.

He flicks on the yellow bug light with the assurance of a pro-
prietor as they step out. Behind the building on a little strip of
unevenly cut grass a picnic table is planted beneath a small
clothesline. They slide onto the benches on either side of the table.

"So what's up?"

This part, looking Bud in the eye and delivering the story, is
going to be even more difficult than he'd expected. Clark glances
once over his shoulder, wishing to be back in the midst of the noise
and distractions. He presses his thumbnail into the soft wood of
the table and studies the tiny scores it leaves behind as he begins.
"It's just that I saw Marie the other day." He raises his eyes. He
wonders how it's going.

Bud's face softens at the mention of his wife. He smiles. "Yeah,
I heard you guys were hanging around on the pier, while I was out
practicing."

Clark blinks. Of course, one of the neighbors must have told
him, or maybe Marie herself. After all, they'd just been talking.
Still, he feels as guilty as if he's been kissing her. And he also feels
slightly, unreasonably insulted that Bud doesn't seem to mind.

Bud looks shyly, almost coyly, at him over the rim of his glass.
"She tell you about the baby?"

Had she told him? Then or before or ever? Wasn't it Hattie
who'd told him?

"Yeah. Congratulations," he says, holding his hand out across
the table. Then, while they're still shaking hands, he blurts it out,

just wanting to get it over with. "The thing is, I saw her with Walter Fleischer."

"Yah?" *His tone is encouraging, expectant. Next he would ask if she'd told Walt about the baby. Clark will have to be more explicit.*

"They seemed, well, very close, if you know what I mean."

Bud furrows his brow, baffled. And then he seems to realize. "You mean you think they were fooling around?" *He snorts.* "You've gotta be kidding me! Clark," *he leans forward and reaches his long arm all the way across the table, setting a square hand on Clark's shoulder,* "I don't know what you think you saw exactly, but trust me, you didn't see that. Where was this?"

He hasn't thought of an answer for this question; for all his worry, he hasn't thought through the details of his story at all. He'd assumed the suggestion would have been enough. More than enough. He says now the first thing that comes into his head, the name of another tavern. "At Musky Bill's."

"Oh, well, then, they were probably talking about the cottages. You know we rent our place from Walt's dad, and Marie's been thinking maybe she could manage all his properties for him. Get free rent for us. Best case, maybe even a little more. It would help out with the baby, especially now when I'm really just getting started with the golf. Here, let me tell you the big plan, Clark. See what you think." *He pushes his palms, one right and one left, along the table, as though spreading out a map.* "The plan is ... well, OK, you can call it a dream, but Marie thinks I can do it, and you know her, whatever she decides on is pretty much a done deal." *He nods and spreads his invisible map again.* "The plan is, I go professional, spend a couple years on the circuit. Tough on her, I know, home alone. But my idea—the part she doesn't even know about yet—is that once I got the credentials, then I start in as a pro at the country club, you know, giving lessons, running tournaments. Mr. Fleischer is all for making the place more* *attractive to the serious golfer. He's thinking of buying a field or two from Hanke, making it eighteen holes, a real course. I could do a good job as a club pro and make a nice life for a family."*

"Bud! We're rollin'!"

Bud extricates his long legs from the space between the bench and the table. He holds out his hand for Clark to shake again. "I've got to keep up with these guys," he says. "Thanks, you know, for looking out for me, but you see there's nothing to worry about, don't you? I mean, Marie and Walt—you're talking about the two people I trust most in this world. Believe me, them two would never hurt me."

Clark, trapped between the table and the bench, doesn't know how to respond. He doubts that Marie would approve of Bud's goal—she's more ambitious than that, but it certainly isn't his place to say so. He sees that Bud doesn't understand his wife, not the way Clark understands Marie, anyway. But probably things are different between husbands and wives; probably there are understandings he can't fathom. The thing he has to do is not disappoint Marie, and he seems to be failing at that.

He's standing now but still caught in the table, so that he has to twist his body to call after Bud. "It's just that I did see them together. They ... they were together."

Bud gives him a wave over his head and disappears through the doorway.

nine

"You're not taking 94?"

Freddi asked casually, expressing no more than mild surprise, but her question tugged Jon out of the vortex of preoccupation into which he'd been sinking for several miles. His anger with Ginny had propelled him to Freddi's, and his excitement at being with Freddi had propelled him to commit to a full day and half the night with her, but somewhere along East Washington, as they drove out of town, the heady rush of both those sensations had evaporated, leaving a slick of depression and anxiety. He'd been thinking of turning back.

"I thought we'd take the scenic route," he said, letting her wonder whether he was being sincere or sarcastic.

The state highway, which he picked up now going east, had no spectacular views. It was, however, a part of the landscape it cut through, not removed from it, the way the interstate was. It paused in the middle of towns and curved around churches and steep hills. Driveways along it led to colorful destinations—a drive-in movie theater and a prison and a tractor-repair business whose yard was packed with machines in various states of wholeness. Mostly it passed fields and stands of trees delineating the edges of fields, just as the interstate did, but close enough that you could see more than green. You could see what people piled on their porches and hung on their clotheslines. Those were Ginny's observations, though. It was Ginny who hated the interstate. Jon realized he'd veered south to pick up the highway without even thinking about it, because that was the route she preferred.

"We can get on 94," he offered, "if you'd rather."

"I've just never gone this way before. I didn't know it could be done." Freddi leaned her head against the back of the seat. "Big old jet airliner," she sang with the radio, "don't carry me too far away."

He looked at her. "Is that what it is?"

"Sure. What did you think?"

He shook his head. "Oh, I don't know. Not that exactly."

Back in high school, he and Ginny, listening to the song in Beth's Pinto, had agreed the opening phrase was "You can sleep with the light on." The song, they'd reasoned, must be about the intensity of dreams.

Freddi was poking at the tuner. "OK if we listen to something else?"

It wouldn't be fair to tell her now that he wanted to cancel the trip. He'd heard her on the phone leaving a message before they left, saying, sorry, she wouldn't be able to make it that evening, after all. They'd argued about this before—he wished she wouldn't change her plans for him.

"You think I should like you for that," she'd said. She was

kneeling on the floor of her office, inserting papers in the bottom drawer of a file cabinet. She wouldn't leave work out on her desk, no matter how late it was. "You think it makes you sound like you're not possessive."

Her tone was matter-of-fact, almost gentle, but he could tell it was a trap. She gave the file drawer a push and it slid closed with a bump.

"Well . . ." he'd begun. He hadn't thought at all about the image his words projected; her changing plans for him just made him feel uncomfortable.

"You don't want me to change plans for you because you don't want to guarantee that you'll show up. In fact, you don't want to plan to see me at all. You just want us to happen to be in the same place at the same time. Can't fight serendipity." She was still on the floor, her skirt stretched snugly over her thighs.

He extended his hand to help her up.

"News flash, bud." He hated it when she talked like that, when she acted as if she were too hard and mean to be hurt. "My plans are none of your business." She ignored his hand and rose gracefully, rolling back on her heels. "I can take care of myself. I'm not your responsibility."

Naïvely, he had indeed thought at first that this was going to be true. Her extreme independence, her ability to identify what she wanted and to go and get it for herself, had been among the qualities that had drawn him to her. She'd chosen to work at Nielson Gray, for instance, not the other way around. Others had had stronger portfolios, but she was obviously the one to hire. She'd impressed Gray with some spiel about Warhol's influence on the table tent and charmed Kaiser by admitting that what she'd said to Gray was bullshit. Her black sheer patterned stockings and minidress had sold Nielson, and the fact that her firm had worked on Ben & Jerry's had wowed that twit

Jimmy Ryan. Somehow it never came up that all they'd done was name a single, limited-edition ice-cream flavor and she had not even had anything to do with that. Not that she wasn't good at her job. She had a real way with words and a feel for what would grab a client and what would resonate with the public, and, maybe most important of all, she knew how to make those two often oppositional goals come together.

Jon sighed.

"You don't like this?" Freddi had settled on the interminable world music.

"It's great." No, he couldn't tell her he wanted to go back. She'd be angry, and justifiably so. And it wasn't as if Ginny would be happy, either, if he showed up now.

Kaiser, Jon realized, had been right. All he'd had going for him was that he was a good guy, a responsible guy, a man of integrity. He had no natural gift, as his father had had; he wasn't a charmer, like his brother; he didn't have Kaiser's ability to tell people to go fuck themselves. He didn't have his mother's ruthlessness or Freddi's will or Ginny's adaptability. He'd been a guy who did the right thing, that was all.

Except, in all honesty, he hadn't been that, either. He'd aligned himself with his mother, when he should have taken his father's side; he'd done nothing to save Kyle from the cops; he'd slammed on the brakes that night for no reason other than jealousy and rage. Maybe betraying his wife was merely acting in character. And, as far as that was concerned, there was by this point no longer a right thing to do. Either way he went, he'd be doing wrong to someone. Ironically, the only person with whom he could imagine discussing a problem like this was Ginny.

He glanced over at Freddi. She was still fooling with the speakers, frowning at the radio, her pink baseball cap pulled low over her forehead. "What are you thinking?" he asked.

"That we should have the Henshaw account."

"That's Kaiser's baby. He'd never give it up. Anyway, they love him."

"I know, but his ideas are getting kind of stale, don't you think? That last thing with the elevator and the crocodile? Kind of amateur hour."

"Well, no one's going to hit it out of the park every time."

"I know that. And I'm not saying Mark isn't a genius. The stuff you guys did for Black Cow was one of the main reasons I wanted to work at the agency. Well, I've told you all this before."

She had. Jon remembered the night, not long after she'd been hired. They'd gone for drinks after work with Kaiser and Patterson and a couple of others. Ginny had joined them. He'd been half embarrassed that night at the way Freddi had gone on about the Black Cow campaign, unsure of her sincerity. But he'd been impressed that she got what made those ads good. She'd hit unerringly on the various considerations that had gone into them, which made him feel close to her, as if she'd burrowed into his mind. She'd said that campaign could have come out of Chicago or L.A. or New York, and that made him think of himself in a way he wasn't used to, or hadn't been used to since he was a child and his mother had made clear that she thought he belonged in a bigger pond. He hadn't taken Freddi's opinion seriously, of course. She was young; what did she know? But it was gratifying to hear. And probably true, at that. No reason why he and Kaiser couldn't be producing top-quality work, just because they chose to live in a city of human scale.

"You want to tell Mark he's washed up, or should I?" he joked now.

"Look, all I'm saying is that account needs a fresh approach. The agency has a responsibility to the client. And to Mark. He should have an opportunity to produce his best work and this project obviously isn't doing it for him anymore."

"But it would be a good account for us?"

"Well, yes. I think so."

If he was honest with himself, he had to admit that he liked hearing this kind of talk, her confidence in him, in them, as a team. The idea of knocking Kaiser out of the way, though, made him feel almost physically ill.

On an impulse, he reached over and pulled off her cap.

"Hey!" She grabbed for it, but he switched hands, opened the car window, and dangled it out.

She shook her head at him, indulgent.

In the rearview mirror, the sun glinting off some metal part on the car behind them caught his eye, distracting him so that he relaxed his grip on the cap long enough for an updraft to snatch it and toss it over the car into the weeds beyond the right shoulder.

Jon pulled into a tavern's gravel parking lot. They got out of the car, gasping in the spongy air that replaced the crisp climate control, and began to walk back along the shoulder. Had he been with Ginny, Jon knew he would have been irritated with himself over the delay, but with Freddi he didn't care. It was only being with her that mattered, not where they were going or what they were doing.

Suddenly she grabbed his arm and made a little hop to the left.

"What is it? A snake?"

"No, I was afraid . . . Isn't that poison ivy?"

"I doubt it. Where?"

"Right there! Right where I was about to step." She pointed, although holding her finger well back, toward a stalk of chicory that had not yet bloomed. "Look! It's all over the place!"

He laughed. "Have you never been outdoors?"

"Don't laugh at me! I never said I was nature girl."

"I'd hardly call this nature."

"So it's not poison ivy?"

"No."

"Or poison oak?"

He gave her a little hug. "I wouldn't let you walk into anything poisonous."

He knew poison ivy. He'd spent an afternoon killing the stuff when he was nine or so on a day very like this in the heat and in the weeds. His father had dragged a can of chemicals with a little hose attached to spray along the edge of the fairway, where the woods was always threatening to trespass on the course. "We're poisoning the poison ivy," his father had sung gleefully, making up a little tune and sometimes doing a dance step and twirling the spray attachment as if it were a cane. It wasn't the way his father normally behaved, and Jon recognized even then that he was glimpsing the man the way he must once have been before something—Jon had been egotistical enough to consider his own existence a strong possibility—had changed him. Where was Kyle? It was unusual for the two boys and their father to be off doing something together. His father worked or sat in the tavern; the boys hung around at home or with their friends. Jon couldn't remember even one other time when he and his father had been together alone. His father let Jon squeeze the sprayer. "Here," he said, pulling the work glove off his hand and slipping it over Jon's, "don't let it get on your skin."

Concentrating on getting it right—not spilling, not squirting too much, not squirting too little, not tipping the canister, any of which might cause his father to swear and scowl and yank the hose back—Jon didn't hear the whir of the golf cart's electric motor until it had driven past.

His father stood watching as the cart and its toad-like driver, plaid-panted knees splayed, climbed the gentle hill on the third fairway and then disappeared over the rise. "There goes the son of a bitch who made me what I am today," he said.

Jon wasn't sure if he should say something or go on spraying or just stand and wait to hear what his father might say next. He settled on a compromise, tapping the nozzle with his gloved finger, as if he were trying to dislodge a clog.

"You know I used to play a decent game." His father was hacking at the roots of a burdock plant as he spoke, driving a pronged instrument deep into the soil, pulling it back out and driving it in again.

"Sure," Jon said. That his father had once been good enough to win money in local tournaments, that he could have made a career of golf, was legendary in their family.

"That's the fellow who killed it for me." Jon's father stabbed the air a couple of times with his tool in the direction the golf cart had taken.

"Mr. Fleischer?" Everyone knew the owner's son.

"Yeah, Walt and I grew up together. Like you and Kyle, really, close as brothers. Believe you me, we had a heck of a lot of fun. But, looking back, I can see your mother was right." Jon's father nodded, as if confirming this for himself, and then turned back to chopping at burdock roots. "You see, Walt was always jealous of what I had with his old man. The old man was always saying things like 'Walt, you oughta take a lesson from Bud here.' He liked the way I presented myself, you see. I had some manners; I didn't make a spectacle of myself the way Walt did, throwing money around, always having to be the center of attention. And I knew how to really work on something, how to follow through, while Walt . . ." He drove the prongs so deep into the soil, it took some effort to pull them out again.

"Well, you know the type: everything's always been handed to them. They don't know what it means, they have no *idea* of the kind of commitment that's required." He looked at Jon, as if expecting confirmation.

If he could figure out what his father was talking about—commitment required for what?—Jon thought, he might possibly have some chance of knowing the type. Anyway, he wanted his father to go on thinking that he did. So he nodded in a way that he hoped expressed world-weary resignation.

"Anyway, I was a favorite in the Butter Cup. They don't play that one now, but it was a big deal back in '63, believe you me." He was swinging the pronged stick idly beside his foot now, swishing at the grass, and staring out across the course. "Everyone thought I'd win it. The old man. Walt. Your mother. The competition was quite a bit tougher than they thought, but I had a decent chance to win, and winning would have done a lot for me. For our whole family. But then that son of a bitch rolls right off the bridge."

Jon knew the story. It was the night before the tournament was to begin. His father had been driving home from the kick-off party at the country club when he'd seen Walter Fleischer go off the bridge into the lake. He'd jumped in, smashed the window under water with a nine iron, and dragged Fleischer out.

"You seen this." His father rolled up one sleeve.

Of course, Jon had. The jagged scars along his father's arm that ran from above the elbow, like a bolt of lightning, nearly to his wrist were unmissable, even though his father nearly always wore long sleeves buttoned at the cuff. It was no secret that they'd come from the broken window.

"So that's why you couldn't play anymore?"

"Oh, I could play all right. At least by the end of the summer, I coulda been right back on top. But I couldn't finish the

Butter Cup, and that was the one I'd put my money on. Only it wasn't my money, you see. I'd borrowed from Walt to make my bet and it turned out he'd taken it from his old man's safe." He rolled his sleeve back down then, buttoned it neatly at the wrist. "Well, the old man gave me the job here to pay it off, which was decent of him."

"But you saved his son's life! He should've given you a reward."

His father shrugged. "Yeah, I suppose I did." He laughed. "But I busted the window on his Caddy."

"And you and Mr. Fleischer aren't friends anymore?"

His father stabbed the prongs into the ground again. "Walt turned out to be a weasel."

"Kyle and me call him 'the Toad,' " Jon offered.

His father laughed again. "Yeah, that's about right."

Emboldened, Jon pushed beyond what he would normally have dared to ask his father. "Why couldn't you have played after work? Kept up your game. You coulda been the Midwest champion."

His father shrugged again. "I maybe could of. But Kyle came along and then I started working over to the gas station nights. And your mother—well, I didn't have to impress her anymore, I guess. That was part of it. A big part of it. Anyway, you better get that poison going."

Had Jon not believed that afternoon that he was being granted a privileged glimpse of the complex transactions that went into being a man, he wouldn't have felt so betrayed later when he discovered that this version wasn't the whole of the story.

ten

The front hubcap of Nora's Passat wagon scraped against the curb as she pulled up. A sort of keening issued from the open back window.

Nora leaned across the passenger seat and spoke up at Ginny through the window. "Hey, sorry about this." She turned toward the small, howling form in the backseat. "Can you stop the song for a minute, sweetie, and say hi to Aunt Ginny?"

Rodney quieted and stared at Ginny. "No, I cannot say hi to her at all."

Nora sighed. "Do you think you should just go by yourself, Gin?"

"No, he'll be fine," Ginny said, sliding into the car. "Won't you, Rodney?" She looked over her shoulder at him, as she reached for her seat belt.

He tipped his head back and bellowed at the ceiling. "I will not be fine!"

But then she snaked her hand behind the seat and tickled his bare feet and he had to laugh. "I remember what Anthony was like at this age," she said. "Believe me, Heidi'll understand." She turned again to face the road. "Did you ever dream you were trying to hold a baby while sitting in a car, but it kept dissolving in your hands and slithering down the crack at the back of the seat?"

Nora laughed. "Not that exactly, but when I was pregnant I dreamed I kneaded a baby, pushed it into a bread pan, and popped it into the oven. And I don't even bake."

"So it doesn't mean anything?"

"Like what?"

"Like that I'm unfit to be a mother?"

"Well," Nora said, tilting her head back to indicate Rodney, who was now touching the window with the tip of his tongue, "you can judge for yourself whether I'm fit to be a mother." She looked at Ginny. "It might mean that you're pregnant."

Ginny rolled her eyes. Nora knew better than to push that line.

On Wisconsin Public Radio a pleasant-voiced man was delineating the highlights of his book on the Irish tin whistle.

Ginny pointed her finger at one of the preset buttons. "May I?"

"Of course."

A Who classic leapt from the speakers with a comforting thump. She remembered Jon once in their Indiana apartment dressed in nothing but his air guitar belting out "G-o-o-o-o-d morning!" to this song, and then developing an elaborate theory—"no, listen, listen," he kept saying, trying to shush her laughter—to explain why such an impossible lyric could make sense.

"Who-o-o-o are you?" she'd sung back at him, taunting.

He'd made a grab at her and she'd run, shrieking, although

there was nowhere to hide but under the sheet, and the bang of a broom handle on the ceiling downstairs made them giggle.

The apartment Ginny and Jon had rented in Indianapolis had been under the eaves of their landlady's house.

"I'd prefer an older person," she'd said, narrowing her eyes at them critically, as they sat at her gingham-covered kitchen table filling out the application. "One older person. Someone who doesn't walk around much."

"Oh, when we're inside, we stay put," Jon had said.

"We mostly read," Ginny had clarified.

"Or watch TV."

"Very low volume."

"Reception's terrible," the landlady grunted.

"And we never wear shoes in the house."

Ginny had given Jon a grateful glance when he'd said that last one. It was a good and believable touch. With its sloping ceilings and honey-colored wood floor, the apartment had a charm that the other places they'd seen in their price range were distinctly lacking. They'd both been raised to make themselves accommodating at almost any cost and had yet to outgrow the habit.

"Well, you do seem like a nice young couple," the landlady had said finally.

They had been a nice young couple.

They'd actually begun housekeeping together, after a fashion, a year earlier, when her father had finally consented to let her live on campus in the all-women's imposing stone dorm on the lake. Just as he'd feared, she, in fact, lived mostly in Jon's tiny, single-windowed room in the shabby blocks of the city where students mushroomed every fall among the two-story wood-frame houses. The room was furnished with a twin mattress without even the refinement of a box spring, which covered nearly the entire expanse of the worn floorboards; a series of cardboard boxes, into which they did their best to organize their clothes; and an orange milk-crate night table she'd plucked the previous spring from a pile of worn-out and makeshift furnishings some other student had shed on the sidewalk like an outgrown carapace. Whereas outside she stuck stolidly to blue jeans and the ubiquitous puffy down jacket, in that room she wore over her tights and turtleneck (the underbits necessary for warmth) a silk Chinese robe he'd bought for her at a secondhand store. In another secondhand store—he knew them all—he'd bought himself a tweed sport jacket to wear over his T-shirts and a black wool overcoat. He tried and rejected clove cigarettes; she took up knitting and ruined the style of his overcoat with a raggedy striped muffler.

They did much of their work while sitting on the mattress in the light of an architect's lamp clamped to the milk crate. Only the decreased frequency of slamming doors and flushing toilets in the rest of the house indicated the passage of time. Often they labored nearly through the night in that capsule-like room, sustained by a turkey sub and a bag of Fritos, the daily rhythms that governed adults and children meaning nothing to them, the window revealing of the outside world only a black rectangle of space. She lived in terror of a midnight phone call to her dorm room from her father, which, as far as she knew, had never come.

The apartment in Indianapolis had been the scene of their awakening from this larval student life, with the sense of adulthood the wedding rings and real jobs carried with them providing a sort of frisson. They'd invested in a futon and, more adult still, a frame to fold it over to make a couch. They'd hung an Indian-print bedspread over the bedroom window for privacy and covered cardboard boxes in wrapping paper to use as coffee and end tables. She lined the windowsills with potted herbs and he used their hatchback to carry home in triumph the two wooden desk chairs, discarded by his employer, that they still used in their home offices.

Heidi Dubchek, formerly Heidi Kaiser, was at a very different stage of her life. "I warn you, it's a cliff!" she trilled, as she led them from the back of the house—the only convenient entrance, if you chose not to arrive by boat—to the front. As if swimming up from the bottom of a well, they moved from dimness toward a brilliant wall of glass that opened onto a wide, redwood deck.

"Isn't the view to die for?" She looked proudly at her husband, Alex, who was, Ginny believed, some sort of VP at Oscar Mayer, as well as the view's procurer.

Alex had been lounging on the deck, a magazine resting limply on his stomach, but as they stepped into the bright and, there at the water's edge, remarkably fresh air, he swung his moccasined feet over the edge of his chaise, rose, and strode toward them, hand outstretched. "Gorgeous day, isn't it?"

Ginny agreed, praised the view, the house, the lot, the hickory that spread its branches over the deck, and generally tried to make herself and Nora collectively agreeable, since Nora was distracted by Rodney, who was trying to pull his hand free of hers and run toward the widely spaced rails, presumably to launch himself down what was, if not quite a cliff, a slope that plunged for about twenty-five yards before giving way to the water. It was obvious why the Dubcheks wanted landscaping. Whoever had put in the evergreen shrubs and crumbling cement stairs had done so with an eye for little more than economy.

"The people we bought from admitted this place was impossible to landscape, so we're giving ourselves entirely over to you," Heidi said, slipping her hand into her husband's and tucking her body against his to emphasize their united front. "I couldn't even grow a Chia Pet, could I, Bugabear?" She looked coyly at him, a teenager with the beginnings of crow's feet and lip lines.

"No, Squeezebug, I'm sure you couldn't," he said, kissing her head.

Ginny, storing the exchange as a tidbit for Jon, walked to the railing to hide her face. "Gosh," she said, "there're wonderful possibilities here, if you're willing to get rid of the shrubbery and the cement." Already ideas were popping pleasantly in her mind, like the opening volleys in a fireworks display.

"Well, we did have one thought, honey, remember?" Alex said. "We don't know anything about landscaping," he added, looking at Nora and then at Ginny, commanding attention for his punch line. "But we know what we like!"

"That's great," Nora said, letting Rodney slide down the length of her leg onto the deck. "What are you thinking?"

"Well, we honeymooned in Italy, you know," Heidi volunteered. "Did the whole Tuscany thing and then went down the Amalfi coast. Ah, so romantic!" She paused and added, rolling her eyes in an aside to Ginny, "Mark and I went to the Dells. Anyway, the terraces of lemon trees, that lush green and then the sparkling blue sea. It was just so . . . ." She stopped, unable to attach a word to the scene.

"Mediterranean?" Nora suggested.

It was Ginny who spotted him first, one foot already over the topmost rail. "Rodney, stop!" she barked, in a tone that froze everyone and seemed to halt time long enough for her to leap or run or somehow hurl herself to the spot, Nora one step behind her. She grabbed the child with both hands around his waist, her panic, combined with exasperation at the notion of having to plant a citrus grove slightly south of Canada, making her a bit rough.

She expected him to wail and try to pull free, but he looked at her and explained in a tone that suggested she was the unreasonable one, "I was just climbing the ladder to pick some apples."

"Get out of that tree!" She could hear her father, the sharp anger in his voice that she'd not expected, that had made her freeze against the branch like a cornered squirrel.

She'd summoned his attention when she'd seen him come out the front door. She must have been about nine, and she'd climbed the box elder, not just as far as the first two or three branches, but way, way up, until the branches began to narrow.

"Dad!" she'd called proudly. "Look at me!"

From up there, he'd looked to her unaccustomedly vulnerable, small, and, she'd noticed for the first time, slightly stooped. She could see the bald spot just beginning at the back of his scalp. His tone, when finally, peering up between the branches, he'd located her, restored his stature. "I mean it. Get down now!"

She'd felt so graceful climbing up; she'd almost swung from branch to branch in an easy rhythm. On the way down, though, in what she could tell by his voice was his glare, she stiffened. Her sneakers scraped the trunk and pinched in the forks. Her hair tangled in twigs. She couldn't seem to get a firm grip on the branches or her clutch was too tight and kept her from moving. When, finally, she'd made her way awkwardly to the bottom, he lectured her. How could she not know better? She was a fool. Irresponsible. Did she want to end up paralyzed? Dead? If she fell, it could hardly be called an accident, could it? Could it? His voice was unyielding. She'd have no one to blame but herself.

"What about an orchard?" Ginny suggested. "An orchard of Montmorency cherries? The dwarf ones. It would be breathtaking in the spring. Oh, and imagine in the winter, with the snow lacing the branches! And, of course, you'd have the fruit in the summer and fall. Or," she went on, when the Dubcheks made no response, "another option would be to do something open and sculptural in keeping with the style of the house. We could keep the outlines of the path the way it is, even use cement again—it would look very modern—which would keep the cost down."

"Well, we were thinking something more like the Spanish Steps," Alex said. "You know, very grand. Symmetrical. Sort of commanding."

"And then for summer parties," Heidi said, "we'd take everyone out on the lake at dusk and then, after dark, dock the boat and then lights . . ." She reached one arm out in front of her and moved it across the horizon to indicate sweep. "I'm thinking those big balls, like Christmas tree ornaments, would be hanging everywhere, illuminating this magnificent stairway."

Unbidden, the scenes from *Battleship Potemkin*, in which the baby carriage plummets agonizingly down the stairs, rose into Ginny's mind. "Well, we might be able to do something like that if we terrace it and build retaining walls. It could be beautiful, but it could also get very expensive . . ." She let her voice trail off and then started again, a fresh approach. "Let's talk about how you want to use the space. Will it just be a means—"

"Mo-o-o-m!" The sound of a door slamming followed. "Mo-o-o-m!" The demand was loud and insistent enough to travel clearly through the house and the double-paned sliding glass doors, tightly sealed to trap the air-conditioning.

Heidi rolled her eyes again, but her exasperation this time was obviously mock. She was smiling as she stepped lightly across the deck toward the door, slides snapping against her well-kept heels.

Alex kept his attention on the water. "I want to get a martini boat," he said to no one in particular; probably, in fact, to himself.

"Anthony!" Heidi had pulled one of the doors open far enough to fit her face into the space. "I mean, Marlin! We're out here!" She looked back over her shoulder at Ginny and Nora. "He prefers to be called 'Marlin' right now. Just warning you."

She slid the door open farther as the boy approached and put her arms around him on the threshold. "How was your night?"

"OK," he shrugged, tolerating the hug but not returning it. "Dad wants to talk to you."

"Say hello to Mrs. Kepilkowski, honey," Heidi prompted.

The boy scowled. "I was going to, Mom. Now you ruined it."

"Hi, Anthony," Ginny said. "I think you've met my friend, Mrs. Blom, at our house."

"That time that kid hit me with a dart?"

"Uh, yeah, I'm afraid that probably was the time. And you might remember Rodney."

"Hi, Rodney." Anthony looked at the much smaller boy and raised one hand in a solemn greeting.

Rodney, who was now standing beside Nora, mirrored the hand gesture. "Hi."

"You can call me Marlin, if you want," Anthony said to all of them. He regarded Rodney thoughtfully for a moment. "I've got some dinosaurs in my room," he said, finally. "You can look at them, if you want to. But you can't touch the skeleton ones because I made them before I was allowed to use real model glue and they break very easily."

Rodney narrowed his eyes. "Do you have a parasaurolophus?"

"Of course."

"Then I'll see them."

"Mom, Dad's waiting. I told you he wants to talk to you," Anthony said, as he turned to open the door again.

"He's waiting here? What does he want to talk about? For crying out loud, we're busy here!" Heidi glanced at Alex, who had not, throughout any of the previous exchange, ceased pondering his property, but who now turned to his wife with eyebrows raised. "I'll be right back," she said. "I'll tell him he can call me."

"Bring him out here," Alex said. "He knows everyone. Bring the guy out here and give him a drink."

"He's not going to want to come out here," Heidi said.

"Well, offer anyway. And don't be long."

Heidi sighed and disappeared into the house.

"When these things happen," Alex said, gesturing vaguely in the air to indicate forces beyond any mortal's control, "and when there's a kid, you've got to get along. That's my belief."

eleven

Kaiser had stayed in his car, using the Camaro as a shell to protect himself from the forces of Heidi-dom.

When she stepped out, squinting against the glare, he felt a
sort of cocktail made of equal parts regret, longing, and fury
slide from his throat to his bowels. The usual. He trusted that,
over time, it would diminish to a trickle and eventually subside
altogether. Emotions had only so much oomph, after all. Someday, impossible as it now seemed, this woman he'd been mixed
up with for thirteen years, inhaling her very exhalations as
they lay in bed, aware of and unembarrassed by her bodily
secretions, would be a perfect stranger to him. Already she'd
replaced her almost blowsy ponytail with straight, flat hair. All
twenty nails, indifferently kept in his time, had obviously been
recently manicured, the toes and fingers polished in comple-
mentary pinks. Heidi's favorite summer outfit had for years

been one of his shirts, worn open over a bikini top and a pair of
very short cutoffs; she was tall and broad-shouldered enough to
escape drowning and instead appear graceful and fluid, but
she'd abandoned that casual look when she'd left him and
replaced it with de rigueur capris and the sort of form-fitting
silk-blend T-shirts that turned out to cost a hundred dollars.
He'd seen them in the catalogs addressed to her that through
some trick of mail order lists occasionally appeared in slippery
heaps underneath his apartment mailbox.

He pretended to be engrossed in his car's manual, made her
come over and tap on the window with one of her pink nails.

"Mark!" Her voice was impatient. Impatience, exasperation: the only emotions he could count on being able to get out
of her anymore.

He smiled up at her. His smile used to disarm her, but now it
made her scowl. He let it collapse, touched the automatic window button. "What's up?"

"What do you mean, 'what's up'? Anthony said you wanted
to talk to me."

"You mean Marlin."

"For Christ's sake, Mark, turn the damn car off. The exhaust
is going to kill us."

He did as she asked, opened the car door, and stepped out.
He didn't really have anything specific to say to her. He'd just
wanted to get her to come to him, an impulse that felt now, as
he stood beside his burning car, pathetic.

"Listen," she said, "Alex wants me to invite you in for a
drink. I told him you'd be busy, but I said I'd ask, so I'm asking."

You could trust her to follow through with little promises; it
was big ones like 'til death do us part that gave her trouble.
Kaiser smiled at his own private witticism. Obviously, she didn't
want him to come in. Obviously, the sensitive, thoughtful

response would be: Hey, some other time; I'll take a rain check. But Kaiser felt a perverse compulsion to get a rise out of her. Maybe he couldn't make her happy, but he could still irritate her. He made a show of studying his watch. "A drink?" he said. "Sure, I could use a drink." He'd resisted an urge to say "wet my whistle," but he gave in to the impulse to mutter, "Decent of old Alex," in a Nick Charles sort of way.

She frowned at him, shaking her head. This sort of behavior had been one of her complaints about him, something she might never have been fully aware of had the marriage counselor not articulated it for her. "Be real!" the counselor had insisted. "Stop hiding behind your act!"

He knew what they both meant. He was sorry, sincerely sorry, that he couldn't oblige them. But for Pete's sake, they didn't know what they were asking. His "act" had won Heidi in the first place. Performing it was the only way he knew how to negotiate the world. He wasn't sure there was anything else about him that was remotely likable.

He stayed close to Heidi as they stepped into the dim, cool house. He'd always liked watching her from behind, but he was aware that he was no longer allowed to enjoy that view. Also, he didn't want to look the way he felt, like a puppy, tagging along with its tongue hanging out, eager for any droplet of attention. Halfway through the cathedral-ceiled living room, he remembered that he was permanently furious with her, despised Alex, and, whenever he came to within a mile of this neighborhood, felt his bile rising with such force that he had to clamp his teeth together. Having a drink in this house to spite his ex-wife was hardly worth the agony it was going to cost him. He glanced around; maybe he could relieve his feelings by accidentally knocking something fragile and expensive onto the unforgiving slate floor.

She touched the glass slider—he noticed that it slid open at the merest flex of her graceful bicep, unlike the piece of junk in his piece-of-shit apartment that was perpetually lunging off the track. Stepping out, he shut his eyes for a moment against the glare and stumbled, misjudging the height of the threshold.

"Care to wet your whistle?" Alex asked, lifting his own glass and shaking it slightly so that the ice chattered. Kaiser had noticed that he and Alex didn't use each other's names if they could help it.

"Very generous of you, sir." He registered Ginny's presence as he was delivering this inane reply. He'd always liked Ginny, always felt a little more alert, a little funnier in her presence. And since he'd become aware of Jon's perfidy, he'd had an overwhelming chivalric urge to rescue her from her husband. Now, caught off guard, he feared for a single, excruciating moment that somehow his attraction to her had been divined. By Heidi? By Alex? By Ginny herself? Had she been planted there to embarrass him? He raised his eyebrows toward her, relying on his act. "You? Here?"

"Ginny and Nora are going to do an Italian garden for us," Heidi said.

"Well, I don't know—" Ginny began, but Kaiser cut her off.

"I thought you and Jon were on your way to Summerfest."

"Oh . . ." She looked flustered and touched her forehead just above the eye with two fingers, half hiding her face. "That was the plan, but . . ." She shrugged. "It went awry."

Alex was handing him the promised drink, a Pimm's Cup in a glass that had once lived in a kitchen Kaiser and Heidi had shared. Kaiser considered dropping it, but then he'd end up squatting on the deck with a roll of paper towels, not exactly the image he was striving for. "Thanks," he said, instead, and treated himself to a large swallow. You had to hand it to Mr. Boloney: he wasn't stingy with the booze.

"God! I haven't been to Summerfest since that year it rained. Remember that, Mark? Jackson Street was a river! And the—" Heidi broke off abruptly and looked at Alex, slipping her exquisitely manicured hand into his. "God, it was awful."

She was lying, Mark knew. That night had been a trip, the warm water, entirely inescapable, gushing onto their faces, instantly soaking their hair and clothes, surging over their ankles, almost to their knees in places. "Imagine," Mark had said, when he described that night to some friends, "suddenly being crammed against a thousand women in wet T-shirts." But that was only a line he'd come up with for the act and, while it may have been factually accurate, it had nothing to do with his actual experience. He had been physically exultant, true, and helpless to sensation, but it was of a purely wholesome variety. His communion with the women around him, and with the men, was of the shared-wonder type. He and Heidi tipped their heads back and opened their mouths to let the water sluice their teeth. They splashed and lost their footing and fell against each other. They laughed with the delight of children. Even if he ever found another woman to love, Kaiser reflected, now that he knew how it could end up, he would never again have the wholly unguarded pleasure he and Heidi had been capable of. It gave him some satisfaction to know that she would not either. Certainly not with Weiner Boy. Or, if she did, she was not someone he knew at all. Of course that might be the worst part of the divergence of their lives: the realization that he did not know her any longer. That the person he had known had somehow evaporated.

"So, what, you guys got halfway there and changed your minds?" he said. They all looked at him blankly. "I talked to Jon," he explained, glancing at his watch, "must have been about an hour ago by now. He said you were halfway to Summerfest."

"Oh," Ginny began, but Nora broke in.

"Ginny had too much work to do," she said, "but Jon decided to go anyway. By himself. He was going to meet up with his cousin there, right, Gin?"

"His brother," Ginny said. Nora was brilliant with a story.

"You know," Kaiser said—he'd begun speaking with just a tendril of a thought in mind, not knowing where it would end up, but the hell with it. He was quite sure that Jon had said "we." "When you're done here, if you still want to go, I'd be up for it."

"Oh, no." But she'd responded so fast, there was no weight behind it.

He pushed. "Why not? It would be fun. We'll call Jon on the way, figure out someplace to meet up with him."

"Maybe we'll go, too," Nora said. "Peter would love to have us out of the house for the evening."

"Great," Kaiser said. "Yes, you come, too. Let's all go. Heidi?" He raised his glass in Alex's general direction to indicate that he, too, was included.

"Go where, Dad?" Anthony had silently slid the door open and was distorting his face by pressing his nose against the screen. Rodney, his head at Anthony's waist, stood beside him doing the same.

"Anthony! Stop that! You'll break the screen!" Heidi said.

"Rodney, stop that!" Nora echoed.

Both boys grinned. "Go where, Dad?" Anthony repeated.

Alex walked firmly across the deck and thrust his fingers into the handle of the screen. "In or out, boys," he said. "You're letting the air-conditioning escape."

Anthony dropped back obediently at his stepfather's command and Rodney stepped back in imitation of Anthony. Alex opened the door and extended one long arm, inviting them wordlessly, inarguably, onto the deck.

"Summerfest. Wanna go?" Kaiser said.

"Right now?"

"As soon as Mrs. Kepilkowski is finished here, yeah."

"We have an appointment in Winnesha after this," Ginny said.

"Well, that's on the way, isn't it? We'll go with you."

"Mark, I don't think——" Ginny began, but Heidi was also speaking and her tone was firmer.

"Mark." She spoke slowly, enunciating each word deliberately, as if communicating with someone with limited mental capacity. "We. Have. The. Dinner."

It wasn't until then that he remembered that he was handing Anthony over early because of Heidi's party tonight for Alex's mother and some cousin who was visiting from some Scandinavian country, possibly Denmark. "Sorry, Atom Ant. I forgot your mom's dinner."

"I hate having dinner!"

"Anthony," Heidi began.

"It'll be great, Anthony. You'll have a great dinner with a great Dane."

Heidi turned so fast to glare at him that her sunglasses flew off her face and fell onto the deck.

"Let Anthony go, Heidi," Alex said, putting his hand on her shoulder.

Well, that was a mistake, Kaiser thought, telling her what to do, especially about Anthony, not to mention touching her when she was feeling cornered. Kaiser retrieved the sunglasses and folded them in his palm. He smiled grimly into his glass. Someone—he, Alex, or Anthony, maybe all three of them—was going to get hurt.

But Heidi relaxed under her husband's hand. Her new husband's hand. "You sure that's all right with you? You wanted him to meet your cousin."

"He'll be here for weeks, Squeezebug. Anyway, time with his dad is more important for Anthony right now."

Kaiser wished he could hit the man. He tipped his head back, coaxing the watery liquor down his throat, letting what remained of the ice cubes bang against his teeth.

"And Ginny? This is really all right with you?" Heidi said.

Who did Heidi think she was? Room mother?

"Well, sure. If they don't mind wandering around an old golf course first for an hour or so."

"I don't mind," Kaiser said.

Heidi glared at him again.

"Will there be golf balls?" Anthony asked.

"I don't know, maybe. If they've turned any ground over, it's possible there might be arrowheads."

"Cool! What tribe? I wish they could be Crow, because I like the Crow. They were the most ruthless."

Kaiser lifted his hand to his heart. Discreetly, he dropped Heidi's sunglasses into his shirt pocket.

1963

The wind comes up as the sun goes down that night, which doesn't happen often. Wind is Marie's favorite weather, especially wind at night. She luxuriates in the whip and rush of it, as she and Bud climb the steep, twisting, packed-earth road, under the bowing trees. Leaves stream along their branches and her hair flutters like feathers against her face. She'd been surprised to discover that she'd actually felt more sexy pregnant than she had ever before, her body the focus of her whole self.

"I wish I didn't have to do this thing," Bud says.

"What? This party? It'll be lovely. You look so handsome." She tips her head to look up at him encouragingly. Sometimes, around certain people, he can be shy, her Bud. She thinks it's sweet.

"Not the party. The tournament. I'm not going to win, you know. Everyone thinks I will, and Mr. Fleischer's bet a lot of money on me—shoot, I bet a lot of money on me—"

"You did?" She stops. "You didn't tell me that."

"I was going to surprise you with the winnings. It seemed like such a sure thing."

"Well, of course, it's a sure thing," she says, swinging his hand, giving him a little pump. So he bet some money, it's what men do, and he's the best, everyone says so.

"No, it's not a sure thing." He looks back through the trees, toward the dark lake. "Actually, it's a pretty sure thing that I'm going to lose."

"Lose!"

"Well, come in second. Maybe even worse than that. I haven't seen everyone practice. There could be more of 'em."

"More of who? What are you talking about?"

"Did you see that guy from Dubuque?"

"What does he look like?"

"I don't know. Tall. Brown hair. What matters is what his swing looks like. I can't beat him. Marie, this guy is like a pro!"

"Oh, for Pete's sake, Bud. You're practically a pro yourself. You're just nervous, that's all."

"I am nervous, but I'm not just nervous. Look, I think I know enough about this to be able to tell if someone's better than me."

"I don't see how you can be sure from one little practice."

He doesn't answer. He turns and begins climbing steadily up the hill again, his eyes on his shoes.

The Lakeview Country Club makes most of its money as a venue for parties—graduation parties, anniversary parties, wedding receptions, post-burial lunches. You can have all the doors open and make one big room or close off rooms for smaller functions. In high school, Marie had worked parties. It was an easy job, arranging a relish tray, carrying plates of chicken Cordon Bleu or prime rib, potatoes O'Brien, and a side salad, a fruit cup or *a slice of cake, but no tips. She'd been to some small-room parties at the club and she'd worked a couple of "all floor" parties, but tonight is the first "all floor" party she'll attend as a guest. The occasion is the Butter Cup, the first tournament the club has hosted, the event that had "drawn 'em up from Chicago, drawn 'em down from Minneapolis, drawn 'em over from Indianapolis and Dubuque," Adam Fleischer is saying as they step in.*

He reaches out with his long, thin arm as he speaks, opening and then closing his palm, as if gathering clutches of tiny men in plaid pants, and then pulls his hand smartly back toward his body. "And here's our star," he beams, flinging his arm toward Bud and opening his hand wide. "Bud, c'mere. C'mere." His fingers, long and gnarled, beckon. It's his son Walter Fleischer, though, who steps forward and draws Bud in, grabs Bud's right hand in both of his and pumps it. "The man of the hour!" Walt announces.

Bud looks around him. A nervous smile flickers across his face, an expression Marie has never seen on him before. She doesn't like the feeling his lack of confidence gives her. She's worried for him, and that part is all right. But she also detects within herself a faint sense of revulsion. She'd felt the same as a child when her kitten's leg had been crushed and had had to be amputated. Her sisters and brothers had cooed over the damaged kitten and nursed it. It almost seemed the more precious to them for the pity and extra care it evoked. She'd done her duty, kept its bandages clean, petted and fed it, but it had seemed sullied to her and she'd secretly wished she could somehow throw it away. She isn't proud of her reaction; she knows it's a defect in her character. But there it is, nevertheless. Bud had been a star since she'd known him. But if his superiority doesn't extend beyond Winnesha, he isn't the man she'd believed she'd married.

After Walt's introduction, the others press in, talking weather and equipment. Marie sees Walt disengage from the crush and drift toward the hallway that leads to the bar.

Back when she was working those parties, Walt, in his summer off from the military academy, was busing, washing, peeling vegetables, and doing whatever else his dad wanted him to do. She was simple to woo. He flirted with her; impressed her by joking with the handsome young chef and handing out Cokes from the refrigerator. He began waiting for her shift to end so he could drive her home. He gave her whimsical, special gifts—a model soldier that he'd painted gold and turquoise, her favorite colors; a wren's nest filled with polished rocks. Like a boyfriend from a book, he wrote poems for her and played a borrowed guitar, badly, under her bedroom window, his voice quavering with emotion at his own lyrics. And he professed to find her beautiful.

She knew she wasn't. As her father used to say, "You ain't the prettiest, but you sure are the smartest." She would smile at this, as her father expected her to, but she felt hurt every time. To hear Walt praise her looks was water in the desert. That she was not, in fact, pretty perhaps didn't matter, if he found her so.

And so when he wanted her to unbutton her blouse and let him see her stiff white bra, she felt proud. She was pleased to let him press tightly against her until his eyeballs rolled back and only the whites showed, proud of what just touching her did to him. The night he unzipped his pants, though, was different. First of all, it was different out than it had been when it was safely held back by his jeans. It seemed a thing with its own alien life, poking up at her. She felt she should look away, but it held her eyes, and she reached a tentative finger toward it.

"Kiss it," he whispered. "Please." He'd thrown himself against the back of the car seat, his legs open, his arms spread wide, his head hanging back, eyes closed, mouth slightly open.

She didn't want to, but she did it. She held her breath and dove down quickly—it was awkward to bend so low—and gave it a quick peck. She was surprised by how velvety it felt, and she might—that was the worst of it—she might even have kissed it again to confirm that impression, if he had not suddenly lunged forward, throwing her down onto the seat, pinning her shoulders with his own, so that it was poking at her stomach, like a giant blunt finger. With her head turned sideways, she could see on the floor, half underneath the front seat, the reproachful crumple of pink that had been her blouse.

"Walt! Stop!" she said, fiercely, angrily. She tried to slide herself out from under him, but his whole weight was on her, pressing even the air from her lungs. His face was buried in her neck and he seemed not to hear her. His fingers shoved under the crotch of her underwear, the nails scratching.

She brought her knee up hard against his groin, and she grabbed his shoulder in her teeth and bit down, not hard enough to draw blood but hard enough to make his eyes open and hard enough to make him scramble off of her.

He claimed to be sorry, as he clutched his shoulder and zipped his pants. He explained himself in terms flattering to her. He didn't know what had come over him; he couldn't help himself. Even though no one had ever used those words with her, she'd read enough to know they'd been repeated by thousands of men, thousands of times.

But now that it was over, she wasn't scared. "Well," she said, "we won't do that again."

When he didn't call the next day, she told herself it was only

because he was so ashamed. But he didn't call the following day,
nor the day after that.

Not until the Hoffmans' party on Friday night did she speak
to him again, and by then she was wild with anxiety.

"Where have you been? Why didn't you call?" she pleaded,
pulling him into the larder the moment she saw him, abandoning
half-composed canned-peach and cottage-cheese salads. She felt
herself beginning to cry and she wiped at her eyes impatiently.

"I guess I've just been busy."

She could see that he was not himself, not the boy she'd known
and kissed, but a different, colder person.

"Well." She sniffed. She reached for his arm and rubbed it,
trying to warm him. "Where shall we go tonight?"

"I've got plans tonight," he said, "with Irma Dalquist."

She laughed, she was that stunned. "Irma Dalquist? Why?"

"Irma and I, we got together last weekend. I like her."

"But what about me?" She'd grabbed at his hands and wrung
them, begging. "What about me?"

Carefully, coolly, he'd extracted his fingers from hers. "I guess
I just think she's pretty."

"Prettier than me?" She wanted to yank the words back the
moment she'd said them, the way he'd looked at her, the pitying
smile he'd given her. What had she expected? A promise that he'd
never find another girl more beautiful?

"You're really not all that pretty," he'd said. "You're so smart,
I'm surprised you don't know that." And then he slipped out the door.

His friend Bud found her weeping, her face pressed into a
stack of clean tablecloths. It was just the sort of scene that would
cause a man like Bud to love her, and she was aware that for years
it colored his view of her for the better, so she had something for
which to thank Walter. That summer she made use of Walt's
proximity to stoke her scorn. All the qualities that had won her—

his easy charm, his quick enthusiasms, his generosity, his open-ness—she dismissed as childish and fickle. She noted his bravado now and the weaknesses it was intended to shield. She saw, too, that he had got his way so often that he'd come to expect it as deserved. And, because it was her nature to do so, she often probed the sore remains of the shame and hatred that had once made her almost unable to breathe when she thought of what she'd done willingly and what he'd done to her. Oh, she knew Walter Flei-scher, all right.

She trails him now to the bar and hoists herself onto the stool beside him. They'd behaved as friends for years now, their history minimized as part of the trial and error of being teenagers. "You ready for tomorrow?"

He smiles. "Easy to get ready to lose." He lifts his glass to his moist lips.

"How about this guy from Dubuque? Bud seems to think he's going to be hard to beat, but I told him that was crazy."

"He's OK. He's got a good drive. But he doesn't know the course the way Bud does. Keep me company?" He taps the side of his glass.

She can see that, already in his twenties, he's beginning to soften. The muscles in his face are slackening, his middle widen-ing. Maybe he'd been right to grab a lot of girls as quickly as he could. His years of even moderate attractiveness are obviously lim-ited. "You know what I'd really like is a walk." She touches the back of his hand just briefly with one finger, but long enough to remind him that she's a woman. "Would you want to review some of the course once more before the tournament starts? Bud is busy being worshipped," she adds, her tone ever so slightly dis-paraging.

Walt swallows the remainder of his drink and slides off his stool. "What could he be thinking, letting his pretty wife fend for herself?"

She bristles. How dare he use such a line on her. How dare he forget precisely how he had hurt her. But she's also happy he's said it, happy to feel the hate flare again to urge her on.

twelve

Ethan had watched for the black Explorer to lumber by and leave the coast clear. It had never occurred to him that Winifred might be in its passenger seat.

Obviously, she was being pressured to give the firm big chunks of her weekends. Ethan knew all about that sort of pressure. He'd put in those hours to make partner so that when he had a wife, he could say, "No, Winifred and I have plans this weekend. She likes me home. You know how it is." On Saturdays, *they* would fix up the house, work on the garden.

Ethan had felt a little sorry for the guy, who he knew had a wife, a house, and a garden. He obviously hadn't planned things very well.

Of course, Winifred was young yet. She'd have to put in her time. And while she did, he'd use his free time to support her, bring thoughtful little snacks to her office, encourage her to take a break to join him for an afternoon run. He could handle the housework. He'd have beautiful meals under way when she finished for the evening, all the scut-work preparation done and just the fun bits left, the last-minute sautéing and seasoning, the tossing and the garnishing, and she would sit at the dining bar with a chilled glass of Lillet, so that they could talk while he took care of those. He was elated, always, when he thought of the ways he would care for her, the means by which he would make her happy.

If she played her cards right—and he could show her how— she could slow down at work in a year or two, start to delegate. The higher-ups respected that, which was something women didn't always understand. Something else he could help her with.

There was no point in driving to her office and hanging around outside, waiting for her to finish up. He'd done that a couple times, brought flowers once, a bunch of tulips, colored the pale, creamy peach-pink of the inside of a seashell, their heads still furled tightly on their fresh green stems. She'd been surprised to see him, had done an actual, movie-quality double take. She'd been with others, a squat blond woman, a man large enough to have played college football, and the guy, although Ethan hadn't known he was "the guy" then. He'd stroked his shirt front, preparing to meet them, a habit he'd developed as long ago as middle school, but she'd left them with a little wave and come to him alone. He decided he was pleased about that. He approved of keeping work and home life separate.

"Well, thank you!" she'd said, when he'd produced the flowers. "They're really beautiful. But I didn't get anything for you."

"That's all right," he'd said, before he'd realized it was a joke, and then he'd tried to think of something amusing to say in return, but he couldn't, so they just stood there, both studying the bouquet as if they'd never seen a flower before.

Finally, he said, "You'd better get them in water." Which wasn't what he'd hoped to say, but it was true that the blooms were beginning to nod.

"You're absolutely right," she'd said. "I'll take them right home."

But she hadn't. He'd noticed her car parked on Gorham—he hadn't followed her, he'd just been driving around aimlessly, enjoying the spring air as it streamed into his windows, and thinking over how well the encounter had gone, and he'd seen the Mustang, an absurdly unreliable car. When they were married, he would buy her something safer and more suitable. Maybe a Camry.

He parked about half a block on, walked back, and stood near her car. For no reason, really, just because it was such a pleasant coincidence to have found her there. Why not say hello? He looked around, assuming she'd stopped to do a quick errand and would be hurrying back, but he didn't see her. He bent to look into the car window, cupping his hand over his eyes to counter the glare of the setting sun. The tulips in their plastic sheath were wilting on the seat.

She'd locked the doors, but anyone with a little patience and manual dexterity could spring that sort of lock with a coat hanger. He put the flowers in a large paper cup of water he'd begged from a restaurant two doors down and propped the container up with a pair of cross trainers she'd left on the backseat.

The Explorer had signaled right, away from their office. Well, he'd reasoned, maybe they were making some sort of site visit. Maybe they were picking up lunch. There were any number of plausible explanations. Ethan had glanced at his car clock. Really not too much time before they were to meet for their walk to Picnic Point, and he'd planned to put together a little salad with fresh peas and mint, with maybe a thick slice of pâté and a side dish of curried peaches. He still had to buy and shell the peas and he wanted to chill some champagne. And he had to make a special trip for the bread.

He'd slowed to turn left, to follow his own course. At the last minute, however, he could not. The problem was that he didn't entirely trust the guy. He had a furtive, jumpy look. And the long hair. That other creep had had the long hair, too.

Ethan had drummed his fingers on his steering wheel, checked his clock again. At that point, he could have followed them for another half hour, turned back, and still have had plenty of time to prepare the picnic and, he raised his arm a little and sniffed, shower. All of the tense time in the car had made him sweat despite the air-conditioning. Where the hell could they be going?

His knee had twitched and he'd begun to rock, subtly, pulling and pushing on the steering wheel. What he'd really needed was a good hard run to pound out the stress. If he turned around then and compromised the meal—bought a pre-pared salad, maybe, instead of doing the peas—he probably would have had time to do a fast eight miles.

They'd driven east on the old highway, past tire and truck-rental stores, past frozen-custard stands and offers to "Try Our Walleye," crumbs of commerce collected along the rim of the city.

The picnic had to be perfect though, after the way their last meal had gone.

"Someone broke into my car the other week," she'd said as she buttered slipper bread. She buttered the whole slice at once, he noticed. And she used the knife from the butter dish.

"You know I'm really not surprised." He tore off a bite-sized morsel of his own bread and deposited a pat of butter on his plate, setting an example. "You need to get a new car with real locks, not those push-button things. Anyone could get in there. Anytime."

"Well, that's what I like about it. I never have to worry about locking myself out." She chewed her bread cavalierly, her elbow propped on the table.

"You know, don't you, that you really shouldn't leave anything valuable in a car. Even a car with a good security system. These guys just break a window. Or they have one of those sticks the police use; they jam it in—"

She interrupted him, trained her eyes on his face as she spoke. "No. He . . ." She paused. "Or she, I suppose, just put some flowers . . . the flowers you gave me, by the way, in water. Isn't that strange? Don't you think that's incredibly strange?"

Ethan raised his eyebrows, sat back in his chair. "Really? That's . . . well, it's not so strange. I mean, he—or she—was probably just walking by and noticed them wilting. Maybe the door wasn't even locked. Maybe it was like, you know, when someone leaves their headlights on and you try the door in case you can just turn them off, just take care of the problem." He snapped his fingers. The sound was louder and sharper than he'd intended.

"You mean you think someone was peering into car windows looking for an opportunity to be helpful?"

"Well, maybe not looking for it . . ."

"But seizing it? Carpe Samaritan, so to speak?"

Had no one ever taught her how to use a fork? She was jimmying it under a wafer of cucumber, as if it were a backhoe.

"Well . . . sure," he said. "Why not? I'd think you'd appreciate it."

She leaned toward him over the table. "It creeps me out, thinking of someone in my car like that."

"It does?"

"Yes, it does."

"Well, I very much doubt it'll happen again."

"Do you? I'm not so sure." She was gazing around the restaurant now, studying the other patrons. "There's a small-town quality in this city. Everyone seems to know everyone else's business."

She dug into her salad again. The tines of the fork would stab her in the chest if she wasn't careful.

"You know it really works better like this." He neatly poked a small cluster of arugula.

She said nothing for a long moment. "Are you my mother?" she said, finally.

"I'm sorry," he said quickly. "I'm sorry. I shouldn't have said that. It's just . . . you're so perfect and I want to help you and . . . God, I'm an idiot. A total idiot."

She stared at her plate, lifted her napkin from her lap, and set it on the table. His chest clenched. His ears rang. He had to grip the edge of the table to keep upright, to keep breathing. She was going to leave! She was going to push her chair back, thread her way between the tables, and walk out the door.

"I'm sorry," he gasped again. "Winifred, listen to me. I'm so sorry. I didn't mean it." He reached across the table for her hand, but she drew it into her lap. "Here," he said. "See?" He picked up his own fork in his fist. "I'll do it your way. It's better." He meant it seriously, said it sincerely, and he could see by the way the corners of her eyes lifted that she was smiling a little. Good, all right, good. "Listen," he tried again, "I'm obviously an open-mouth-insert-foot kind of guy, so I shouldn't be telling anyone what to do with a fork."

She sighed and turned away from him to look around the dining room.

"Forgive me," he said. "Please." He waited, watching her, his knee bouncing steadily under the table, jiggling the ice in the water glasses. "Please."

"Your method seems to be the favorite around here," she said. She didn't smile again, but she didn't leave.

"Winifred," he breathed. She was miraculous.

Her fork, however, lay untouched on its green bed, until the waiter took the plate away.

They talked about—what?—the ubiquity of summer road construction, the blessing of growth versus the curse of sprawl, the weather. When the waiter set their pizza in the center of the table, she teased a wedge free with her fingers.

"Good choice, huh?" she said.

The motion of Ethan's knee threatened to topple his wine. In future, he would have to be more careful with his comments.

Now, miles from where he needed to be, Ethan reminded himself that the future would be this evening, his first opportunity with her since that awful meal. It was a big mistake to waste precious preparation time following her out of town. But he couldn't turn around.

thirteen

Freddi could tell Jon had been preoccupied almost from the minute they'd started driving and she knew what he must be worrying about, and wasn't it great to be reminded of why it felt lousy to be in love with this guy just when they were setting out to spend about twelve hours together? "I guess I'll use the ladies' room," she said, "as long as we've stopped."

She pushed back through the weeds. Mosquitoes had bitten the front of one ankle and the back of the other and she must have brushed against something poisonous, despite his assurance, because the skin on her forearm was beginning to tingle and sting.

The tavern wasn't as off-putting as some of the ones you passed on roads like these, low brick bunkers with shaded windows and crumbling cement stoops. This one was two stories of limestone with an apartment up top that had curtains in the windows. Freddi stepped into the cool dankness, into the sour smell that always signaled home.

"I grew up in a town of taverns and taxidermists." That was the line she'd used at parties the years she lived in Chicago. Back here it didn't make her so interesting. Too many people came from the same sort of places.

She'd tried it anyway one Friday night at a table in the Back Room. Six had squeezed into a booth meant for four. She'd been aware of Jon's thigh next to hers, the masculine smell of the jacket—leather, Speed Stick, and Irish Spring—he'd crushed between her shoulder and the wall when she'd complained that the brick was chilly. The two of them had been a creative team for three weeks.

"Where exactly?" someone had asked. Mark Kaiser, probably. She'd said it just for a laugh, but Mark had a disconcerting habit of pursuing even the most offhand information. She'd named the town and then, oh yes, it had definitely been Mark, directing his alarmingly steady gaze across the table at her, asking what her parents had been doing in that little town in the middle of the state.

So she'd been forced to be specific, which made her slightly uncomfortable. Not that she was ashamed of the facts—she would actually have enjoyed presenting them, in rather heightened colors, on a date, or to a friend, intimately, one on one—but she'd never figured out how to make her childhood into an amusing anecdote for a crowd, how to establish her distance from her mother's world without sounding callous.

"My grandparents owned a tavern." They laughed. "My mother was the bartender."

"I bet she knew my father," Jon said.

"And your father stuffed squirrels," someone suggested.

This was where you had to hit the right tone, or people got

uncomfortable with the sordid details. Lots of people grew up without their fathers, but very few had no idea who those fathers were.

The apartment above the tavern, where she and her mother lived alone, had been her grandparents' way of providing for their prodigal daughter. It was dim by day; the curtains were shut against the morning light so that her mother could sleep in and then stayed shut later because no one bothered to open them. "Just have to shut 'em again in a few hours," was her mother's attitude.

Downstairs, in the tavern itself, daylight was even more diffuse. Freddi often played down there on days when there was no school, putting a family of four—mother, father, sister, brother—through its paces in a cupboard her mother had given over to her as a dollhouse, while decades of sour beer and stale smoke hung around her in a miasma. There were two windows in the tavern, high in the wall, remnants of the building's former glory and set with squares of chartreuse glass. They gave the light an underwater cast and greened the faces of those who drank early in the day.

Whenever she was in one of her periodic wistful moods, Freddi's grandmother, whose face seemed to have melted into her neck as she aged, would sigh and rub the ball of her foot against the tavern's floor, as if to scratch away a swatch of the brown indoor/outdoor carpeting. "This was really something," she would say, and then she'd describe once again the mosaic of green and cream tiles that had covered the floor when they'd bought the place, picturing draft horses—"Belgians, I betcha any money"—pulling a wagon overflowing with hops. But the grout had been mildewed and weakened and a fair number of the tiles had been missing. She'd wanted to replace them and fix the floor up, "but that," she'd said, and Freddi's mother had chimed in with bitter glee, imitating husband and father, "woulda cost money."

Aesthetics had never moved Freddi's grandfather. "If he coulda sold them tiles," her grandmother said, "he woulda ripped 'em out." As it was, he covered them over to save on their upkeep. Freddi had once used her Wonder Woman ruler to pry a bit of the carpeting up to take a peek at them, but underneath was plywood and she knew that any tool she could wield was useless against that. When she was seven, her grandfather sold the bar itself, a magnificent piece of mahogany and chrome, along with its matching stools to an antiques dealer from Chicago, who paid not only for the pieces but for their removal. Sometime in her twenties, Freddi realized that she could date her longing to live in Chicago from the day two men arrived and removed to that mythical city what was clearly, even to her very young eyes, the most beautiful and substantial fixture in her home.

Her grandfather replaced the bar and stools with cheap, ugly versions constructed of beaverboard and Naugahyde.

"No one gives a rat's ass about the decor," he used to say. "No one in there can see straight anyway." He wasn't thinking about his daughter, who spent more time in that place than anybody, but she was like him, not caring how things looked as long as they functioned.

At night—here was another story she liked to tell—the atmosphere was altogether different. Freddi could feel the driving pulse of it through the floor and the walls as she read by the glow of the Pabst Blue Ribbon rosette that buzzed outside her bedroom window. Often she would slide down the stairs, her bottom bumping on each rubber-covered tread, and sit for a long time just behind the pale yellow door that separated her quiet, dreamy space from the rough-and-rollicking public one.

She surfed her mother's voice whenever it rose from beneath the music and the laughter and the occasional shouting, the crack and roll of the billiard balls and the thud of thick glass against the top of the hollow bar. Sometimes she fell asleep there, propped between two worlds.

Which was becoming a habit with her, Andrea had pointed out. "You know," she said, "I sometimes worry that you don't want a real relationship."

She wasn't even talking about Jon. This was back when Freddi and Jon were only friends, friends whose pulses freshened in each other's presence, different sorts of friends, in other words, from the type she and Andrea were, but still "just friends." Andrea was talking about the unsuitability of Ethan, just then, and also of Paul and Jack and Richie, all the men who hadn't stuck for one reason or another.

"In my family women don't marry." This, too, was a line, one she'd begun to use after she turned thirty, which seemed to be older in Wisconsin than it had been in Chicago. As with the taverns and taxidermists, she exaggerated for effect. It was only her mother who had not married.

"He and I come from the same background," she'd reported of Jon to Andrea. "He knows what it's like to have to make yourself up from scratch." The lunches she and Jon took had been getting longer, and they talked less about work. "And his wife—"

"Don't tell me," Andrea interrupted. "She doesn't understand him!" Freddi had laughed; the idea that she would have an affair with a married man was so ridiculous. Andrea knew it, or she wouldn't have made the joke. That was, however, essentially what she'd been about to say.

Freddi considered herself a moral person. She was practically a vegetarian (she wasn't a fanatic, of course); she voted in

every election, even if she despised all the candidates or knew
nothing about them beyond the stuff of their ads; she walked to
stop AIDS, gave blood regularly, and, back when she lived in
Chicago, she would always give up her seat on the el to the
elderly and the infirm. In fact, she often found it more relaxing
to stand for her entire commute, rather than continually worry
about whether she ought to relinquish her place. No one could
deny she was a nice person, an unselfish person. She cared how
others felt; she would not willingly, knowingly, hurt someone.

"Oh, c'mon," Andrea had told her. "He's the one who's hurting her, not you. You don't owe her anything. You barely know
her."

She'd appreciated Andrea's point of view. It was true, after
all, that *she* was not cheating on anyone. Still, she felt guilty.

In the tavern, the bartender pointed her down a dark hallway,
and she had to stand, blinking for a minute, letting her sun-
struck eyes adjust to the dimness. She squinted now at the toilet
seat. What was that? Dried blood? Or worse? She balanced herself in the air over the bowl.

Ginny had been standing near a makeshift bar—the end of a
picnic table crowded with oversized bottles—the first time
Freddi had seen her. She was—what was the French phrase for
those women who were ugly, if you considered their faces one
feature at a time, but still somehow beautiful, when you put the
whole picture together? *Jolie laide.* Her eyes were uneven and
her nose too long. Her hair was clamped heedlessly in a clip in a
way that emphasized the extreme width of her mouth and the
length of her face. Still, there was something magnetic about

her. Freddi was conscious of wishing that this woman were her friend. A volleyball game had begun, and they were both turned toward it, watching it absently as they stood there, sipping their drinks.

A little kid raced over and planted himself in front of the woman. "I've got a great one!"

"OK. Shoot."

"What should you do when cats..." he paused, breathed deeply. "No." He began again. "What should you do when it's raining cats and dogs?"

The woman screwed one eye shut and aimed the other dramatically into the branches.

"Give up?" asked the kid, hopefully.

"No, I'm thinking."

The kid hopped up and down impatiently. "I think you have to give up."

"OK, you're right. I give up."

"Be careful you don't step in a poodle!" the kid shouted.

"Ahhh!" The woman emitted the sort of fake laugh adults resort to with kids, but the kid seemed perfectly satisfied.

"OK, I'll be back," he said and raced off.

"How old?" Freddi had asked. Parents liked it when you showed an interest in their offspring.

The woman put her hand to her forehead. "I can never keep track. Seven, I think. Somewhere in that golden period when they're both able and willing to talk in full sentences." And then, registering Freddi's puzzled look, she'd exclaimed, "Oh! You thought he was mine! No, that's Anthony Kaiser. I'm Ginny Otto. Are you at Nielson Gray or are you a significant other, like me?"

"I'm a copywriter. I only started about a month ago. I don't remember meeting..." Freddi had frowned, stumbling over the word "husband." What if this Otto guy was someone important whom she ought to know? Or what if he and Ginny weren't actually married? Could he be a woman? She'd already presumed about the kid and been wrong. Was she thinking too conventionally and bumbling into another mistake?

"Jon Kepilkowski," Ginny said. "I'm married to Jon Kepilkowski."

"Oh, Jon!" Freddi wasn't yet working with Jon, but of course she knew who he was. Her interest in this woman deepened. "You're like me?" she said, lifting her plastic cup to indicate the ruckus around the net. "Not a team player?"

"Oh, I'd play if they'd let me. But they like to win."

They talked about the city, about their careers at the university, about leaving the area and coming back again.

"My wife always attracts the weirdos." Jon was there suddenly, one arm around Ginny, claiming her, the other hand raking back the hair he let grow over his ears, not quite long enough to pull back into a ponytail but a little longer than less "creative" men would dare. For whom was he preening? He'd grinned at Freddi. The way she remembered it, she'd felt, even then, a little shot of espresso in her veins.

Freddi leaned toward the mirror as she washed her hands. She seemed to have aged since the morning. It was the driving; she couldn't help squinting at the bright road despite her sunglasses. She pulled gently at the corners of her eyes, trying to smooth out the lines.

If she was going to have to hurt someone—or, as she preferred to think of it, if she was going to be involved in a situation in which someone got hurt—Freddi would rather that person be a vague, anonymous entity, not a lousy volleyball player who'd loaned her a sweatshirt when the weather turned.

"What do you think, Vanderheiden?" Mark Kaiser had said in his disconcerting way a couple of weeks ago. "Is it more important to be happy or to be good?"

He was practically hanging in the doorway of her office, long arms over his head, fingers hooked on the doorframe.

Freddi had felt herself blushing. Did he know something or was he just fooling around the way he did?

"Well, Kaiser," she'd said finally, emphasizing the name to show she could play like one of the boys, "what if you're the sort of person who can't be happy unless you're good?" She had a small stack of manila folders in her hands and she tapped them smartly on the desktop, as if to demonstrate that she was the sort of person who kept things in order. She *was* that sort of person.

"Maybe you're the sort of person that thinks being happy is the ultimate good. Many people are." He'd smiled so she couldn't tell: Did he know something? Was he mocking her? Should she tell him that her happiness and goodness were none of his business? But if he knew nothing, if he was just being Kaiser, pitching right at her face to see if she'd duck, then she'd be being hostile, a crybaby, no fun, for no reason other than his goddamn irritating manner, which everyone at Nielson Gray seemed to find so clever, so attractive. Well, she'd found his provocative manner attractive on many other occasions, hadn't she?

She'd shaken her head, deflecting him. "Nah. Happy isn't my thing."

He'd turned suddenly serious and dropped his hands from her doorframe to his sides. "Mine either, I guess," he'd said wistfully.

And then he'd disappeared down the hall, leaving Freddi to muse about how likable and how elusive Mark Kaiser was when he revealed himself and about whether she ought to put some effort into pinning down that manifestation of the man.

The paper dispenser was empty so Freddi dried her hands on the back of her shorts. The dim coolness and the melancholy of nostalgia had soothed her irritation. Jon would have found the cap by now. He'd be wearing it, looking silly in pink, as he leaned patiently against the car, arms crossed, everything under control. Already, as she thought of him, she felt the need to pull him toward her, to press against his warm skin.

Someone new had come into the bar. She remembered that two had already been there, a man and a woman, but now there was a third. He was sitting at the far end, close to the window, so his features were shadowed and indistinct. As she drew even with him on her way to the door, he suddenly swung around on his stool, reached out, and grabbed her wrist. "Winifred! Hi!"

fourteen

He'd startled her. Her eyes were round with fright and she'd yanked her wrist from his hand.

"No, no, Winifred. It's me." Ethan reached for her again as he slid off the stool.

He didn't intend, exactly, to block her feet with his. He didn't mean to close his hand so tightly around her arm. He just wanted her to stand still, to stop eluding him, but instantly he saw it was a mistake. Women, he knew, were like wild creatures; you had to wait for them to come to you.

"Ethan, please!" She stepped back firmly and pulled away again, crossing her arms over her chest. Her fingers rubbed a little circle at the spot where he'd touched her. "Your hands are freezing!"

He saw her glance toward the door, which made him want to grab her again, but he crossed his own arms, holding himself back.

She shook her head and laughed a little then, squinting her eyes at him and smiling. "What are you doing here?"

He'd scared her—that hadn't been his intention, although, to be honest, he hadn't really thought about how she'd react to his appearance. But now she was recasting him, softening him with her look, with the tilt of her head. She was pushing him back into the form she'd long ago established for him, the form with which she was comfortable, even (he supposed he should be grateful for this—he *had* been grateful) fond. He was the dear friend. The man who was not really a man.

He tried to return her smile, tried to be a dear friend, as she demanded. But he was tired of it. It was not how he wanted to be with her.

She was waiting for his dear-friend-like answer. If he said that he'd been following her, probably she would think he was joking.

Tailing her had felt perfectly legitimate. After all, why should he not be on that particular road at that particular time? And then, too, he did not fully trust the guy, and if anything happened, even something as innocuous as a flat tire, he wanted to be nearby to help—all right, to rescue—Winifred. Although she wouldn't like to hear that he thought she might need rescuing, protecting her seemed to him a natural inclination, something other men would understand; something other women might even appreciate. It had been necessary in the past, after all.

But then, when it had looked as if they did indeed have a flat, he hadn't stopped to help, had he? Instead, he'd driven by, parked on the gravelly shoulder, and watched them through his binoculars. He couldn't explain that behavior or, at least, could not explain it in any way he liked to admit.

It was the guy. He didn't want to have to talk to the guy. He certainly didn't want to see the guy with Winifred, not up close.

His feelings didn't entirely make sense. After all, this was just some fellow Winifred worked with. A married man, at that. But still, he felt safer, better about everything, keeping his distance when the two of them were together.

And then, when he'd seen her go into the tavern alone, he'd thought it a good opportunity. He had an image of himself, larger than life, like a Macy's Thanksgiving parade balloon, popping up with his arms spread wide, between her and the guy, obscuring her vision of that other man. He just wanted to remind her that she already had an important relationship, lest she be distracted. Was that something he dared tell her?

"Where're you going?" he asked, instead. He'd intended it to sound casual. It was the obvious question, wasn't it?

But she frowned and slid one foot in the direction of the door. "Listen," she said, "you know, it's good I ran into you. I left you a message. I don't know if you got it? I've gotta work and I don't know . . . I mean I doubt I'll be able to get back in time for our picnic. This account is . . ." She let the words trail off and shook her head again, raising her eyes to the ceiling in mock exasperation.

He felt panic begin to cloud his brain. He flicked his thumbnail and fingernail together several times—snap, snap—to relieve the pressure. "Wait," he said. "No. You can't work all day on a Saturday."

"I know," she said. "Sometimes I wish I'd gone into law." She smiled at her own joke.

Was this because he'd scared her? Snap, snap, snap went his nails. He had both hands going now. Because he'd shown up there? "How about later? A picnic was probably a bad idea, anyway. Sand in the tapenade, room-temperature Pinot Grigio, West Nile virus, who needs it? We could have a late dinner at my place. Or your place. Or go out. Whatever. What time do you

think you'll be done? Nine? Ten? I think Lulu's serves until
midnight. I could check." He pulled out his cell phone, in part
to stop the nervous clicking of his nails.

"Oh, God, Ethan." She lowered her head and then pushed it
up again with her hands, splaying her fingers through her hair.
"This is really lousy of me, I know." She stared toward the door
and expanded her cheeks with air that she expelled in a long
sigh. "It's just . . . you know . . . it would be wrong of me to
promise anything for tonight." She looked him full in the face.
"You never know how long these things are going to take and if
we're not finished by Monday . . ." She drew her finger across
her neck and made that wet, back-of-the-throat sound that was
supposed to stand for cutting, but that really didn't sound anything like a knife slicing through flesh. "Next week, though,
I'm totally free. How about Wednesday? Do you want to meet at
the Back Room for dinner on Wednesday?"

No, he did not want to meet on Wednesday. Or, rather, he'd
be happy to see her on Wednesday as well as this evening, but
not instead. He'd envisioned the afternoon. A formless, open-
ended, anything-could-happen afternoon, lounging in the
warm air with the soothing sound of water against the rocks.
He would not replace that with another chaste meal, sitting up
straight opposite each other, shivering in some over-air-condi-
tioned restaurant, their connection neatly severed when they
sealed themselves in their own cars at ten o'clock.

He said, "No, Winifred, it would not be 'wrong' of you to
make a promise for tonight. What would be wrong would be to
break the promise you've already made to me for this afternoon."

Her cheeks reddened, instantly, brilliantly. He longed to
touch them, to feel the hot blood under her cool skin. She
drew herself up and squared her shoulders. Her reaction

disappointed him. Most people, he'd noticed, got aggressive when confronted with their mistakes, but he'd credited Winifred with more self-awareness.

"Ethan," she was saying, "I'm sorry you feel I've wronged you. But when I have a deadline, I have to work."

He pressed on. He was ruining everything. He knew it, but pushed impatiently past that knowledge as if it were a cobweb. He could not let her twist everything up like this. She was making him seem unreasonable, as if he were injuring her with his crazy demands, when it was she who was not behaving the way a girlfriend should. "I don't 'feel' that you've wronged me," he said, keeping his voice calm, the argument logical. "You have wronged me. But it's all right. I understand why you can't meet me this afternoon. I just don't see why we can't get together later. You can't work all night."

She sighed, jutting her lower jaw out so that her breath blew the strands of hair on her forehead into the air. Her face was not at its most attractive contorted like that. "Tell you what," she said, "if we get done at a reasonable hour and I'm not too tired, I'll call you, and if you still want to do something, maybe we can. OK? But don't count on it. OK?"

"It's OK if you're tired. I'll make some pasta; we can eat it in front of a video. I'll pick something up. How 'bout a screwball comedy? Would you prefer Jean Arthur or Barbara Stanwyck? Or I'll just choose, shall I? But nothing with subtitles. And no letterbox, right? We don't want that kind of thing tonight. Nothing you have to work to watch."

"That sounds nice, Ethan. Really, it does. But just don't . . ." She paused. "You know, if something else comes up . . . if you want to make other plans . . . you know . . . just go ahead and we'll do it some other night."

He shook his head at her and smiled. It was sweet of her to

worry about him. "I'm not going to make any other plans, Winifred. You give me a call later and I'll bring everything over to your place. Or I could even head over there on my own this evening, have everything ready when you get home. I remember where the extra key is. Would you like that? Is that a good idea?"

"No, don't do that. Don't do that." She straightened up again, her voice firm. "Ethan, listen. I'll call you. OK? I will call you tonight. But I've got to go now."

She slipped away as she spoke, so that the closing door punctuated her final words, and he was left standing in the gloom.

fifteen

Absently, out of habit, Jon, still thigh deep in Queen Anne's lace, flipped open his cell phone to check the time. Four missed calls. Ginny, Ginny, Ginny, and a 414 number it took him a moment to place. Kyle. What the hell did he want? He pressed End hard for several seconds and the phone piped its cheery little goodbye tone.

Growing up, Kyle, older by little more than a year, had been the bad one; Jon, the good one. Very often, as it turned out, being bad was good. With girls, for instance. Also, their father obviously preferred Kyle, but that might have been because their mother preferred Jon. That was one of Ginny's theories, anyway.

Kyle had charm, which also made bad good. Charm trumped everything. Standing next to Kyle when they were nine and ten or so, Jon could feel himself fading, the force of his own personality overwhelmed by Kyle's. When they were together, Kyle talked for both of them. Jon's role was to smile and nod. Kyle lied for fun, just to see what he could make other people believe. But people were delighted to be tricked. "That Kyle! What an imagination!" they clucked. Jon, cautious and direct, seemed not sensible and honest but slow-witted. By the time they were teenagers, Jon was taller and broader than Kyle, but this only meant that Kyle was quick and graceful, while Jon was ungainly. Jon might have hated his brother had he not, of all those Kyle charmed, been the one most thoroughly enchanted.

"Kyle, wait!" he cried nearly every morning when they were young, as his brother thundered down the stairs, and then periodically throughout the day as Kyle reappeared to eat or to snatch some mysterious item from their room. Kyle had his own friends, boys even older than he. Sometimes he waited for Jon, more often he did not.

"Probably for the best," Ginny had said more than once. They used to talk about Kyle a lot in the early years, and Jon had always been grateful that Ginny seemed immune to his brother's spell. He'd recovered from it himself very abruptly one afternoon his freshman year of high school.

It was late October or early November, the sky, gray all day, was beginning to darken outside the second-story windows of his last-period history class. The skin on his fingertips had already begun to crack, as it did every winter, so that it was painful to wash his hands, excruciating to eat French fries. World History was normally a sophomore-level course, but his mother had pushed for it in their scheduling meeting with the guidance counselor.

"Is there any reason Jonny can't take it?" his mother had asked. She kept raising her hand to her face to hide the neat square of cellophane tape that secured the earpiece of her glasses. Here, at this table, Jon noticed for the first time that this gesture merely called attention to the flaw.

He'd slumped in his seat, trying to indicate with his posture that he disapproved of his mother horning in on his life—which, as far as he was concerned, should remain comfortably indistinguishable from those of his classmates—without actually showing overt disrespect. "Jon," he'd corrected her.

His mother had looked at him. "If Jonny can enroll in the course, I think we can assume they'll take Jon," she'd said.

The counselor had glanced up from the thick computer read-out she'd been paging through and looked at them over tiger-striped reading glasses. "Do you have two boys in this year's class, then, Mrs. Kepilkowski?"

This line, and Jon's mother's imitation of it, had made Jon's father laugh so hard at dinner that he'd had to push his bridge-work back into place with his thumb. Mostly, though, his father objected to his mother's attempts to bend the rules. Another evening, when she'd been scanning the course list, circling with a red marker the classes she wanted for him all the way until graduation, his father had pounded his fist on the table. "Leave the boy alone. He's a good boy as he is; he doesn't need to be better than everyone else."

She didn't bother to look up from the page, though she'd jumped involuntarily along with the table when his fist had come down. "Jon doesn't belong with the hoi polloi. If you expect too little of him, Bud, he'll amount to nothing."

"Like me, you mean."

They could hear the soft scratch of her marker on the page.

"Your expectations, Marie, are poison." He tipped his head back to drain his can of beer—to spite her, he refused to use a glass—crushed the can in his fist, and hurled it against the kitchen wall. Then he pushed his chair back and left the house.

Jon had worried about Kyle.

"Cool, man, you can help me study," Kyle had said the evening it became clear that, although he was a year ahead of Jon, they'd be taking most of the same classes.

Jon scowled at his mother, who was working a strand of chicken thigh away from its bone, oblivious. "See?" he wanted to say. "You really think shoving me ahead is worth it?" But he only stared with righteous hatred at the top of her head, where white strands rose twisting from her smooth, dark hair like wire-thin snakes. He would take the classes she required, but she couldn't make him perform well in them.

He and Kyle weren't in the same period. Their mother at least made sure of that, probably further confusing the counselor. There was one other freshman in the sophomore history class, a girl, who explained loudly and with a roll of her eyes that she was there because of a "scheduling conflict," an inspired story, he'd realized later, far too late for him to chime in, "Me, too." It was mostly OK, though. Someone noticed his last name and pretty soon the other kids knew he was Kyle's brother and liked him for it, or wanted him to like them because of it, and although he felt more like a pipsqueak mascot than a classmate with those guys, that was a lot more than he'd hoped for, which had pretty much been that no one would pay any attention to him.

Mr. Pikna was going on about the Han dynasty that afternoon. For notes, they were expected only to copy what he wrote on the board and he hadn't written anything in a while, but was just leaning against his desk, going on about peoples coming together along the Silk Road, cultural exchanges, and the kind of junk that filled out the picture but wouldn't be on the exam, so Jon was listening, but also pressing the tips of his fingers one by one against the desk to test when they'd begin to hurt and how much, when the police sirens started. There were two, maybe three cars, it sounded like, as close as the school's parking lot. Their classroom didn't face the road but the swath of tall grass in back and the woods beyond, its paths trampled and littered this time of year by trippers, field and otherwise.

Several kids were out of their seats, headed for the door and Pikna was going in that direction, too, whether to bar or lead the way, Jon couldn't tell, when a bullhorn sounded just outside.

"Stop running. You're under arrest. Stop running now."

The kids, like iron filings drawn by a magnet, rushed to the row of windows that formed a long, narrow stripe of sky along one wall. Jon, hanging back, expecting Pikna to say, "Sit down, there's nothing to see," was the last to press his forehead to the glass. He didn't know what he expected, gangsters or bank robbers, maybe, the kind of people that pounded down alleys and scaled chain-link fences on TV. Certainly he did not expect Kyle.

The police had already caught Paul and Lee and Stinks. They were walking toward the building with their hands behind their backs. Stinks was wiping his nose on the shoulder of his parka. Jon registered their surrender in the same moment that he saw Kyle, moving like a jackrabbit toward the woods, the tail of his flannel shirt flying, his wafflestompers clearing the mounds of matted grass and weeds in enormous leaps. There were three cops after him, two converging from the sides, a fat one charging straight up the middle.

Jon gripped the window ledge, willing speed into his brother's legs. At first, the words—"Go left, Kyle! Left!"—were only in his head, but within moments they burst from his mouth. He couldn't hold them back. "Go, Kyle! C'mon, run,

Kyle!" he pleaded. "Those pigs'll never catch him. They'll never catch Kyle." He said it partly to the class, partly to himself. He believed what he was saying, could envision Kyle sprinting the last stretch, dodging among the trees, until the police, winded and disoriented, were merely chasing shadows.

But they did catch him, before he'd even reached the woods, which would not have saved him anyway. The tall one on the right and the fat one in the middle reached him at the same time. They pushed him so that he sprawled facedown in the dry, bleached grass.

Jon blinked and took a step away from the window. He knew the school had its share of troublemakers, kids who spent a lot of time with the dean, kids who'd been suspended, kicked off athletic teams, had their parking privileges revoked, but those kids were all just breaking school rules, not the law.

The cops helped Kyle to his feet. He stumbled, off balance with his hands behind his back. His watch cap had come off, but his hair retained the shape of it, pressed close at the crown of his head and forming a ledge just below his ears. His corduroys—the gray ones, his favorite pair—were nearly sliding off his slim hips, but because of the handcuffs he couldn't pull them up. That wasn't fair, Jon thought, they should have let him pull his pants up.

He wanted to beat those pigs back. He imagined opening the window and heaving a desk out, two desks, perfectly aimed, so that they knocked down the tall one and the fat one. The tall one was stooping to retrieve his hat. In a movie, Kyle would have kicked him over and sprinted for the parking lot where he would have jumped into a squealing getaway car driven by a girl with streaming hair.

When he could no longer see Kyle from the window, Jon ran out of the room, down the hall, down the stairs. He leaned on the rail and jumped four steps to the landing, six to the bottom. He pushed through the front doors of the building just in time to see the fat cop cover Kyle's head protectively with his hand as he folded him into the back of the squad car.

He ran after the car. That was, at least, his first instinct. He watched the cop car's brake lights redden at the street and saw his chance to pour it on, catch up with the car and, if not hurl himself on the hood, at least hammer his fists against the trunk to register a protest, something Kyle would certainly have done for him. But he slowed his pace imperceptibly but enough to keep the car out of reach. He was not Kyle and for the first time he saw clearly, and somewhat shamefully, that he did not want to be. When the brake lights went out, the car turned the corner, and it seemed okay to stop running.

At some point during the long, gray walk to the sheriff's office, it occurred to Jon that it was one thing to break the law—of course, he didn't yet know what Kyle had done, but illegal activity might, in certain circumstances, have some honor to it, or at least demanded some daring—but if you were going to skip sixth and seventh periods to go into town to break the law, then you shouldn't be scurrying back to campus at three o'clock to catch the school bus home. He didn't want to think this; he tried, in fact, to push the thought away, but it nudged at him insistently, like a dog that wouldn't go lie down. Was his older brother, his idol and his nemesis, just some punk kid?

He'd been sitting in the sheriff's office facing an unmanned counter, behind which no one had appeared for half an hour, when his parents came in together.

"What are you doing here?" his mother said.

"Waiting." At last, an excuse to speak, to stand. "I saw them grab him. They pushed him and they didn't let him fix his pants. I didn't see them read him his rights. I'm pretty sure they didn't read him his rights."

She held up her hand to shush him and went to the counter. She rapped her knuckles on the Formica and called into the space behind it. "Hello?"

This would be it, then, Jon thought, his body still tense, but his mind beginning to unclench. In a minute, his mother would plow through the door behind which he knew Kyle must be and drag his brother back out. This was only Winnesha, after all, and the sheriff, Jon knew, had been in his mother's algebra class.

A woman appeared, her hair blown back and shellacked, her uniform made of a material so stiff it could hardly bend around her breasts. His mother talked quietly to her and then came to sit in the chair between Jon and his father, dropping her face into her hands.

"Marie, it's all right," his father murmured, his hand rubbing her back through the puff of her winter jacket. "It was just some joyriding."

Jon felt alarm, like an electrical current, sizzle along his skin. He could not remember another occasion when his father had comforted his mother.

"No, it's not all right," she said through her fingers. Then she straightened—her usual self regained—and turned to his father. "You know, I'm sick of your saying that everything is all right. Not everything is all right."

"He made a mistake," his father insisted. But he'd dropped his hand from her back. "Everyone makes mistakes."

"Bud, this was not a mistake. I see what he's doing. Afraid of the future, wrecking things so he doesn't have to face it. I'm not going to let him be like you."

His father's face hardened. It was a look Jon and Kyle had

learned to dread, but his mother didn't seem even to notice. Jon
wanted to warn her, throw himself between them, vomit on his
shoes to create a distraction, but, as he had for hours now, he just
watched. "Like me?" his father said. "You were the one who
destroyed my future, Marie. Remember?"

"Bud, I think you know better. I certainly know better. By
now, I bet even Walt Fleischer knows better."

The plastic chairs were bolted together, six of them in a row,
so the best his father could do was lift one end of the line and let
it drop down again, hard, onto the linoleum. Then he opened
the door with a kick and left them.

That night Jon waited until his mother was sitting alone under
the light of a single lamp, her head bent over a new issue of
McCall's. With a studied nonchalance, he sat on the arm at the
opposite end of the couch. "You know, Mom, you probably
shouldn't mention Mr. Fleischer to Dad." He felt wise then, full
of understanding of the subtle, secret interlockings of the
world.

"Why not?" she said sharply, lowering her magazine to her
lap and looking at him straight on.

"Well, he ruined Dad's career," he prompted.

She frowned. "What do you mean?"

"Well." Jon shifted uneasily and drew his hands from his
pockets. How could it be that his mother didn't know this essential piece of information about her husband's life? Had she forgotten what the Butter Cup had meant to him? And to her, too.
To all of them. "You know," he insisted, "when Dad cut up his
arm pulling him out of the lake?"

She looked at him for a few moments, beginning with the
top of his head, then lowering her eyes to his feet and lifting

them to his face again, as if to assess whether he was full-grown enough to receive the information she was about to impart. "It was your father's own fault Walt was in that water," she said. "I bet he didn't tell you that."

Jon looked at her, unable to answer. His father hadn't said anything about the accident being his fault, had he? No, Jon would remember that.

"No, it wasn't," he said. "Dad was just driving home from the country club. He saw Mr. Fleischer go off the bridge."

"I see," she said. "I suppose in those days the bridge was on your father's way home from the country club."

"Well . . ." he began.

"Where do you think we lived?"

"Here, I guess."

"That's right. In this lousy cabin that he promised me would only be for a few months. Not that I cared then." She sighed. "He wasn't just driving home. He was in one of his crazy rages, chasing Walt, eighty miles an hour. It's a wonder he didn't kill someone. He wanted to kill Walt, I can tell you that. Well, you know your father." She lowered her eyes to her magazine again, as if she'd said all that needed saying on the subject.

Jon had been in the car often enough when his father had sworn, slammed his palm on the horn, gunned the engine until he was riding the bumper of the car ahead of him, a car whose driver had offended him by being too slow, too fast, too indecisive, too assertive; offended him, in other words, in some unpredictable but definite way. He did know his father. "Well, however it happened," he conceded, "he still did save him, and it still did wreck his career. Who knows what he could have become."

"Yes, who knows?" She closed the magazine and leaned forward to align its spine carefully with the others piled on the coffee table. "Sometimes I think things happen for the best. You see, this way your father can be a great golfer who never had a chance, instead of a mediocre golfer who couldn't make the grade."

Jon knew that his father had gone down to the tavern and that Kyle wouldn't be released until the morning, but he glanced over his shoulder and, when he spoke, his voice was almost a whisper. "Are you saying he wasn't good?"

"I'm saying we don't have to know," she said briskly, rising from the couch. Her hand snaked under the lampshade and she switched off the bulb. "Make sure the outside light's on, would you, Jon?" she said into the blackness. "I think I'll go up to bed."

"Any luck?" Freddi was walking fast across the parking lot, one hand shading her eyes.

Jon shook his head and began to look randomly at the ground around him. While she'd been in the tavern, he'd pretty much forgotten what he'd been searching for.

"How about we get going then?" she said, climbing into the passenger seat.

Jon shrugged. He wouldn't have minded poking around in the weeds a little longer. After all, it had to be here. But it was her hat, her decision. Were this a movie, he thought as he slid behind the wheel, the camera would even now be zooming in on the bright circle of fabric they were abandoning.

sixteen

Freddi slid low enough in her seat to rest her heels on the dash. Ethan was still in the tavern, but if he happened to step out, it seemed better that he not know which car she was in. Not that he would follow her or anything crazy like that.

Jon frowned. "Is your seat belt on?"

She smiled at him challengingly. "No." He couldn't hold her gaze, of course. He had to look at the road. But she was sure he'd understood her message. He could not admit even to being her boyfriend; he had no claim on her life.

After a minute or so, though, she shimmied upright, trapped herself behind the nylon sash, and snapped the buckle.

From the corner of her eye, she studied the side of his face as he drove. He was so right, so perfect for her. "You're it!" she shouted, but silently, inside her head. "You're it!" As if she'd just pounced on him in a game of tag.

. . .

"But how do you *feel* about him?" Andrea had asked. "That has to be the main thing." They were at the condiment counter at an outlet of a local coffee chain, trying to disguise the bitterness of their drinks with various powdered flavors. "What's this? Cocaine?" Andrea shook some white onto her palm and touched her tongue to it. She shrugged and shook some into her cup on top of the cinnamon and the chocolate she'd already sprinkled there.

"Oh, you know," Freddi answered, stirring sugar into her own cup, "obsessive thinking, unrealistic appreciation of random characteristics, compulsion to bore friends with anecdotes." She couldn't deny that she did have all the right feelings—she found herself smiling unconsciously at the thought of him and she did, in fact, think about him excessively. She even doodled his name, like a teenager, to give those thoughts substance. "But it has to be more than love," she said, sipping cautiously at her burning cup. "It has to be true and lasting, the real deal, soul-mate stuff." That was the only way, she'd convinced herself, that it could be love worth waiting for and love worth grabbing for, even if it meant, temporarily, another woman's unhappiness.

Andrea nodded. "I see what you mean." She dipped into her own cup and emerged with foam clinging to her upper lip. "He has to be the one."

Then it would be all right. Then she could not be blamed. Not forever, anyway. In time, everyone would come to agree that while Ginny was a very nice person, she and Jon were just not right for each other the way Freddi and Jon were. It was a fact that maybe couldn't have been recognized back when Ginny and Jon had married. They were so young; how could they have known who they would turn out to be almost twenty years later? They'd grown apart, like twigs forking at the end of a branch. No one could be blamed.

"I'm pretty sure they don't have sex anymore," she'd told Andrea.

"How can you know that?"

"He says they're like friends to each other. Old friends. That's not how you'd describe a sexual relationship, is it? He said he sleeps on the couch."

"Well, I'm sure at least they don't enjoy it."

"We're looking at a condo together on Tuesday."

That shut Andrea up.

She'd introduced the idea two days ago. He'd come over to work and they *had* worked, sitting on her little balcony until the mosquitoes drove them in, and then sprawling on her couch and on the gray-painted wood floor, their productivity accelerating for an hour or so and then deteriorating.

Finally, they were laughing hysterically at nothing—the fact that all the pens in her house were dry, which led him to make some silly comment in a Monty Python sort of voice, which led her to say something else that seemed overwhelmingly funny at the time. They were great at riffing off each other that way, until every word, every gesture made her weep with hilarity. When she'd recovered enough to speak, she sipped her beer and, because she felt so comfortable, so happy, ventured, "I looked at a condo yesterday."

"A condo? I didn't know you were thinking of moving."

"Well, I know *you* love this place. But I think it's time for something more grown up. I want a modern apartment with straight walls and windows that open all the way and closets a person can stand up in. I want to be able to see from the front to the back. No more hidey-hole rooms. No more 'charm.' " She made the quotation marks in the air with her fingers. "I want wide open spaces."

"Oh, give me a home . . ." he began to sing.

She interrupted before he could get them started again. "I

found a place I like a couple blocks down from the capitol. You know, one of the skyscrapers?" The building was six stories high, towering by Madison standards. "The views—"

"I didn't think Madison had views."

"This place would change your perspective." She paused. "In other ways, too." She paused again. "The one I looked at was big enough for a couple."

He shook his head, remaining, willfully, she was sure, obtuse. "I'm surprised they aren't charging an arm and leg for those places."

"Well, it is an arm. Maybe even an arm and a foot. But it's a very good price, I think, for what it is." She began to peel the label off her beer bottle, concentrating her gaze on the corner she'd lifted with her fingernail, trying to ease off a bit more without causing it to rip. "I was wondering if you'd look at it with me."

"Of course. I'd love to see it."

She felt hope, like a bubble, lift her. "I know you'll like it. It would be a good place for us."

Did he close his eyes? Or was that a blink?

He reached for her, stroked the side of her face with one finger. "You know I wish I could stay with you tonight." Normally she loved this gesture and the sentiment, but now she stiffened.

There was no good response. If she said she wished it, too, he would say, "I can't," as if she had been the one to open the subject, which would be infuriating, and then, sooner or later, he would go. If she said nothing, he would sigh, and then, sooner or later, he would go. "What will you do when you get home?" she asked.

"Well," he said, looking at his watch, "I rented this documentary on baseball. I'll probably crash on the couch halfway through."

Reassured, she teased him. "My video store has documentaries. You could watch it right here."

"Here I have better things to do," he said, as she'd intended. "But I really have to go."

He acted as if his obligation to his wife was a force beyond his control.

"You act as if your . . ." She hesitated. She didn't like to say the words "wife" or "marriage." "You're half of it, you know. You have a say."

"Listen," Jon said. His hands were on her shoulders. She loved the way they felt, not sexual now, just sincere. His fingers were always smeared with ink. She loved that, too, the evidence of his passion for the work they shared. "I'd like to take a couple of months to ease Ginny into this."

The name made her turn her face from his, but he continued.

"She's got some big project going right now. And, in general, summer's her busiest time. I don't feel good about throwing this at her in the middle of it."

"Feel good!" she interrupted. "You're never going to feel good about this! I don't feel good! She's not going to feel good! You're not supposed to feel good!"

"Shh, shh," he soothed. "I know. I'm sorry. But in September, when things are quieter, it'll be different. Not good, but not quite as bad. OK? Can you give me three or four months to do this with some decency?"

She sighed. It felt a little odd to be talking about managing Ginny's feelings like this, as if she were a project. But it also felt virtuous and healthy. She wished Ginny well, after all. "I can wait," she said, "until September."

She'd stood on her balcony that night in a silk shift she'd bought back in Chicago and watched him walk to his car. She felt beautiful, the night breeze off the lake lifting the hair around her face, fluttering the silk against her skin, but as far as she could tell, he didn't look back.

. . .

"He's not doing her any favors dragging it out like this," Andrea said. "If he doesn't love her, he should let her move on, find someone else. That would be the decent thing."

It sounded crass the way Andrea said it, but that didn't mean it wasn't true. Besides, Freddi didn't believe that Ginny was the kind of person who would want to stay with a man who didn't love her best. Freddi certainly wouldn't, if the situation were reversed.

"Maybe Ethan and Ginny will get together," Andrea suggested.

Trust Andrea to find the humor.

For some months after Freddi and Ethan had rediscovered each other, Andrea had been rooting for Ethan. "Aside from the fact that he's a lawyer," she'd said, "what's wrong with him?"

Many of Freddi's Madison friends professed to despise lawyers, who, with the possible exception of public defenders, they perceived to be at best gray-suited plodders along the safe, dull path of financial security, and at worst, parasites, feasting on others' misery. Freddi's friends believed a job should nourish the soul, even if it kept the bank account lean. Andrea, for instance, was a librarian who supplemented her income by playing the flute at weddings. They claimed to like Freddi despite her job, although they acknowledged that at least she did something "creative." This disdain of the practical, Freddi had noticed, had begun to ease now that they were all in their thirties and starting to think about home ownership and retirement plans.

Freddi had invited Andrea and Ethan to dinner one evening, thinking she might be doing them both a favor. Freddi was an experimental cook, less interested in perfecting her technique than in trying something new. She kept a binder of recipes sliced out of magazines, organized by occasion—Formal Dinner Party, Brunch, New Year's Eve for Two, Cocktails Before a Show—and protected in clear plastic pockets. For Ethan and Andrea (Casual

Dinner for Friends), she'd chosen a Moroccan chicken dish, with ginger and lemon and small green olives. While she quartered the chicken, she indulged in a mild fantasy about the success of the partnership she was about to initiate. Andrea would relax Ethan, show him how to take life less seriously; Ethan would tighten Andrea's standards and keep her from deluding herself with pop psychology. They would appreciate each other. Grow because of each other. Who but Freddi would have realized, people would say, that such different sorts would be a perfect match?

Freddi was vague about who these people might be. Neither she nor Andrea nor Ethan had a wide circle of friends and acquaintances who discussed their lives among themselves, but she imagined this sort of community at some future date when all of them were settled in houses that invited dropping in on weekends, the way people did on TV shows. Wasn't she, in fact, sowing the seeds for this very system of overlapping friendships by bringing together two of her friends? By the time she discovered that the lemons she'd bought had to be "preserved," which took a week, she was almost envious of Ethan and Andrea's happy future, the independent-minded son or daughter they would raise, the sculpture by local artists they'd collect, their small but thriving company, which would take care of the legal aspects involved in the acquisition of rare books. She substituted lemon juice for the preserved lemon—it would be different, she decided, but equally tasty—and arranged the sofa pillows around the coffee table. They would sit on the floor to eat. It would be fun and an icebreaker.

Andrea arrived early and pulled a bottle of ranch dressing from a plastic grocery bag. "Was this the kind you wanted? I couldn't remember." She opened the refrigerator, exchanged the dressing for a bottle of amber ale from which she sipped as she leaned against the counter, watching Freddi arrange a plate of semisoft cheeses and cocktail toast. "Do I look all right? I wasn't sure about the hair."

Andrea ruefully described her hair as "easy to dye," which meant indeterminate in color and thin in texture. This evening she'd pulled it off her neck in a claw clip.

Freddi pulled a couple of strands loose around her face and neck. "Actually," she said, standing back to give her friend careful consideration, "you look quite stunning. What's going on with your skin?"

"Aha! I've discovered the key to beauty." Andrea tipped her chin back for a long swallow of beer and then grinned. "I finished a forty-five-minute swim exactly one hour ago. Exercise to the point of exhaustion, followed by a quart of water and a quick shower. That's the secret to a glowing complexion. Of course, the effect is transient. Where is this guy?"

By the time Ethan arrived, precisely ten minutes late, as was his custom for dinner parties, Andrea had finished a second beer. Although Freddi had clearly specified casual, Ethan was wearing a dove-gray suit of summer-weight wool and a tie. He'd brought a bouquet of yellow roses. "For the hostess," he said, and gave Freddi a long look as he put them into her hands. He did not acknowledge Andrea until Freddi introduced them. "A friend of Winifred's!" he exclaimed. Then, shaking Andrea's hand: "A friend of Winifred's. A friend of Winifred's. It almost rhymes, but not quite. What is that called?"

"Andrea," Andrea said drily.

"No, no, I mean . . ." but to Freddi's relief he stopped himself. "Andrea, yes, Andrea. The things I've heard about you," he teased, his tone slightly suggestive. Freddi was surprised to feel a pinch, indistinct but bothersome, of jealousy.

She needn't have. The introduction was not a success. Ethan, his suit jacket riding up around his neck, looked uncomfortable and silly wedged on a pillow between the coffee table and the couch. "That's free-range chicken, I hope," he said nervously, when she brought out the main course. His preoccupation with the purity of food was a quirk she found sort of endearing. She shared his opinion in general terms—it *was* free-range chicken—but she also enjoyed the occasional butter burger and enjoyed even more his consternation when she consumed one in front of him. Only with Ethan could one feel like a daredevil for eating a hamburger. She could see that Andrea, however, thought him stuffy and rude, an assessment confirmed when he squinted at the bottle of dressing she'd contributed and passed it on without removing the cap. Before they'd even finished the chicken, Andrea was slightly drunk. She'd stretched her feet out so that they were nearly in Ethan's lap and Ethan eyed with distaste her toe ring and toenails, which she'd painted a metallic purple. Conspicuously, he'd declined to remove his shoes. And he paused before every mouthful to pick the raisins out.

"I'll talk to you tomorrow," Andrea hissed into Freddi's ear, as she pushed her feet into her sandals. From the doorway, she gave Ethan a little wave. He'd raised himself to the couch and made clear he didn't intend to leave first.

Almost as soon as she'd shut the door, Freddi exploded. "You behaved very rudely! Are you aware of that?"

He looked startled. "No, I certainly didn't mean to be rude. It's just . . . well, I really don't think people should wear rings on their toes. And I think painted nails look a little . . . I don't know . . . cheap, I guess."

"Jesus, Ethan! Women wear jewelry! Women paint their nails! Women adorn themselves! It's what women do! You can't object to that."

"You don't."

"I do, Ethan. Look, I do." She held up her hand, fingers splayed, to display the ring, a gift, surprisingly, from her grandfather, which she never took off.

"It's all right on your fingers. Just not on your toes."

"Rings on her fingers. Rings on her toes, Ethan!"

"And you don't paint them."

"What?"

"You don't paint your nails."

"Only because I'm lazy. Look, Ethan, look." She stalked into the bathroom, plucked the bottles from the shelf and threw them onto the couch beside him. "Look! Very Berry. Winky Pink. Cherries in the Snow. Blood on the Tracks. I've got all the colors. I'll paint them right now, and you'll see." She unscrewed the top of one of the bottles as she talked. "I'll paint them right now and I bet, I bet you any money, I'll still be a woman that you like."

"Love."

She heard a swishing in her head, like the sound that came from pressing a shell to one's ear. This was not what she wanted him to say.

Oh, she knew it all right. And, damn it, she liked the attention, liked the puppylike devotion, liked that someone, some man, put her first the way Jon, obviously, did not. But she'd thought it was clear that he was not to say it. She swallowed. He was looking at her steadily, waiting.

"Oh, Ethan . . ."

He cleared his throat. "Let's pretend I didn't say that, OK? It's too soon. You need . . . time. You're focused on your career right now."

She couldn't let him believe that. "Ethan."

He held his hands in front of his face, palms out, making a barrier. "Please, just . . . can you please just not say anything. And we'll just go back." He stood up from the couch and began backing toward the doorway. "We'll just . . ." He broke off, moving his hands back and forth rapidly in front of his face, erasing, until he had to lower a hand to turn the doorknob.

"It's 'rings on her fingers, *bells* on her toes,' " he said, stepping over the threshold. "Just . . . so you know."

seventeen

"Is it 'rings on her fingers and bells on her toes'?" Freddi asked. She was sitting up straight now, her legs crossed at the knees. She kicked one foot up, toes splayed, and studied the effect of her fuchsia polish against her tan.

"Is it what?"

"Rings on her fingers and bells on her toes?"

"Of course. What else could it be?"

"I thought 'rings on her fingers and rings on her toes.' "

"Then how would she make music?"

"I thought it was some sort of wordplay. Rings ringing."

"Well, maybe the rings do ring, but there are bells, too."

Ginny knew nursery rhymes, Jon thought. And the chants that went with the clapping games little girls played. And jump-rope songs. And Christmas carols. Probably she knew lullabies, too. All the things women were supposed to teach their children.

They were nearing the road that led to Winnesha, the house he'd grown up in only a couple of miles away, a walkable distance for a teenager who wanted to hitch a ride to Madison. Hitching was how he'd gotten to the hospital the first night he'd gone to visit Ginny, knowing that he'd ruined everything.

He'd made good progress: a man who sold dental equipment had picked him up within five minutes of his raising his thumb and had taken him as far as Johnson Street, where it turned out to be easy to get a bus to University Hospital. When he stepped into the shadowy canyon between the hospital's entrance and the parking garage, he paused, terrified. Ginny, he felt sure, would rather not see him, and her parents, especially her father, had looked at him on the night of the accident as if they wished they could scrape him off their shoes. Before getting this far, he'd agonized for a week, and in that time had almost managed to make not going at all sit right with his conscience. But he'd known showing up was the right thing to do, even if they hated him. It could be done quickly, however. All he had to do was tell Ginny and her family again that he was sorry and leave the flowers.

Five minutes, five minutes, he repeated to himself, as he went down the fluorescent hallway, trying not to look into the dimly lit rooms he passed and holding the flowers—stiff pink carnations and a spray of baby's breath against a fan of leathery fern—away from his body so they wouldn't get smashed.

As it turned out, she was alone. No glowering father or trembling mother, no duo of wide-eyed, spindly, spookily lookalike little sisters. "I told them to take my grandmother out for a cheeseburger," she explained. "They were driving me so crazy I wanted to pull the plug."

The phrase alarmed him, but she giggled a little, to show there was no question of plug-pulling. He'd seen her smile often before—she had the sort of whole-face smile, even last year when she'd worn braces, that you didn't see very often on teenage girls—but he hadn't known she was capable of joking.

She looked not so much injured as vaguely unclean. Her complexion, tan a week ago, was now a grayish yellow; her hair lay flat and greasy against her scalp. Her eyes were larger than he remembered. Like the wolf, he couldn't help but think. He tried not to look at her hips and legs. Under the rumpled white hospital blanket, they, too, seemed to be far larger than they should have been, grotesquely out of proportion to her upper body.

He ended up staying two hours, leaning at first against the wall just inside the door, one sneaker stepping on the other, and then sitting in the vinyl-covered visitor's chair. That night, in his own bed, he imagined that he'd sat on the edge of her bed, but in real life he'd sat squarely in the chair with both feet on the floor, trying to keep from shifting his weight so that the cushion wouldn't make embarrassing sounds. He'd held the flowers across his knees.

His forgetting to give those flowers and her being too shy to ask for them—because what if they weren't for her, after all? imagine the humiliation!—became one of their stories, a set piece they performed together at parties when the subject of courtship came up.

"I had a good time," she said. This was after he'd made it to the chair, but before he'd been relieved of the flowers.

He frowned. What could she be talking about?

"At your party. I mean until this," she hesitated, "unfortunate turn of events. It was a really good party."

"Well." He was stumped. He hated to think about the party now. "Thanks."

"When I said Beth made me come, I didn't mean—"

"How're we doing tonight?" A nurse breezed in, her shoes

squeaking on the linoleum. She bustled around Ginny efficiently, chatting, wrapping a cuff around her arm, poking a thermometer into her mouth. Jon worried that she might accidentally pull the covers off some part of Ginny that he shouldn't be seeing. He also worried that he wished that would happen. He began to sort and count the colors in the tiles under his feet, a gray, a brown-gray, a green-gray. He tried to determine whether the pattern repeated on each twelve-by-twelve-inch square. He tapped the bunch of flowers on his knee to the beat of an Elton John song that was leaking through the room's thin wall.

"Put a penny on the chest," he sang softly, almost unaware that he was making any noise at all. "Penn-ee-y! Penn-ee-y! Penny on the chest."

"Here, I'll take those," the nurse said, when she'd finished with Ginny. "Before you knock their heads off."

"I don't think those are the words," Ginny said, after the nurse had found a vase and wedged it between a book and a box of Kleenex and left the room. "Penny on the chest."

"I don't know," Jon said. "That's what I thought they were."

"But what would that mean? Why would he be saying that?"

What the words might mean hadn't bothered Jon before. "Maybe," he said, "it's like if you save a little at a time, you'll end up with a lot. Or maybe," he was warming to the subject now, "it's a song about a bunch of guys betting on something? And everyone's supposed to ante up." He liked this idea. He could picture the scene in his mind, the dark, smoky room. Zoot suits. The sort of metal-banded chest pirates would use.

"A penny?"

"Well, maybe a penny means like a hundred dollars. You know, like a dime means a thousand."

She was smiling. "Maybe it's a folk remedy for a cough. Maybe a penny is really a poultice." She laughed, and so did he, even though he wasn't too sure what a poultice was.

"It's not 'put a penny on the chest,' Jon." He hadn't ever heard her use his name before. He liked hearing her say it. "It's 'when he speaks in jest.' " She sang the phrase to the tune.

When he finally got home, Kyle was sitting at the kitchen table, eating a bowl of cereal. "So?" he said. "How'd it go? She like my flowers?"

Kyle had chosen flowers, too. Red roses, their long stems tied together with a red satin ribbon. Jon had left them on a bench outside the hospital on his way in. They were gone by the time he emerged from the building.

Although already he had told the story so many times of the rabbit that had run across his path that he could actually see the thick gray-brown fur, the frightened eyes, the pinky insides of the oversized ears, nothing but his anger with Kyle had caused him to brake so suddenly.

The party had been Jon's idea; he'd planned it; he'd bought the stuff with his own money. Of course, Kyle was invited. And, of course, Jon knew that half the people who'd shown up, the older ones anyway, the girls especially, had come because of Kyle. But Kyle, being Kyle, had to steal the whole show, had to make the rounds as if he were the host, joking and smiling, using his charm in that obvious way that he had, while Jon stood off to one side, holding the plastic cups.

The tractor ride was a bit of entertainment, one cool thing his dad could give him, access to a big tractor and trailer. They'd all piled on the flatbed, screaming and laughing, except for Beth, who was standing behind him, her breasts making him sweat. When they'd started down the steep grade, he'd looked back to keep the ride safe. He wanted to be sure that the trailer hitch was holding. But what he saw was the way his brother was looking at Ginny, the girl he'd been dreaming about, the girl for whom he'd thrown the whole fucking party, a girl his brother hadn't thought about for one second before that afternoon. She was smiling at Kyle, one hand pinning her long, dark braid to her heart. He couldn't help himself. His foot just lifted off the accelerator and stomped the brake.

He wasn't trying to hurt anyone, not even Kyle, certainly not Ginny. He was just mad.

It wasn't a simple matter to become the one who brought homework to her. She had friends, an efficient network of girls who kept lists on small pads of lavender or pink paper, girls who made pop-up cards and tagboard posters to amuse her, girls who had regular access to cars and the combination to her locker. He intercepted Beth, told her to tell the rest of them that he would be responsible. The accident, after all, was his fault. He should be the one to help. It was decided that he could not be trusted with the locker combination nor with collecting the assignments. They would deposit their lavender instructions in a special folder to be kept in his locker, along with any necessary books, and his job would be to deliver them via Badger Bus. The girls did not approve of hitchhiking.

Doing his own homework in her room, while she did hers, transformed his high-school career and, he liked to think, altered the course of his life. The teachers' demands, which he'd long been in the habit of shrugging off, now seemed important. He could not ask Ginny to quiz him on the abbreviations of the periodic table, for instance, and then tell her he'd gotten a C. He had to pole-vault himself into her league. The hours he was not at the hospital, he worked on his studio art project, imagining the night when he would lead her through the series he was calling Shades of Gray, charcoal drawings with occasional spots of bright color in significant places. With her, he saw that he might be better than he'd thought he was.

1963

Once outside, Marie slips her arm through Walt's. It's just a casual, friendly gesture the way she does it, but it lets her fit herself against him, her hip against his, her shoulder tucked into the hollow below his collarbone. She can feel his heart beat against her arm as she directs his drift toward the darker reaches of the course.

"My own father's bet on Bud," he sighs. "Not that that isn't the right idea, if he wants to make money."

She stops and they stand on the unnaturally wide-open land, the wind tossing her hair into his face, pulling at their clothes. "And you wanted him to bet on you?"

"Well, of course." His laugh is rueful.

"That's too bad." She'd assumed his father's obvious preference for Bud would anger him; it had never occurred to her that he might only feel hurt. So he's weak. She's very glad of it, glad that *it makes her despise him and harden her resolve. She slides her hand into his. The gesture could be meant to comfort or it could mean more. She waits to see how he'll interpret it, knowing she has to keep things perfectly balanced to create the right illusion. It won't be enough for Bud to find them talking. They are friends, after all. Talking together on a dark golf course might make him ask questions, but confusion or even suspicion isn't enough. On the other hand, the idea of Walt's fingers on her back or his breath against her neck makes her want to vomit.*

He turns his face toward her, brushes his lips against her cheek. There's no mistaking that gesture. "Bud gets everything," he murmurs.

"Maybe not everything," she says, stepping away from his lips, but pulling him on by the hand. It'll be a simple thing to hold him off, since she no longer cares whether he loves her. She'll wait until she hears their voices, Clark's and Bud's, and then she'll invite him to feel the baby. That, with the seeds Clark has planted and the compromising setting, should be enough. And she won't actually have done a single thing to hurt Bud.

eighteen

"Got it!" Mark shouted from the back of Nora's car, where he sat wedged against Rodney's top-of-the-line car seat. Music for the very young blasted from the speakers. "It's Virginia."

They'd stopped at Ginny's house on the way out of town, so that Mark could swipe Jon's laptop for the account folder he needed. He'd had to try a few of the passwords he knew Jon normally used before hitting on the right one.

"Did you ever see a whale with a coconut tail?" Rodney sang loudly.

"Are there any games on there?" Anthony bounced forward, so that he could see around Rodney.

"Anthony! Sit back and keep your seat belt on or you're going right back to Mom's."

"That house isn't Mom's," he said. His tone was disdainful, as if Mark should know better.

"What are you talking about?"

"That's what Mom says to Alex: 'It's your house. It's not up to me.' "

"Well, you're going back to Alex's, then, if you don't sit back and buckle your seat belt."

Ginny saw that he was grinning. Well, she didn't blame him. He'd suffered for months after Heidi had told him she was finished with him, really finished. She said it wasn't because there was someone else (although there was, in fact, someone else, not Alex, whom she didn't meet for another year, but her orthodontist); she had other reasons, reasons that were precise in Mark's bitter, self-flagellating retelling, but which became formless and insubstantial within days after Ginny had heard them. Certainly, she couldn't recall them now. Well, there were things she'd not been told, obviously, even though, God knows, she'd been told and told and told until she shrank from the phone's ring. Often Jon would pick up, and immediately thrust the receiver at her, claiming to have done his shift all day at work. She understood, knowing the hour she was in for, the same litany Mark had rehearsed a hundred times, two hundred times—why did Heidi, why didn't Heidi, didn't Ginny think that Heidi should have . . . ? She imagined him as he spoke, literally tearing at his hair, sprawled on the single beanbag chair with which he'd furnished his cramped, underlit, tenant-worn box just off Highway 18, the sort of place rented by people without the energy or resources to search for something better.

She and Jon had been startled and a little frightened by his misery. What happened when you were married, she realized, was that, although you began as two independent people, you eventually grew in certain ways to accommodate your partner's weaknesses and let other parts of you atrophy in deference to his strengths. It was a fine system as long as it endured, but if you extricated yourself from it, you couldn't help but be, at least for a time, deformed.

She suspected that Anthony had made that comment about Heidi and Alex to please Mark. She looked into the backseat again. The boy was tying the seat belt into a series of knots. "Anthony, please buckle that. We're on the highway and it's very dangerous."

He did as she told him to and smiled at her. It occurred to her that perhaps her body, in its unwillingness to trust her with a new, tiny creature, did not know better. Perhaps her body was a fool. Or just afraid. She'd not heeded that fear in any other part of her life. Why should she heed it in this?

Outside corn rows formed a corduroy pattern. She'd always found that optical effect mesmerizing from a car, the way the scene would abruptly change depending on the angle at which your eye caught it; one moment, a wall of corn, the next, a vast series of corridors, each one offering to guide you straight through the field. The offer was deceptive, she knew from experience. Lured into the thick of it, she'd panicked more than once, as the stalks closed in, blocking her vision and scratching her skin with their sharp leaves, while the clods underfoot, hard and uneven as stones, had made her ankles ache. Best to stay on the periphery.

"Ninety-nine point nine percent of accidents happen within half a mile from home," Anthony said.

"That's bathtub accidents." Nora turned the music down. "All right," she went on, "I'd like to remind the three Stooges back there that we're here on business. When we get to Meadowwood there's to be no interrupting, no wild behavior. This is our most important job right now, and Mr. Fleischer shouldn't have to put up with any nonsense."

"Whatever," Mark said.

Anthony giggled. Rodney observed the giggling for a moment and then belted out his own laughter.

Nora frowned into the mirror. "Mark. This means you."

"Who is this Fleischer character, anyway? Some local bigwig?"

"He was my boss when I was eighteen," Ginny said, "although all he did was sign my checks. I didn't really know him personally until a couple of months ago. This is the exit, Nora." They separated themselves from the interstate, and the straight, flat stream that rushed, unchecked, from one end of the country to the other went on without them.

She could drive this exit with her eyes closed, knew, internally, the exact degree of its ascent, the precise location of its stop sign. In every season and at every hour of the day she'd driven it and the road onto which they now turned. It was along here on a dark winter evening, her father chauffeuring her home from some activity or other, forensics, probably, or piano, something she could do on crutches, that she'd found out who Walter Fleischer was, the part of him that mattered anyway.

"Did you know that Jon's father was a good enough golfer to go pro?" She couldn't help herself; she had to talk about Jon, even though her father disapproved. There it was, the sour face, as if he'd bitten into a rotten piece of fruit. She fingered the tiny lead sculpture—a person running—Jon had made for her and strung on a chain.

"He tell you that?"

"Jon told me." She knew better than to go on, but she brazened forward, staring out the window and speaking not to her skeptical father but to the undulating carpet of snow, silvered in the moonlight. "But the night of his first big tournament, he wrecked his arm rescuing Mr. Fleischer from the lake."

"After he forced Walt Fleischer's car off the road." He was

waiting, she knew, for her to react with dismay. She would not, although this information had surprised her, as he'd intended.

"If he did, he probably had a good reason."

"Jon tell you that, too?"

"No," she admitted. She looked at him, waiting for him to know more than she did about everything, even about her own boyfriend's family, to understand everything better. That was the way he always had to have it.

"Well, he probably doesn't know. He's only a kid." He sighed and turned to stare for a moment out his own window, as if he regretted having to tell, as if she'd dragged the secret out of him. "Walt and Marie Kepilkowski were—what's the term you kids use?—making out behind a sand trap is what I heard, and Bud caught them at it."

She was silent for a minute, sinking into the drama he'd described. He thought he was exposing deceit and uncivilized fury, a family any reasonable girl would wish to avoid, but what she saw was thrilling passion and romantic hotheadedness. It pleased her to realize how little he understood her.

Downtown Winnesha had recently become picturesque. Two blocks at the center had been bricked to affect quaintness and the newer people who'd moved into the big, turn-of-the-century houses on Main Street and Maple Avenue, people who owned small businesses that supplied large manufacturers with unobtrusive but essential components, like rubber hosing and plastic valves, had the money and the taste to restore them and make them bright. Ginny's parents' house, which had always been one of the best maintained, though never improved, now looked slightly shabby in comparison.

She directed Nora through town and out the other side.

Within a few blocks, Main Street shed its village ways and became County Y, its tight lots and pretty wooden bungalows giving way to a gas station and a couple of taverns before picking up a stretch of little ranch houses spaced well apart along the edges of the fields, their miniature ranches consisting of lawns large enough to justify sit-down mowers. It was beyond these that the radical change began, at least for Ginny. The fields once flat and green with expanses of corn and soybeans and alfalfa, the hilltops left grassy for the cows to graze were covered now with Colonial-style duplexes dominated by convenient garages. Beyond these, incongruously set among a few remaining acres of corn, were clusters of imposing stone manor houses with multiple chimneys and garages with room for three carriages, vulnerable saplings staked in their emerald front yards.

They turned off of Y onto DD to follow the south shore of Lake Winnesha, and then onto Country Club Drive. That road had once been shadowed with maples, but the sun lay in wide patches now, where trees had died and hadn't been replaced. Some new trees, maybe more randomly spaced than the old ones, would be a good idea. Ginny pawed through her bag for her notebook.

The golf course itself shocked her less this time than it had two months ago, when she'd first seen it in its present condition, a meadow of matted grasses, thistle, and milkweed, with stands of intrepid box elders, a weird terrain of mesas and shirred hummocks where the greens and sand traps had been. As a piece of prairie, it was in an awkward, transitional stage, but to her eye, it was distinctly more beautiful now than it had been when it was uniformly brilliant green and cropped.

"Sorry, right here," she said, as Nora nearly passed the entrance.

They were meeting at the old clubhouse, the restaurant

where she'd been a hostess, where her mother had been a salad girl, where her mother-in-law had been a waitress. A place she'd never imagined a child of hers might know.

Fleischer's Excursion was parked directly in front of the entrance.

"Should we hang around out here?" Mark asked.

"Oh, no. Don't you want to look around a little?" She wondered, as she said it, why he would. The place, so rich to her, would be only a derelict patch of weeds and neglected buildings to him.

But Anthony was already halfway to the door with Rodney just behind him. "Yeah, Dad! Let's look!"

The restaurant's entrance was still fitted with a storm door from the fall of 1988 when old Mr. Fleischer had closed the place for good. It shook loosely on its hinges as Ginny knocked. When no one answered, she pulled it open, turned the handle— also loose—on the front door, and pushed in.

The setups were still on the tables in the dining rooms—the salt and pepper shakers, the amber faceted water tumblers, the red glass votive candleholders, the ashtrays stamped with a picture of two crossed golf clubs in green—as if the place were ready to serve meals within the hour, but the tablecloths had yellowed and the light fixtures and ceiling fans were gauzed over with spiderwebs. The letters on the menu, posted in a glass-fronted case, had bleached into illegibility.

"Mr. Fleischer?"

The kitchen was strangest to her, since, in the time she'd worked there, it had reverberated with clanging pots and spraying water, the angry hiss of perpetually frying chicken, and raised voices. Now the only sound was the steady drip of the tap, which had produced a huge orange moon of rust in the enamel sink.

"Dad! Look at this!" Under the sink, Anthony had found a trap, its metal bar bisecting a heap of slender rat bones.

Ginny inspected it. "If you had some model glue," she said, "you might be able to piece this together."

"I have model glue! Dad, can I take it home? Please?"

"Oh, yeah. Your mother would love that. Tell you what, if you can find a box to put it into, you can take it. We'll work on it at my place."

"And I can work on it, too?" Rodney asked plaintively.

Anthony was already slamming cupboard doors open. "How about this?" he yelled, holding up a saucepan.

Nora raised her hand. "Hold everything, boys. Technically, the rat belongs to Mr. Fleischer."

"As do the pots and pans," added Ginny.

"Let's see what he's willing to part with," Nora went on, "before we go any further."

"Well, where is the bigwig, anyway?" Mark asked.

"In the bar." The voice came from a distant room, but the words were distinct.

The bar had been set apart from the hot clatter of the kitchen and the warm hum of the dining rooms by a long narrow hallway, off of which the restrooms opened. It had simultaneously frightened and compelled Ginny at eighteen. Whereas in the dining rooms people leaned back in their chairs and clicked their glasses together in festive toasts, in the bar people hunched protectively around their drinks, sipping steadily. As soon as Jon's father finished his shift mowing and raking, she knew that he settled, unshowered, onto a stool for an hour or two of a different sort of work, his greasy cap on the counter beside him. Her own parents, she was sure, had never sat at the bar.

At eighteen she knew she was expected to understand things as an adult would—what a man meant, for instance, when he looked at her a certain way—but she was still guided far more by emotions than by experience. She was prone to overreacting or underreacting to signals, feeling skittish when perhaps she ought to have laughed, laughing when her hackles should have risen.

As a hostess, she often had reason to visit the bar. One of her jobs, for instance, had been to make sure its refrigerator was stocked with olives and cocktail onions and its bin was full of pretzels. Another was to keep track of patrons who, not perceiving the strict division between bar and dining room that Ginny observed, would have a drink at the bar while they waited for a table. These she needed to summon at the appropriate moment, the correct number of menus cradled on her hip. And on the nights Jon was tending bar she made more trips down the hall than were strictly necessary. He'd gotten her the hostess job and to take it she'd turned down the offer of a secretarial position at the firm of one of her father's lawyer friends, a job that would have given her "something to show for her summer," as her father had put it.

Her hostess uniform was a cranberry-colored dirndl skirt, an ivory blouse with a bow at the neck, and black sandals with inch and a half heels, all items she never wore in her regular shorts-and-T-shirt life. She twirled slightly on her toes when she turned to lead people to the dining room to feel the skirt bell around her knees. She'd cut her hair by then and pinned it off one side of her face with a barrette, and she was aware of its ends swinging jauntily, too, as she turned, light on her feet, happy, grown-up, an integral part of the summer bustle. Working at the club, she felt mature, and she saw Jon, casually mixing drinks in his dress shirt and maroon tie, as an adult, too.

When she crouched behind the bar to check the contents of the mini-refrigerator, she ran a quick hand up his sockless calf. He touched her waist whenever he could, letting his hand slide over her buttock as she stepped teasingly away. With the self-consciousness and self-absorption of adolescents, they were at once performing for and oblivious to those around them who were marking their gestures and their looks.

She was alone in the dark hall the night the man stepped out of the restroom to block her way. Business had slowed for the evening and she'd left her hostess stand to whisper some stray thought to Jon. She'd noticed the man in the bar, a big man in a short-sleeved dress shirt. He'd smiled at her from his table, a smile she didn't like. She'd frowned in response and turned abruptly away. Then she'd touched the back of Jon's neck with her fingertips to show that she was not to be smiled at.

She glanced at the floor now, meaning to skim past. He wasn't stepping aside for her, but she was good at making her body small. There would be enough space, if she brushed the wall.

He, however, made his body larger. He shifted his weight so that his shoulder and hip blocked the hole she'd meant to use. Surprised, she stepped back with a tight gasp. "Hey, pretty girl," he said. His voice was soft, gravel-filled. "Don't run away from me. I don't bite."

She gave him a quick, little smile—a smile! "Excuse me," she said. "I need to get back to the hostess stand."

"Ah, the hostess," he said. "Are you the hostess with the mostest?"

She smiled again. Oh, yes, you are amusing. I am amused. Can we be done now? If she couldn't run, she must placate. She was that sort of creature.

But Jon was not. Voices carried easily down that narrow hall. "What's going on here?" His words snapped. He was with her and then between them faster than she could even register his movements. He was shorter than the man and much slighter, but he leaned forward aggressively, his face in the man's face, his chin jutting forward, his index finger an inch from the man's eye. "I said, what's going on here?"

After her first moment of relief, she felt again the shameful rise of her need for politeness, politeness at all costs. She plucked at his shirt. "It's OK. Jon, it's OK."

The man stepped back, either from surprise or from the sheer force of Jon's aggression. Jon curled the finger he'd been pointing into a fist and pulled it back, even with his own face. "You leave her the fuck alone! You hear me? I said, do you hear me?"

The man raised his hands, stepped back again. "OK, kid. Geez, I was just talking to her. No harm done."

"If I ever see you talking to her again . . . If I ever see you in here again . . ." Jon's teeth were clenched. A fleck of spittle flew from his lips and sparkled for a moment in the dim light.

"OK, I said, OK." The man hurried toward the door, stepping sideways so as to keep Jon in his view. "Lousy drinks anyway," he added.

She was proud when she told her father how Jon had defended her. She hoped this might make him regard Jon differently. How could he not embrace her champion? But he was not impressed.

"I told you I didn't want you working in that place. You need to be much more careful, Ginny. How could you let a man corner you like that? Don't you know how to take care of yourself? What? Did his attention flatter you? Don't you know better than that?"

Ginny couldn't answer. She'd not felt flattered, had she? Or was that why she'd stood there smiling like a fool? Although she'd given her father the impression she'd been trapped, that wasn't the case at all, was it? No, she could always have turned and run back down the hall to the safety of the bar. She could have screamed. But that hadn't been necessary, had it? He'd only been playing with her. Testing what she would do, what she would let him do. She could have run, but she'd been embarrassed to do so. Embarrassed to show him she was still just a frightened girl.

"You're giving notice tomorrow," he went on. "In fact, no, forget the notice. They don't deserve notice if they can't give you a safe place to work. You're not to go back there, you understand?"

In the end, she convinced him to let her give notice, which brought her almost to the end of the summer anyway. But the hostess uniform had lost its power to make her a grown woman.

Ginny sent her voice down the hall ahead of her. "Mr. Fleischer?"

"In here."

He'd unrolled several pages of plans on the bar and had been bent over, studying them. He sat up, somewhat stiffly, and turned as they came in. With his prominent jaw, his wide mouth, and his slightly protuberant, hooded eyes, he distinctly resembled a toad. It was difficult to imagine him a Lothario, until he slid off the stool and stepped toward them with his hand extended. He possessed the sort of self-assurance that arose from a thorough and genuine enthusiasm for something other than himself, in this case, the project before him. He was like a child with a new and long-coveted toy. You wanted, Ginny thought, to be invited to join his game, to help him have his fun.

"I can't wait for you to see these," he said, drawing the women toward the bar as soon as the greetings and introductions had been cleared away. "They'll interest you, too," he added over his shoulder to Mark. "It's amazing to see how a piece of fallow and, really, featureless ground can be transformed into something useful and beautiful."

Mark glanced politely at the papers, but Ginny could see that there was nothing on them to hold his attention and soon he wandered over to study the photos that covered the west wall. At the far end of the bar, near the cash register, Anthony ran his index finger along an ancient display of candy bars and then pressed his palms and face against the glass front of a cigarette machine. Rodney was examining the glass case underneath the register in which packets of tees and boxes of balls were displayed. In the daytime, the bar had been a sunny room, a place to pay for a round of golf and a couple of cans of grape pop for the kids. She'd forgotten that. Was this worn wood floor, these few wooden stools, all "the bar" had been, when she'd found it so thrilling?

nineteen

Jon slowed to turn into a lot marked with a hand-lettered sign. "Summer" had been spelled with a single *m*. The official lots, even those most distant from the grounds, were still several blocks away.

"We'll need a tent," Freddi said, "if we're going to hike from here."

He waved "never mind" to the attendant and backed into the street. It was Ginny who liked to save pennies by parking miles away, not he. Although he'd never objected. It had become a sort of game with them, in fact, driving an extra block to see if they could go one dollar cheaper. They liked to think they were doing their best to keep the world from taking advantage of them.

"This area looks interesting," she said. "We should come down here one day and look around."

"Oh, the Third Ward, yeah." Had they parked where he'd intended, Jon thought, they would have been walking here, looking around, that very afternoon. He tried to shrug off his irritation. After all, she was only trying to be pleasant. "A couple of these galleries have really interesting stuff," he said, "and there are some theaters here, too. It's all very hip and urban. You'd like it."

"Sort of a Midwestern TriBeCa?"

"I guess." He checked his mirrors, shifted in his seat. He didn't like this habit she had of trying to prove her worldliness. He could hear the strain in it; the compulsion to establish her identity as a sophisticate. If she'd ever been to New York, he suspected that the trip had been some sort of package tour. Which was fine! He'd never been at all. He just wished she wouldn't pretend to be more cultured than she was. Or at least he wished her pretense was less transparent.

He and Ginny had considered living in this neighborhood years ago. He'd been offered a position with a newborn company with a high-art sensibility that had just opened its office there. The Third Ward was an area in transition then, somewhere between the warehouses it had once been and the artsy district it had become. The guy who'd interviewed him had told him about some lofts for sale, raw spaces, they turned out to be, with the bathroom a drywall enclosure in one corner and the kitchen a cluster of shiny appliances installed against the opposite wall.

Ginny had wanted to do it. "It's like no life we've ever had before," she'd said. They'd stood in one of the huge windows at the front, a window that began so low that their knees pressed against the sill. The place felt daringly open to the street below. It was a winter afternoon, the sky a heavy gray with the weight of the snow that was beginning to fall. Most of the surrounding buildings were dark and shut up, whether for the evening or forever it was difficult to tell, but here and there another gigantic window blazed with light. The buildings themselves were romantic brick and stone structures, denoting industry in an era before prefabrication and plastic.

But, he'd argued, they were so inexperienced, any life other than returning to their parents' houses would feel new and exciting. They didn't need to be extreme. In the end, he'd accepted the offer from Nielson Gray instead, a long-established company in the city they knew well, and soon enough they'd bought the sort of house in the sort of neighborhood he'd grown up aspiring to. He'd had doubts and regrets about that decision sometimes, sure, but when the start-up folded in three years' time, he knew he'd made the right choice.

"Maybe if you'd been working there, though," Ginny had suggested gently, "it would've made it."

The notion that what he did might matter to someone or something beyond himself had startled him.

"This okay?" They'd reached the official lots and he joined the line of cars inching into it.

She'd pulled down the mirror and was primping. "Sure. Whatever."

That rubbed him the wrong way. "Well, no," he said. "It's not really 'whatever.'"

"Huh?" She was frowning at her reflection, fluffing her short hair with her fingers. She turned to him, smiling. "I'm afraid my hair is DOA. We're going to have to get me another hat."

He looked at her. It was true; her hair was not attractive, pushed down that way against the sides of her head. She had a strangely small head, he noticed for the first time. He felt an urge to give it a little squeeze, as if juicing an orange. "It's not 'whatever,'" he repeated. "You said I was parking too far away, so now I'm parking close."

She looked at him, her eyes narrowed with disdain. "Well, good." She freighted each pronouncement with a long pause. "Great. Thank you. Is that what you want me to say? Thank you." She pushed the mirror up with a jerk. "Why are you making such a big deal about this? I had no idea parking was so important to you."

Why *was* he making such a big deal of this? After all, she'd not intended to criticize Ginny's habit. She'd just been expressing her own preference. What was the matter with him?

"Sorry," he said. "My mistake. Let's drop it. Let's have a good time."

She stared at him steadily, a slight smile on her lips, as if weighing the options, already playful. He appreciated her easy shift, her willingness to be happy with him. How simple it was to be with someone who wasn't helping him to drag along a clanking, groaning sack of well-worn grudges.

"OK." She leaned toward him, pushing her lips forward.

He kissed her but was aware of an unpleasantness on her breath, a hint of ketosis. He could hear other people walking past the car and could feel the heat that was beginning to replace the cooled air, now that the engine was off. He pulled away. "Ready?"

Even so close to Lake Michigan, it was hot. Mirages puddled the stretches of asphalt between the rows of cars. It was a day best spent sitting still, Jon thought, as he straightened his back, which had stiffened during the air-conditioned drive. He turned on his phone. One call from Kaiser. So Ginny had given up. He should probably call her, just to say hi, let her know when he'd be back.

"Invite her to dinner," his mother had said, handing him the phone one day when Ginny, as usual, was on the line.

The thought of exposing Ginny to his mother's scrutiny alarmed him.

A week or two later, he heard his mother say into the phone, "Why don't you join us for dinner on Friday?"

Ginny wore the gray wool skirt and navy sweater in which she'd played Chopin at the state music competition the weekend before. She secured a piece of her dark hair, newly shorn since the accident, with a girlish tortoiseshell clip.

"My mother says to say hello," she said. She shifted her cane from her right hand to her left, so that she could lift from the counter the glass bowl of planted bulbs Jon had carried in for her and pass it into his mother's hands.

"The last time I ran into Hattie must have been, oh, almost a year ago now. At the Piggly Wiggly." His mother settled her large glasses more squarely over her eyes. "And how," she asked, "is your father?"

"He's good." Ginny shrugged. "Working a lot, I guess."

"We were all very good friends once. Did you know that? I know Jon didn't." She rummaged in the drawer beside the stove for a spatula while the potatoes spat and popped in the pan. "It's funny how twenty years can change things," she went on. "I wonder if the two of you will remember each other in twenty years."

Which was the first hint he'd had that she'd decided not to like Ginny.

"Oh," Ginny had laughed, instantly neutralizing the poison, "I'm sure remembering each other won't be a problem."

For which he'd loved her.

His mother served whitefish, as she did every Friday, full of hidden bones. "You look very much like your father," she said, as she offered Ginny the platter.

"Really?" Ginny seemed pleased by the thought. "No one's ever said that."

"No," his mother said, "they wouldn't."

"You cut your hair," Kyle said.

Ginny nodded, looking down at her plate. Jon, himself, had not dared to mention the change, as she'd had it done in those early weeks, just after she left the hospital.

"It looks good," Kyle said.

"Thanks." She smiled, giving her head a little shake. The haircut, perhaps the accident itself, Jon had noticed, seemed surprisingly to have made her less self-conscious, more self-confident.

Her father tapped his horn in the driveway when he arrived to pick her up.

"Why doesn't he come in?" Jon's father said, and stepped out to the car, while Ginny said her thank-yous and shrugged into her peacoat.

"Call me when you get home," Jon murmured, as he shut her into the car.

"She's a nice girl," his father said, when the two of them came back into the house. "Don't you think she's a very nice girl, Marie? That's what I said to Clark out at the car there. I said, you and Hattie have raised one hell of a nice girl, there. Geez, that guy's really losing his hair, though."

His mother was rubbing a dishcloth along the inside of the glass bowl that had, a few minutes before, contained the bulbs. She looked at Jon. "I'm sorry," she said, "but I hate narcissus. I'm sure, if I let these grow, you would agree. They stink."

Jon hadn't remembered how relentlessly hot and loud Summerfest could be. Freddi was holding his arm now, publicly claiming him. He hadn't counted on feeling so exposed. As they converged with the crowds on the ticket booths, people seemed to be coming at them from every angle. Once inside, he knew, more people would be staring down from the tram. Hadn't he run into those he knew every time he'd come here? Grade-school people, high-school people, college people, people he'd gotten to know at the various minimum-wage jobs he'd worked before earning his degree, people from the agency, people from Winnesha, people who knew his mother, who'd known his father, his cousins and second cousins. Any one of them, all of them, could be here today, sharp-eyed and loose-tongued. He'd brought Freddi here without thinking about the consequences, just like everything else he'd done with her.

Freddi elbowed him and nodded with a smirk at an obese woman in leopard-print leggings who was laboring several yards ahead of them toward the entrance. He looked away, pretending to be making a careful choice among the crowded ticket booths. She could be mean sometimes, childish. He'd seen it before, the nasty, admittedly hilarious comments she made about people at work. A lot of them deserved it, but not all of them, and she didn't discriminate. Anyone who could be laughed at was fair game. In fact, she seemed to relish most bringing down the weak. Well, he'd laughed, hadn't he? Probably more often than he should have.

twenty

The woman in leopard-print leggings could have been her mother. Freddi was almost afraid she would turn and reveal her mother's flaccid cheeks and crooked teeth, her too-long hair and too-bright lips, her eyelids collapsing under the weight of too much black mascara. She knew the attitude she showed Jon was unkind, but she had to make clear she had no connection to people like that, even though they were whom she was obviously fated to become, if she wasn't vigilant.

He was pulling away from her. She could feel the buffer of space he was setting up between them. Normally his body would be leaning toward hers, his shoulders sloped in her direction, his gait in sync with her own, his eyes returning to her face, as if directed there by magnetic force. Now she felt as if she were repelling him. His eyes were scanning the crowd and he was walking slightly ahead, not so much that she could reasonably make an issue of it, but enough so that his meaning was perfectly clear. He was acting as if he'd dragged her along as a favor. Well, this whole Summerfest thing had been his idea, hadn't it?

She told herself it should piss her off. She should be pulling away, if anyone should. Who did he think he was, leaving her hanging like this? I want to see you. I can't see you. I want to be with you. I can't be with you. Pulling her toward him and then letting her go. She summoned Andrea's voice into her head, could imagine Andrea's dense curls quivering with outrage. "Who does he think he is? Who does he think *you* are? He should be all over you, and it should be you who decides whether he comes in or has to trot on back home and make the best of it."

That was how she should feel, but instead anxiety unfurled like a tendril of smoke from the base of her stomach, up through her chest. She grabbed his hand, laced her fingers with his.

His hand in hers was not exactly limp, but it wasn't responsive either. Usually, when they held hands, he caressed her thumb with his in an absentminded, comforting sort of way, but now his thumb was still. His hand was tolerating hers; that was all.

Her anxiety was spreading, the tendril of smoke becoming a screen. "Hey," she said again. Her voice threatened to become taut, but she forced it to relax. Now was the time to be coaxing, seductive. "Where'd you go?" She swung her hip a little, nudging his thigh.

For a moment it worked. He gave her hand a little squeeze and tilted his head to look down into hers. "I'm right here."

But, in fact, he was already drifting away again. She was sure he was thinking about his wife—the "other woman," from Freddi's point of view. God, the irony.

If she were honest, she had to admit that she resented Ginny's fragility. Why should she be coddled along until just the right, the least hurtful moment? So far, she'd pretty much been handed everything on a platter as far as Freddi could see—the privileged childhood, the education, the supportive husband, even the talent. That was why she couldn't suck it up like everyone else had to when something didn't work out the way she wanted. It was the first time the world hadn't rolled out a red carpet for her and told her right where to put her feet.

Freddi was proud of the fact that she'd never been handed anything. Well, no, she'd been handed plenty, but all of it was crap—a dead-end town and ignorant, self-satisfied relatives who mistrusted ambition and disdained beauty. She'd defined it all before, countless times, to Andrea and to others. And they'd all agreed that what she'd been given she'd had to push away like a greasy burger for the sake of her health, for the sake of her survival. From the very beginning, she'd had to invent herself, to figure out what she wanted and go for it. Well, she'd wanted him and she'd gone for him, and he'd wanted her, too; she had absolutely no doubt about that. But here they both were, stymied by his inability to move forward with what they agreed would be best for everyone involved.

They had passed through the gates now, along with masses of people who imitated the sounds of cows and sheep as they went. Did they all think themselves original? She and Jon stood still, strangely marooned, each gazing absently in the opposite direction, while other, more purposeful festivalgoers swirled around them.

And then they were like some Abbott and Costello routine, both saying "Which way?" at the same moment, which was funny. And then pointing in opposite directions, which was funnier still. And somehow they ended up walking north, which had been her choice, just randomly, not because she really had any preference, it was all the same to her, but still she took some small satisfaction in the fact that they were going the way she'd chosen, and Jon, for his part, seemed happy to be pleasing her. And so suddenly they seemed to be back in their groove, not touching, but walking with the same stride, walking with an awareness of being together. Maybe it had just been the long drive and the heat that had pulled them apart. Maybe she'd been oversensitive. It was better to try not to think about it now that it was over. That was the way a good day could get ruined.

In Chicago, she worried she'd be found out as the beer-drinking type and had learned to order cosmopolitans and merlot. Now, sitting at a picnic table, her fingers encircling the cool, plastic cup of froth, she knew she didn't truly belong to this world any longer either.

The beer, though, was what they'd needed to smooth their way back to each other. Her lips nearly caressing his ear, so as to be heard above the howl and hammer of the music, she began to tell him that she'd always lived in limbo, that maybe there were people, herself among them, who lived best outside the confines of conventional roles and conventional expectations, people who had the vision and the strength to chart their own course. That she, for instance, didn't necessarily want to be a wife.

They had to concentrate fully just to hear what the other was saying, had to press their bodies together and bow their heads, cheek to nose. Under the table, he rested his hand on the inside of her thigh. They were both relaxed and intense, the air of their own private world infused with the sweet, malty scent of their breath.

Without warning, a man she'd never seen before sat down

abruptly on the bench beside Jon. Startled, she grabbed for Jon's hand. But his fingers seemed almost to dissolve in hers, so quickly did he pull them away. She was nonplussed and then angry. Of course. It was someone he knew. She turned away. It disgusted her to be with him under these circumstances, to see him act weak and sneaky.

"She had to work," Jon was shouting. "Didn't she call you?"

"Plant emergency?" the man shouted back. "That's too bad."

As he spoke to Jon, the man's eyes were on her, but not in a way that betrayed suspicion or disapproval. He tilted his head so he could see around Jon and gave her a small smile, as if inviting her to explain herself. She could tell that she pleased him. She found herself, almost without having willed it, smiling back at him, accepting the compliment. In fact, she felt as if she couldn't look away, as if she were a small mammal mesmerized by a snake. It was surprisingly pleasant to be pinned in that way.

"So you brought a friend?" she heard him say.

"Freddi's from work. She's my partner at work." Jon was struggling to stand now but was thrown off balance by the way his legs were trapped between the table and the bench. "Freddi," he said, "this is my brother, Kyle."

"Your brother!" She lifted her eyebrows.

"Oh," Kyle laughed. "I see you've heard of me."

What had she heard? Ne'er-do-well, father's favorite, drugs. Had there actually been jail time? Looking at him, it didn't seem possible.

The band had started some wailing that increased the already powerful volume. Jon extricated himself from the bench and leaned toward Kyle. "Where's Paula?" he bawled.

Kyle made a vague gesture with one hand. "Crystal screams whenever Paula tries to take her away from the merry-go-round. I was just making a tour to look for you."

"Well, you found me."

"Yeah." He tilted his head in the direction he'd gestured. "So, c'mon." He was still focused entirely on Freddi, so that the invitation seemed to be for her alone. Without hesitation, she began to follow.

But Jon was shaking his head. "Kyle, I'm sorry about this, but I'm afraid we have to work. I mean, since Ginny couldn't come, we decided to make this a work thing."

Jon was looking at her. She knew he expected her to chime in—yes, they were working, the man was riding them hard, had to keep the pedal to the metal, noses to the grindstone, eyes on the prize and all that.

Back a few months ago, she'd actually savored the close calls and artful deceptions, describing them in detail to Andrea, as if reporting the antics of children. Oh, she and Jon were so much cleverer than those they practiced to deceive. But now she felt her insides contorting with embarrassment at this swill. How could he stand to hear himself? It was so obviously fake! She wondered if anyone had ever been fooled.

"Maybe we *should* hit the merry-go-round, Jon." She shrugged and threw in an explanation: "We're working on a milk ad."

"Great. C'mon then." Kyle put one hand gently on her back, so that it was he who was protecting and guiding her through the throng, while Jon followed helplessly behind.

"Hey," Kyle said, looking over his shoulder to include Jon, "I just thought of a great idea for your ad. Instead of beer coming out of a tap, you could have milk. And you could have milk, like on the bar, in steins. And then the slogan could be something like, 'Get drunk on milk.' You know, like 'Get high on life.' "

The carousel was in an out-of-the-way corner, tucked against a fence that enclosed backstage machinery. A few children, some tense, some elated, were perched on the brilliantly painted animals, and their weary parents brightened and waved as their own came around, and then sagged as they rode off again. One little girl who was watching, rather than riding, broke away from her mother and ran toward them.

"Daddy! Mommy! It's Unca Jon! Look, it's Unca Jon!"

She was a messy girl, with orange powdered cheese smeared around her mouth and tangled black hair and thin brown ankles. Jon grabbed her and swung her into the air without hesitation. He kept his focus on the girl while Kyle introduced Freddi to his wife, and when Paula asked about Ginny, it was Freddi who had to answer, and it was Freddi who had to riff about the stupid milk campaign for which they'd apparently come to a beer-greased rock concert for inspiration. No matter, she was self-possessed enough for them both. She glanced at Jon, the messy little girl tall on his shoulders now. She could imagine one like that for the two of them. He saw her looking and gave her a nod, grateful for the way she'd carried off their fiction. That sweet communication, that special moment of attention that tied them together, reassured her. He loved her, after all. It would work out for them in the end. She felt sure of it. And a year from now, two years, how they ended up would be all that mattered.

1963

Clark hasn't come up with a plan, but it turns out he doesn't need one. Bud comes to him.

"Have you seen Marie?"

All he has to do is lead the man onto the golf course. But he worries she hasn't had enough time and so he dawdles in the entryway, slowly finishing his drink, waylaying an acquaintance, even retying his shoelaces. Now that they're finally out here in the darkness, their shoes scraping along the narrow dirt road that skirts the first hole, while the wind pushes roughly through the woods on their left and the gully gapes on their right, he worries that too many minutes have passed. If Marie has seduced Walter, and if he's as insistent and forceful as Hattie maintained, can she hold him off? He shouldn't have let her do it; he should have insisted he'd have no part of such a scheme. But then what would she have done? Something even more risky? Something crazy all on her own?

He glances at Bud. Doesn't he wonder why his wife is wandering around a golf course in the middle of the night? But Bud's face is relaxed, impassive. This is his territory, after all. Perhaps for him stumbling around in the dark out here isn't an extraordinary thing.

Marie had said the third hole and had described its position in relation to the woods at the southwest corner of the course. One evening a week ago Clark had made sure that he knew where that hole was, but he'd come at it then from the road, like a kid hunting golf balls. He'd never approached it from the clubhouse.

They're beyond the trees now, which means it should be on their left, just a little ways up. Or is it farther over and farther up? The long rolling spaces, the unnaturally flattened greens, all of it looks different in the grays and blacks of the night.

If she screams, they can run toward the sound and rescue her. Does he hear voices over there? That rise, the sand trap might be behind it. Or is it over in this direction? No, it has to be the rise.

"This way," he whispers. "I think they went this way." Too late, he realizes that he cannot have known this from observing them leave the clubhouse together. Cannot have known unless he's in on a plot.

twenty-one

"Are you going to keep this crater?" Nora asked, when at last they'd made their way outside. Several thin silver bangles jingled as she flung her arm out to indicate the gully near what had once been the first hole. Mark had declared that as long as he had Jon's computer he might as well work, and the two little boys had followed a rabbit halfway to the third hole, leaving the landscaping party on their own in the long grass behind the clubhouse.

"This has always been a trouble spot," Mr. Fleischer said. "I remember my dad wanting to get truckloads of soil to fill this thing in, flatten it all out, but my mother wouldn't let him. She said it was the only interesting feature on the property. Anyway, it would have been prohibitively expensive to fill it, even back then."

"It's great for sledding," Ginny said. Standing in the heat, it was impossible to recall the relentless bite of the wind on her cheeks and the incipient ache in her toes and fingers. But she did remember the safe feeling of her father's legs, holding her and her sisters snugly on the toboggan. They went fast enough to scream, but with her father in charge she'd never had to be more than pleasantly afraid. With him back then, she felt more than safe; she felt as fully protected as she'd been when still enwombed.

She studied the ground about a third of the way down. Somewhere there in the blackberry brambles and honeysuckle was the place where she'd lost her balance.

She'd tried a couple times to ditch the beer Jon had given her, as she'd intended. But whenever she set it down, she felt too self-conscious to walk away. She didn't want people to know she was a goody rule-follower, didn't want people to see she hesitated to do what everyone else did without a second thought, scared she might get in trouble. What did that mean anyway, getting in trouble? Scared her father would look at her, shake his head, and look away, disappointed. Scared she would not be the person he expected her to be. That was what it came down to. But that was a powerful thing.

Once, she did manage to leave the cup next to a bowl of nacho-flavored Doritos, but Lester Darkcloud, sweet, officious, smitten, retrieved it before she'd gone three steps. And she was glad to have it back, glad to have something in her hand that she could raise to her lips when she couldn't think of anything to say or anywhere to look.

She drank some finally. It was tedious not to. She didn't mind the yeasty taste, liked it, even.

"If I don't pee now, I'm gonna wet my pants." Beth had already downed two plastic cupsful. "Be right back."

The sun began to set and the mottled evening sky softened the hard edges, making it easier to talk to people she hardly knew. Ginny sat on the grass with some others, sipping what was by now tepid liquid. When someone suggested they try the wapatuli, she finished her beer, so as not to be wasteful, before getting up, brushing her rear in case of grass, and matching the others' languid gait as they made their way to the card table on which rested the vodka-soaked watermelon bristling with straws. There wasn't enough room for all of them at once. By the time Ginny bent over the fruit, most of the others were wiping their mouths on the backs of their hands and wandering off toward the food. The vodka tasted even better than the beer, somehow icy and burning at once. Ginny drank some more.

"You like wapatuli?" It was Kyle again. He hitched one buttock over the edge of the table.

"I guess," she said. She giggled. She felt she'd made a witty reply.

"I've got some better stuff inside," he said. "Amaretto, peppermint schnapps. Can't offer it to the hoi polloi, but I could get a glass for you."

Ginny blinked. Her lids seemed to stay closed a fraction longer than usual. The liquor didn't tempt her, but having something special, something Kyle Kepilkowski had given her secretly, made her giddy.

He pressed her. "What can I get you?"

"I don't know." This answer seemed to lack something. Not knowing how else to dress it up, she giggled again and stroked her braid, pulling it forward over one shoulder.

"Should I surprise you?"

It was the way he looked at her that did the trick; she recognized that even as she fell for it. He had the knack of concentrating his attention, not staring but focusing, so that you felt yourself to be dead center in his sights. It was very flattering.

She wished he would stay where he was, but the strain of trying to think of things to say to keep him hooked on the table edge was unbearable. His offer solved all problems. He would go, but he would come back. "OK."

She leaned against the table and watched him stride toward the house, stopping to lay his arm over a girl's shoulders, poking a boy in the ribs, playing the host, and then she looked away. She didn't want to stare after him, didn't want him or anyone else to know she was eager for him to return. While she waited, she tested her blink. Her lashes were definitely sticky.

From the top of the hill a horn tooted a festive salute. Jon was driving a green tractor that pulled a flat trailer and behind him stood Beth, her hands on his shoulders. Ginny waved at Beth, her hand dipping and swiveling in front of her face. Beth raised her own hand, cautiously, just for a moment, before setting it securely back on Jon's shoulder. Later, with irony, Ginny remembered noting that this wasn't the safest place to ride.

Jon braked and, with what looked like some difficult maneuvering of the shift, disengaged the gears. "All aboard!" he shouted.

Like clusters of debris flushed loose in a stream, his guests began moving across the yard toward the trailer.

Ginny glanced at the house. No sign of Kyle. Feeling foolish waiting, she pushed herself away from the table and started toward the tractor.

"Bonfire, that's what I heard," someone said near her.

A couple of boys had lifted the keg between them and were staggering awkwardly across the grass with it.

"Ginny, sit with us!" A boy from her history class reached a hand out to her. She took it, hyperconscious of his grip, of her footing, of the narrow strip of trailer bed beside him onto which she'd have to squeeze, of her long bare thigh pressed against his jeans.

She didn't start out so very close to the edge, but people kept getting on the other side, squeezing her over. She worried about splinters as she shifted, but the gray wood had been rubbed to an almost powdery smoothness by the thousands of items that had slid over its surface.

The tractor lurched as it started forward and people shrieked with pleasure. They swayed exaggeratedly and clutched at one another.

She was facing the back, and, as they climbed out of the depression in which the little cabins huddled, she saw the shabbiness of the place fall away. What had been junk up close—gas cans and tires, engine parts and rusty metal cabinets—became shapes in soft colors; the pitted-dirt drive became a gray ribbon. The lake, which up close had been a yellow-green, silvered.

They crossed the road and drove onto the golf course. Someone tugged her braid, accidentally, she assumed, the result of the soft crush and grind of swaying bodies. She pulled the hair forward. A hand snaked over her shoulder and pulled it back again, just when the angle at which she was sitting suddenly shifted as the trailer tipped forward over the lip of the gully. She turned with a playful "Hey!"

Kyle.

She smiled, her involuntary response. But would it have been better to look aghast, to give his hand a playful slap? What would Beth have done? Or Tracy? What would Jean Arthur have done in one of those movies? Her mind scrambled for an alternative, but she just continued to smile. Crowded, noisy, rolling along as they were, there was really no need for repartee.

The jolt, when Jon hit the brakes, surprised her, surprised everybody. "Whoa, whoa!" people shouted, laughing, grabbing at each other. Her body pitched backward and then forward, and that would have been all right, would have been fine, except that the boy beside her, in his similar pitching was shoved against her, which pushed her shoulders to the left just enough that, off balance and crowded as she was, she couldn't right herself. She grabbed at arms, hands, the huge treads of the tire, anything, but already she was too far over the edge. Her fingers brushed a fold of someone's T-shirt, but they caught nothing but air.

At the beginning of her fall, she felt a pound of adrenaline like a bolt of lightning, so strong that, for the flash of an instant, she was amazed it didn't lift her up onto the trailer again. And then a dizziness overwhelmed her, as her body kept moving in a direction it couldn't make sense of.

She hit the ground with her back, which knocked the wind out of her. That part was startling, but hardly even painful. The bad part came afterward. She stared up at the looming wheel, saw the dirt packed into the cracks in the rubber and the rust along the rim. She saw the wheel rise up, as if it were rolling over a branch, and she heard a ferocious crack, as if a fire-cracker had exploded much too close. The sound made her feel like vomiting; it would have made her scream, if she'd had the breath to make a sound. Others screamed for her, while she gasped like a fish on the beach. Although they swore she stayed conscious, she couldn't remember anything that happened afterward, until she found herself in a hospital bed.

After that what she remembered was Jon. She remembered the way he stuck his head in the room first to make sure it was OK to come in; she remembered his sneakers with bolts of ball-point lightning penned on the rubber toes; she remembered his ugly flowers, dear to her because he'd chosen them for her. He'd stayed with her for more than an hour, even though she couldn't think of anything clever to say—that silliness about the lyrics!—even though she wasn't wearing the shorts that made her thighs look less wide, even though her hair was filthy and she was wearing the pale-blue-rimmed glasses she'd replaced with contact lenses two years earlier. She wished he'd come back, and he did, night after night, came to her house, too, and politely drank the orange Shasta her mother served because she didn't think teenagers should imbibe caffeine, and let her father's comments about raising the driving age and the irresponsibility of those who would let a high school student operate heavy machinery glance off him like Nerf balls.

She'd been a track star the spring before it happened. She ran the hurdles, because it felt closest to flying, and anchored the mile relay. She wasn't the fastest sprinter on the team, but she could sprint the longest. Full-out from gun to tape, that was the way she raced, her long legs taking huge, inefficient strides, gulping up the cinders. She would have had to give it up the following year anyway, accident or no. She could feel herself slowing toward the end of the season, her speed undercut by the womanly widening of her hips and by the lunches she skipped to curb that widening. Her coaches recommended cross-country in the fall, explaining that she had to learn discipline and strategy for the following year, for the long haul. But she wasn't interested in pacing herself, in hoarding her energy and meting it out in careful increments. That was only the work of running with none of the joy. If that was all that was left to her of the sport, she was done with it. After the accident, she'd told herself it didn't matter that she couldn't race; she'd already put away such childish things.

Standing at the brink of the gully now, she was surprised to realize that the place held no terror for her. The feelings it excited centered on the challenge of transforming its awkwardness with wildflowers and crab apple trees. Her coaches had been right, after all, it seemed. What mattered in the end was the discipline and strategy, the slow, steady accretion of the miles, not the burning, full-out dash. Was she to think of herself forever a careless person? Was the world to be forever an intolerable risk because of a single thoughtless, unlucky moment? Or mightn't she define herself instead by her resilience? There was, as her doctor had said, no earthly reason why she should not give birth to a baby and safely raise a child, and it was time, she said sternly to herself, that her body recognized this fact.

Walter, who'd hung back to examine some evidence of trespassing in the wooded section, was slightly out of breath when he caught up with her. "I've been meaning to ask about your mother," he panted.

"You know my mother?" She wasn't surprised. It was a small town. Probably he'd given some money to the music center or they were both involved in the nature conservancy.

"I once thought Hattie Sorensen was the love of my life." He said it lightly and then laughed wistfully, as befitted the declaration.

"Really?" Ginny smiled. "When was this?"

"Oh, a long time ago, obviously. Almost too long ago to remember." He reached down and tugged at the tough stem of a cornflower, which bent but refused to break. He straightened, abandoning the blossom. "I was a jerk, only thinking about myself—well, I'm sure you know how boys can be—and then she found your father. And lived happily ever after, I hear.

"Say," he went on, staring out at the blue bits that sparkled beyond the screen of leaves, "isn't this spectacular now that I've taken out those hideous pines? So close to the lake and no water view . . ." He shook his head. "It would have been a crime."

twenty-two

Kaiser perched on a stool at the far end of the bar. He had a good view through the window and the back door at the weeds behind the building. He was neither a golfer nor a developer, but the place in both of its manifestations struck him as small-time. And who were these people who would choose to live in grand houses in the middle of nowhere?

He'd used Jon's computer many times when they were partnered, so it was simple to find the old notes he wanted on the Lacey project. The file was a disappointment, though, thinner and less inspired than it had seemed when they were in the middle of it.

He double-clicked a few more files randomly, aware, as he did so, of breaking a personal taboo: he didn't spy on people he knew well. That was straying beyond voyeurism into betrayal. Anyway, there were things even he didn't want to know about his friends.

He'd been right to stay clear of Ginny. In keeping Jon's secrets, he was lying to her, too, and that made him furious with Jon and himself. Altogether, he was uncomfortable near her, as if forever perched in the starter's blocks, balancing on his toes and fingertips. He longed to rat his friend out but feared that desire came from nothing better than the hope that she might then fall into his arms.

Vanderheiden crowded the in-box of Jon's e-mail. He avoided those at first and, warming up, opened a few other messages at random: a shipping confirmation for a set of Sinatra CDs, a note about one of their company's accounts from another artistic director, one from a graphic designer. The tone of those, he noted, was slightly different from that which they used when they wrote to him, more chatty, less smart. Jon was obviously their buddy, not someone they strove to impress.

Outside the window, Ginny was talking to the toad-like little man. She looked like a colt or a deer from this angle, long-legged and delicate, someone the wind could stagger.

He positioned the cursor over a wvanderheiden and clicked. "I like the sans serif with the caption." Innocent. Another. "Tuesday 10:30." Could go either way. Another. And there they were, the strings of secret emotion. He looked away, sickened by a surfeit of feeling, Jon's and Freddi's on the screen, Ginny's incipient agony, his own confusion and shame. But he shut the top against the keyboard without closing the windows he'd opened.

He would tell her later, after Summerfest. He would call her, if he had to, if he couldn't get her alone. Of course, they might see Jon and Freddi there. Then there would be nothing left to tell.

twenty-three

Kyle leaned close on the pretext of steadying his daughter on Jon's shoulders. "What the fuck are you doing?" he hissed.

"*I'm* playing with Crystal. What are *you* doing coming on to a woman practically in front of your wife and kid?" Jon shot back. He broke away from Kyle and spun the little girl, so that her feet flew in the air, making a circle around them. "Dizzy? Are you dizzy yet?"

"Maybe you should wonder why your woman is so interested in me."

"She's not my woman. We work together. We're working. If you understood the concept, you might not need to hit me up for a loan every six months."

"Daddy! Now you spin me!"

Kyle snorted as he stepped close to retrieve his daughter. "I guess Mom was right about you, after all," he said lightly, infuriatingly.

Jon frowned. "What are you talking about?"

"You know, the night before you and Ginny got married? How she said you would fuck it up?"

"Daddy! You said a very bad word!" Crystal reached up and slapped her palm over her father's mouth.

"I don't know what you're talking about." It came out too loud. Paula and Freddi looked at them.

"What's going on over there?" Paula's tone was peevish.

"We're remembering Jon's wedding." Kyle smiled at Freddi, who looked away.

Jon did know the conversation Kyle meant, although his brother had it wrong, as usual. They'd been out drinking, ful-filling minimal expectations for the night before a wedding, and it was two in the morning by the time they'd come home for what would be for Jon a final night in their childhood room. It was early June, warm summer during the day, chilly spring at night. The tireless mating call of the peepers rose from the marshes when Kyle shut off the engine.

They sat for a moment in the dark car. Jon let his head fall against the back of the seat. He wanted it to be this time tomorrow, the slick tuxedo and the stiff shoes long ago stuffed back into their bags. He wanted to be alone with Ginny in the room they'd reserved in Door County, this life behind him, that life beginning. He had no desire to go into his parents' house, even for the night, had not wanted to since a similar evening of semi-drunken camaraderie more than a year ago, when Kyle, always generous with secrets like which door to the high school didn't lock automatically when you stepped outside, had told him why their father had been angry enough with Walter Fleischer to chase him until he flew off the road.

Kyle let his head fall back against the seat, too. "I thought by now, I'd come up with something serious to say."

"But no?"

"No." He sighed. "But, hey, you and Ginny are great together. I thought so from the beginning, you know, the way she kept looking at you at that party . . ."

Jon turned his face toward the dark window. The memory of himself on that occasion still made him feel sick to his stomach.

"It worked out in the end, didn't it?" Kyle was saying. "It worked out great."

They closed the car doors as quietly as they could and stumbled, laughing, onto the porch. The door emitted its familiar creak. Two steps beyond the threshold Jon reached for the newel post in the darkness, knowing just where it would meet his hand.

"I've tried not to say anything." Her voice rose from the far corner of the living room, the place where she always sat with her needlepoint and her magazines.

"Shit!" Kyle exclaimed. "What are you doing down here, Mom?"

"Believe me, I have tried," she said.

Jon could hear her thumb flicking at her lighter, until a small flame shot up. She lit a cigarette and the orange dot that intensified as she sucked in the smoke seemed to draw him and Kyle into the room. She had a knack for the commanding and dramatic.

Jon wanted to say, "Try harder," but after a lifetime of training he couldn't summon sufficient lack of respect. Besides, he wanted to hear what she had to say, so that he could slam her. He saw the cigarette move, knew she was picking a crumb of tobacco off of her tongue.

"She's never going to be right, Jon," she said, "just so you understand that. Even though she can walk now, even if she can still have children. Maybe you don't care about that, but there's something else to consider." She took another long draw on her cigarette and coughed. His eyes had adjusted to the darkness and he could see her now; her eyes looked black behind the screen of her glasses.

"Sit down," she'd said, motioning in the air before her toward the couch with her cigarette. "You, too, Kyle. I want you both to hear this. I want both of my sons to profit from their mother's experience." She pulled on the cigarette again. "What I worry about, Jon, is that you care too much, that you think now, because of an *accident,* this girl is your responsibility."

"Ginny," he interrupted. "Her name is Ginny."

She ignored him. "You've always been such a responsible boy! I think you believe that you did this to her and that now, forever, you have to make it up." She leaned forward, her voice suddenly filling with emotion. "But that's too big a burden for a marriage. Marriage is a heavy thing already. This load will break it. I can tell you that. Believe me, it will ruin you. And her, too, Jon! Think of her life, if you won't think of your own. Let her marry a boy who's had nothing to do with this!"

"It was my fault, but—"

"Don't say that! It was an accident! She shouldn't have been sitting there anyway. This is not something you did!"

"It doesn't matter, Mom. I'm not marrying Ginny to make anything up to her. I'm marrying her because she's the love of my life." It sounded stupid, even to the ears of a twenty-two-year-old, but it felt true, nevertheless. "She's the love of my life," he repeated, making it stone. "Something you couldn't understand."

Freddi giggled, a sweet, girlish sound, at something Paula was saying. It made Jon feel queasy. What was she doing chatting with his brother's wife? And if Kyle told Paula, as he certainly would—they were married, after all—wouldn't Paula feel it was her duty to tell Ginny, her beloved sister-in-law? Panic seared him at the thought. His mother had been right about the heaviness of marriage, but he saw suddenly, vividly, that that heaviness, that fabric of understandings and misunderstandings, of events witnessed, celebrated, and mourned, of dependable support and casual betrayal, of happy occasions of agreement and of never-ending accommodation both willing and grudging, that union, enduring despite insults and neglect, relentlessly invested with hope, had become the bulk of his life. Maybe he did love two women, but he had only one marriage, one history. If he gave that up, then what would be left of him? A man he wouldn't recognize. A man he would despise. A man as insubstantial as that girlish laughter. He nodded, suddenly resolved.

"Hey, Freddi." He crossed the few feet of matted grass to where she stood and put his hand on her shoulder, forcibly enough to signal that he wasn't interested in discussing the matter. "It's too hot here. Let's take a walk by the lake." He began to steer her away from Paula, saying over his shoulder, "Gotta get to work. We'll meet up with you guys later."

"Wait!" Paula said. "Where are we meeting you?" She turned helplessly toward Kyle. "Did you guys set something up?"

Jon waved his hand over his head. He had to end it now, immediately, before it was too late.

Freddi giggled again. "Wasn't that sort of rude?"

"He was rude to me, to us. Don't worry about them. Right now, I want to see you."

He led Freddi through an opening between an Italian sausage stand and one selling Harley-Davidson T-shirts, so that they emerged on the bicycle path along the lake that ran behind the main activities of the festival. The fresh breeze blowing directly off the huge body of water dissipated the greasy smells and muted the blares and jangles of the bands.

"This is nice," Freddi admitted. "I guess I'm not really a carnival girl."

"C'mere, then," Jon said, tenderly, trying to cushion what was to come. He felt calmer and more generous now that they were moving toward what he knew would be the end. Would she be tearful or angry? Both, maybe. He didn't know her well enough, he realized, to say for sure. Whatever her response, he was determined to be kind, to help her in any way he could. It was his fault, after all. He had made promises. How was she to have known he'd never meant them, when he hadn't known it himself? They were well out of sight of anyone but the gulls and a few misfit teenagers, who were preoccupied with their own self-important, illicit activities. He slipped his hand around hers and led her gently off the path toward the water. In a few yards they were scrambling up the piled rock that formed the seawall.

On the far side of the wall, the wind grabbed bits of spray and tossed them playfully at their feet. "Oh, look!" she exclaimed, pointing. Among the graceful yachts and frolicking small craft that seemed to exist merely to further animate the summer festival scene, there was a large, old-fashioned sailing ship with three masts and rows of square white sails. "I wish we could ride on that."

He pulled her down beside him; they were alone on this side of the wall. Wedged deep between the rocks like treasure were scraps of paper and plastic in brilliant colors—an empty Doritos bag, a wad of napkins, a cup still partially full of orange drink—and a crazy number of broken bottles, so many that people must have been throwing them there for years for the perverse pleasure of hearing the crash.

He remembered that when he and Ginny had climbed over this wall as teenagers, he'd been certain they were the only ones ever to have done such a wild thing. They were, after all, inventing the world; no one who had come before could possibly have felt or experienced the things they did. It might be possible, even at this age, to reinvent the world with Freddi, but it would be, he felt now, a version paler than what he already had. He could not bear the loss.

He wrapped his arms around her, wanting to hold her as he talked, hoping his comfort would ease the sting. Ashamed, he hid his face in her hair, hesitating, trying to begin to tell her with his body alone. There was the long drive home to consider. And beyond that, there was their partnership at work. Nevertheless, he knew what he'd decided and that now was the time to speak.

The first blow was to his kidney. He heard a shout and felt confusion before he registered pain. The punch pushed him forward into her. Her scream threw him back.

twenty-four

Ethan had run over the rocks, scrambled, really, on hands and feet in some stretches, when he'd seen what was happening: Winifred and that man, pressed together, his arms and legs wrapped around her. Not working. They were not working.

He'd twisted an ankle, scraped his shoulder, bent his fingers backward as he ran; pains for later. When he was close enough, he leapt and landed in a crouch, his left hand clawing at a rock on the upward slope to steady him, the side of his right fist coming down like a mallet in a soft spot.

The man fell forward, groaning.

Ethan grabbed him by the shoulders and pulled him back again, trying to tear him off of her.

He had no notion of how to fight, no plan other than a fierce, overwhelming desire that they—this man and his Winifred—not be together, that what he had just seen be dissolved. What he'd imagined, hurtling over the rocks, was that the force of his punch would send the other sprawling, bouncing down the few feet of the seawall into the lake, but he turned out to be harder to move than that.

He drove his knee as hard as he could into the other without falling himself. Ribs or kidney or whatever it was he hit was a harder mass than Ethan had expected; there wasn't much give. But maybe it was enough. The guy tumbled off the rock he'd been sitting on and banged against the one below.

She was pushing him; her thumb pressed into the base of his neck.

This felt right, finally. Not good, but right. She was seeing him now. She was taking him seriously.

And then the guy was on him, flying uphill, throwing Ethan down so that his head cracked with a strange, hollow sound against a rock. Pain streaked through him and, like a battering ram, it opened something inside him, a fury he'd kept banked for years, waiting to be released. The fury made him reach for the bottle he only half knew was there. The fury closed his hand around the long neck, a perfect handle. The fury raised him up, lifted the bottle high.

The jagged edges connected with a skull, an ear, a cheek, a neck, and the blood appeared as if by magic, an incongruously brilliant, shining red against the browns and tans of his hair and skin, the mottled blue of his shirt.

Someone was screaming. Winifred, probably. Her mouth was open and her eyes huge. The man too was staring at him, his hand moving slowly through the air until it pressed against his head, trying to cover the red. Ethan felt suddenly dizzy, an agony radiating from the back of his skull. He tried lowering his head to push the blackness back, but it kept spilling in along the edges, filling in what was left of the light, until everything was dark.

1963

Bud doesn't like the way Clark keeps after him, saying things about Marie and Walt. Or not saying things exactly, but almost saying them, making Bud think things he doesn't want to think. Why is this any of Clark's business? But Bud is used to people trying to help him, bringing him his cleats, a glass of ice tea, offering to let him borrow their new fishing rod or their car, proffering useless secrets about another team or another player, all so that when he wins, they can say, "I know Bud Kepilkowski." Or even, "I helped Bud Kepilkowski."

He glances sidelong at Clark in the darkness. The man looks like a weasel with his pointy face and long, narrow body. He's pushing his nose forward into the wind like he's trying to sniff out Marie and Walt. If he saw Walt come out here, it was probably to practice his putt. More than likely, though, neither one of them is out here. Marie's most likely in the ladies' room and Walt's *probably sitting out in his car, sampling his private stash, trying to forget that he can't putt to save his life. Bud shakes his head. What's he doing out here with this weasel? If anyone has a thing going on with Marie, maybe he's the one. That day at the pier wasn't the first he'd heard of this weasel hanging around his house. He wonders if he should punch him.*

And then he hears her voice, or thinks he does. Was it her laugh or just a trick of the wind? He's had that happen before, heard her voice call his name when she wasn't even at home. There it is again, not words, but the rise and fall of hushed voices, hers and, yes, maybe Walt's slightly nasal tones.

"This way. I think they went this way," the weasel says. He obviously hasn't heard anything; he's heading off on a tangent toward the eighth hole.

Bud ignores him, holds still to listen. Suddenly, the voices stream at him, hers and his, and hers, again.

"You're not scared of a baby, are you?" That's her. Near the third hole.

Immediately he begins to run, his smooth-soled loafers slipping a little on the shorn ground. In seconds he's covered the distance to the third hole and then, in four steps, is across the springy green. He stands above the sand trap for an instant, looking down. Their bodies are dark against the light sand. They're reclining, each propped on an elbow, not quite lying down but not sitting up either. Walt's hand is on Marie's belly; her hand is on his wrist.

He leaps and lands with a grunt half on top of Walt, and grabs him by the upper arms, digging his fingers into Walt's flesh. He flings Walt out of the sand so that he spins like a cartwheel, his legs whipping in arcs one after the other.

Sand flies into Bud's eyes and between his teeth. For a moment he's blinded, and he spits and blinks.

"You see, Bud!" Marie is shouting. "Now do you believe Hattie? Now do you see what he's like?"

He looks at her, his love, and feels tears, unexpected and hot, washing the sand from his eyes. For a second, brief as a breath, his muscles are dough; he can't gather himself, can't even think which way he wants to move.

But she's on her feet. She's pointing into the darkness. "Get him, Bud!" she shrieks. "Get him! He's getting away!"

Walter has never been much of a runner, but he's moving quickly now, his white shirt glowing, bobbing with every step. Finally, Bud is back on his feet. Finally, he's running, too, rage washing over the confusion and hurt, filling his blood with oxygen. At last, he's flying over the grass, down the road, up the drive, gravel shifting and crunching under his shoes, his breath booming in his ears.

When he reaches the parking lot, he hears the slam of a car door and then the growl of an engine. The lights of Walt's Thunderbird flick on. Bud runs back and plants himself at the entrance to the lot, arms outstretched. Walt's lights are on the gravel in front of him, then at his feet, then directly in his eyes. He squints. He stands firm. Walt swerves, his car rocking as it moves over the lumpy grass, his head practically hitting the ceiling as he bounces past before swerving back onto the drive again.

Mr. Fleischer's pickup is parked in its usual spot, near the entrance to the bar. The bartender hardly glances at him as he palms the keys off the hook above the cash register. He's Bud Kepilkowski, after all; he's driven that truck for Fleischer plenty of times.

At the top of the road, he has to guess and goes left. Within a mile, he can see the Thunderbird's taillights from the top of the hill. The T-bird is the faster car, but Bud is the better driver. He guns it, careening down the hill, braking just enough to make the hard turn at the bottom. Walt is not far ahead of him around the bends into Sandy Hollow. Bud can see he's having trouble control ling the car; he slides into the oncoming lane and then overcompensates and nearly goes into the woods, but he rights himself and screams on, past the little houses and the taverns, down the narrow road where someone might easily be walking.

"Stop!" Bud shouts, his head out the window of the cab. "Stop, you son of a bitch!" Walt has his windows rolled up tight, as if that thin sheet of glass can protect him.

The road turns sharply to the left again, following the contours of the lake. Soon they'll be on the little bridge that spans the neck of water between upper and lower Winnesha. Where does Walt think he can go? How does he think he's going to get away? Are they going to go on roaring through the night until one or the other of them runs out of gas? Bud glances at the gauge. Full. Mr. Fleischer never lets the tank get below the halfway mark. Walt, on the other hand, typically runs on fumes.

"Stop, for Christ's sake!"

But Walt only goes faster, turning left and then right, shooting up onto the unlighted bridge. His angle is wrong; Bud can see it. The road has straightened, but Walt is listing right. Metal screeches against wood, a headlight explodes with a pop, as Walt flies through the low barrier. For a moment, his car is airborne, as if traveling on an invisible road, and then the heavy engine pushes the front end down and the taillights tilt up, as if someone's hooked the back of the car from the sky.

Bud barely hears the splash above the squeal of his own tires. Mr. Fleischer's clubs are in their bag on the floor on the passenger side and, almost by instinct, he reaches in and pulls out an iron. He doesn't hesitate, doesn't for a moment doubt. In the same way he'd known when the football in his hand would fly straight to the receiver's, or that his club would connect smoothly and powerfully with the ball, so he knows now that he'll dive into the black water and come up with Walter Fleischer. In minutes, it'll be done. Standing on the road, he can already feel the slick water on his skin, can sense Walt's weight in his arms.

Where the car went off is obvious from the break in the barrier and even in the darkness, Bud can see the bubbles rising from the spot where it sank. He deepens his breaths, steadying himself as he steps out of his loafers. Then he dives as far as he can, the iron tight in his fist.

It's darker under the water than he imagined, the lake too murky for moonlight to penetrate, but after a few strokes, his knuckles bang against metal and he can vaguely make out the car's pale-blue form resting on its side on the black lake bottom.

With his left hand, he grabs hold of the door handle and uses it to pull himself against the car. He plants his feet on the frame and yanks, but the door doesn't give, and the window is still shut tight.

In his right hand, he has the club by the neck. He drives it as hard as he can against the glass. The water, though, pushes back. It won't let him build enough force. He's running out of air, his lungs burning. He has to get up. He has to get air.

He breaks the surface, gasping. Three breaths and he's down again. This time he knows just where to go, just how to concentrate his strength. One, two, three, four furious strokes and the glass at last gives way. A long shard cuts deep into his flesh from his knuckles to just above his elbow, as the iron and his fist plunge through.

He works the iron around the window, banging and scraping, knocking out the glass to make a space big enough to admit him. Once again, desperate for air, he shoots upward, gasps, and dives back down.

Squeezing in the window gives him his single moment of panic—what if he can't get out again? But he pushes the panic down as he puts his arms and head through the hole and shoves his shoulders after them. He waves his hands wildly in the cavity, feeling for Walt. Almost at once he touches a limb, a leg or an arm, what difference does it make? He pulls—it's an arm—works his own shoulders out the window again, and then Walt's. His lungs burn.

One more trip to the surface, one more dose of oxygen, and he's grabbing Walt under the arms, heaving him out the window. Walt's belt buckle catches on the window frame, but Bud jerks it loose. And then he's shooting for the surface again, his fist tangled in Walt's shirt.

He drags Walt out, presses on his chest, and breathes into his lungs. He's taken his share of lifesaving courses and seen enough movies to know the basic drill. Although, when Walt coughs and vomits, he's half amazed that it works.

They both lie spent for a good while on the marshy grass. It's Walt who first notices Bud's bleeding arm.

"Damn! Look at this." He lays a gentle finger on Bud's arm, just above the spot where the cut begins, and then takes off his wet shirt and wraps it tightly around the wound.

In the truck on the way to the emergency room, he glances down at the golf bag, crowding Bud's feet. "See you lost the nine iron."

Bud is thinking about how his arm is probably bad enough to justify forfeiting his spot in the Butter Cup, maybe bad enough to justify giving up golf altogether. He doubts he'll have the heart for another game.

"Leave me here," he says at the hospital door. "I don't want to see you again." He slams the door when he gets out and then leans back in the open window. "If I ever see you near my wife again, I'll kill you." He knows it's a foolish thing to say, but it seems necessary.

twenty-five

Though his attacker was sprawled over the rocks, obviously unconscious, possibly dead, Jon could hardly keep from stumbling forward to kick him until he could no longer raise his leg. Then, too, he could clearly see himself lifting a stone high into the air and bringing it down upon the man's skull. But Freddi clung to him, pinning his arms against his body, pressing him back against his own rock bed. He tried once or twice to pry her away, but his efforts were feeble. From his right eye, he could see nothing and blood was sluicing uncontrollably down that side of his face. Freddi seemed to be bleeding everywhere, from her ear and chest, her neck and arms.

This, at last, wrenched his attention from the man who lay unconscious, possibly dead, a couple yards away. "Are you hurt?" Frantically, he touched her body, searching for the gashes that must be causing such terrible leaks.

"Ethan, what have you done? What have you done?" she was screaming and then keening, and then she was merely sobbing.

The viscous red dripped everywhere he touched her. Eventually, it dawned on him that the blood was likely to be all his own. Although he remembered that the day had been especially hot, he was shivering now.

He recognized the name Ethan and now the man himself, whom he'd seen once or twice in the parking lot at work and driving in Freddi's neighborhood. She'd told him, disloyally, about this guy, and he'd lapped up her cruelly amusing stories, because he could claim the girl and shamefully enjoyed the pity and contempt he'd felt for the man who could not.

Gradually he became aware of the squawk of an ambulance and a police car, bullying their way through the crowd he now saw had gathered on the grass. Had Freddi called them? Or had some of the teenagers? How had all these people known there was something worth witnessing going on out here?

Someone peeled Freddi off of him. It was a relief to feel her weight lifting, to assume that she was being taken care of somewhere else and by someone else. A woman covered him with a blanket and began pressing gauze against his cheek. She bent so closely over her work that he could see, through his left eye, the fine, dark hairs that grew over her lip. He wanted, for some reason, to touch them, and began to raise his hand.

"Hey, lie still there, buddy." She gently pushed his arm back down.

He heard what must have been Ethan's voice, faint, but pleasantly baritone. "What happened?" he was saying. "What's happening?"

So he wasn't dead, after all. Wasn't even unconscious. "My eye," Jon said. "I can't see out of it."

"Well, you got lucky," the woman was saying to him. The

fine hairs moved as she formed the words. "This laceration missed your eye by a good half inch. Once we get the blood cleared away, you'll be able to see just fine."

"I'll have a scar, though, won't I?"

"I wouldn't worry about that." She lifted the soaked gauze and pressed a fresh layer to his cheek. Her tone was more disapproving than reassuring.

He felt light-headed, but also a lightness of another sort. He felt clean, as if whatever had remained of his obsession for Freddi had drained out of him with his blood. He relished the pounding itself, the clear, clean physical pain of it. He ought to thank this Ethan guy for giving him the beating he deserved. He could start fresh now with Ginny, if she would have him. He was pleased to be scarred in a place that he could not hide. He and Ginny would be a matched set now. His carelessness had damaged them both. He laughed giddily at the thought.

"I think this guy's going into shock," he heard the woman say.

"No, I'm all right. I need . . ." He ran his palms over the tops of his thighs and his chest. "My phone. Have you seen my phone? I need to call my wife. I need my wife!"

"Your wife is right over there, sir," the woman said. "She's just fine. Can we get another blanket over here?" she shouted over her shoulder. "And the stretcher. He's ready to move."

"No! I need my phone! Or your phone. Anyone's phone. Can I get a phone over here, please!" he shouted.

"Sir, you need to stay quiet. You need to hold your head still. I'm happy to call anyone you want, once we get you to the hospital."

She was lying, placating him, he could tell.

He spotted Freddi's phone out of the corner of his right eye, despite the blood that still seeped a little from the wound to cloud his lens. Its silver case winked at him from between two rocks. When the woman turned away with some order or other, he shifted his body, strained his arm toward it, trapped the antenna between two of his fingers and pulled it close. He held it under his cupped hand tight against his chest, waiting for his chance, while they rolled him this way and that, expertly settling him onto the stretcher.

twenty-six

"Well, I couldn't eat one every day," Ginny said.

"I could!" Anthony licked the grease from his fried Twinkie off his fingertips.

They were climbing into their seat on the sky tram, which would carry them suspended from one end of the Summerfest grounds to the other and back again.

"It's not really a ride, you know," Mark had frowned. "It's not going to go fast or anything." He was distracted, scanning the crowds.

"That's OK," Anthony insisted. "I want to see the boats from the sky."

There being room only for two, they decided that Ginny would ride, and Mark and Nora would take Rodney down to the carousel.

Ginny had ridden the tram once before, that first time she'd gone to Summerfest with Jon, just because they'd wanted to try everything then. Now the fun would be in going with someone for whom most experiences, however mundane, were still new and exciting. As they would be for her own child, Ginny thought, putting one hand protectively over her belly. She would take the test that was waiting in her vanity drawer, she decided, as soon as Jon came home.

As they ascended, she sensed the weather changing. It was still broiling, unusual so near the lake, but the wind was beginning to shift. By night, they'd be shivering in air blowing off the water. In early July, summer in this northern place had hardly begun; the truly sweltering days and balmy nights were still all before them. Nevertheless, the approaching weather blip was a reminder that the days, while still so long, were already on their downward slide. Two months and change was all, really, and then the summer, the precious, glorious, burgeoning summer would disintegrate as if it had never been.

She'd told her father that she intended to marry Jon as they drove home from Madison together in a blizzard. It was only afternoon; classes had been canceled, his office had closed. The highway was crowded with people trying to beat the weather and already far too late. The snow drove at the windshield, thick as ash from burning paper. When she said it, he braked, perhaps more abruptly than he'd intended. The car fishtailed slightly; his hands clenched the wheel.

"Why?"

She'd been startled by the question, too startled to answer in any but the most predictable way. "Because I love him."

"Hmmph," he'd said, and she could not say she was surprised.

In fact, in some small but fundamental way, his response satisfied her. Obviously, she did not want to marry Jon simply to defy her father, but the fact that he disapproved was all to the good. Her new life would be all her own then, her own to share with Jon.

Below and off to the left, near the bike path, she saw an ambulance pulling away from a knot of people. What terrible thing had happened while everyone was supposed to be having fun? Had a bike collided with a pedestrian? Had someone had a heart attack brought on by the heat? Or by the horrible food? Had someone OD'd? Half these Goth kids had to be on something, although, in fact, most of them looked strikingly innocent, their hideous clothes hiding awkward adolescent bodies too fat or too thin, their painful-looking piercings and shavings incongruous in their soft, youthful skin.

Anthony grabbed her arm, pulling her attention to the endless stretch of water. "Look!" he said. "An old-fashioned ship!"

As their chair swung around for the return trip, her purse began to ring.

"F-o-o-o-d for you! Ooo, ooo. Ooo, ooo." Anthony sang to the ringtone, the Who song Jon, fooling around, had put on her phone.

She dug the phone out and flipped it open. When she saw the name below the number, a bubble of relief raised her spirits. So Freddi wasn't with him then.

"F-o-o-o-d for you!" Anthony belted.

She pressed Talk, a smile giving her voice a lilt. "Hello? Freddi?"

1963

Clark stands at the window staring at her squashed red face under the tiny pink cap, her fist, small as a walnut, curled defiantly beside her head. They tell him that her eyes can't focus so far yet, but it seems to him that her gaze is trained on him commandingly, that without question she's choosing him as her protector, her knight.

Two nurses come down the hall, brisk and starched. As they pass, the one he's not seen before whispers to the other, whom he's seen in his wife's room. "Another miracle baby," she says, giggling. "Think, if she'd gone to term, she'd have been fifteen pounds at least!"

"Shhh," the second nurse hisses.

Do they imagine he doesn't know? He almost wants to run after them, to assure them that he isn't such a fool. Or that he's done playing the fool anyway.

Whatever spell had held him to Marie had broken when he'd witnessed that wild run across the dark grass and learned what had followed. How could he have consented... no, how could he have wanted to be a part of her drama? And how could he have believed she was in control of events? There was no telling what a person might do when his—or her—emotions were aroused. As his are now.

What difference would it make that he would probably never know for certain his wife's state of mind at the moment of this baby's conception? What counted was that Hattie had returned to him. And if Marie hadn't so entranced him, he would have recognized sooner that Hattie had come to him for help because he was the one she wanted, for herself and for her child. In choosing him, she had plunged back in and finished her piece with a flourish.

The giggling nurse, now serious, comes toward him. "Do you want to hold your daughter, sir?"

He makes a cradle of his arms, ready to accept the flannel bundle. "Yes."